On the Run with Love

On the Run with Love

J.M. Benjamin

www.urbanbooks.net

Urban Books, LLC
97 N 18th Street
Wyandanch, NY 11798

On the Run with Love

ISBN 13: 978-1-62286-765-3
ISBN 10: 1-62286-765-3

First Mass Market Printing July 2016
Printed in the United States of America

10 9 8 7 6 5 4 3 2 1

This is a work of fiction. Any references or similarities to actual events, real people, living or dead, or to real locales are intended to give the novel a sense of reality. Any similarity in other names, characters, places, and incidents is entirely coincidental.

Distributed by Kensington Publishing Corp.
Submit Orders to:
Customer Service
400 Hahn Road
Westminster, MD 21157-4627
Phone: 1-800-733-3000
Fax: 1-800-659-2436

On the Run with Love

by

J.M. Benjamin

To all those who continue to support
my bodies of work.

Thank you!
J.M.

Prologue

The first bullet whizzed through the air, shattering the bottle of Rémy Martin Grand Cru VS on the table and piercing the soft flesh of Freddie's upper left side, separating two of his ribs. The burning sensation ignited his insides letting his intoxicated mind know he had been shot. But he wasn't surprised. How could he be when he saw it coming, saw them coming, from across the crowded club.

The second shot caught him in the neck. His blood splattered all over a screaming female beside him who was scrambling to get away.

Yes, he saw the bullets coming. He could see them in his eyes before he saw the glint of the cold steel in the shooter's hand. When their eyes first met, his instincts went into survival mode. He saw murder and knew he was the victim. As he reached for his pistol, something happened. Something just made him stop, and he accepted what was taking place. He was tired.

His whole world as he knew it had come crashing down around him. Everything was gone and the only thing that remained was the fact that he was a wanted man. Not only by the police but by everyone it seemed. They all wanted him out of the way. Freddie couldn't eat or sleep without the incessant thought that he was running out of time.

The third shot that hit him like a sledgehammer in the abdomen was the welcoming committee that told him it was all over. And he welcomed it.

Freddie embraced the warm sensation he felt creeping over his entire body. He welcomed the way everything and everyone around him began moving in slow motion.

The sound of screaming voices and the tempo of the popular club mix by Adrian Sykes warped in Freddie's ears to match the steady rhythm of his heartbeat as it slowly got drowned out. His heartbeat was pounding loudly in his eardrums over all the commotion.

Even the fourth bullet, the last shot he felt, seemed to move in slow motion. From the barrel of the gun, he followed its *Matrix*-like trajectory as it zeroed in on him. He watched it come dangerously close to a woman's ducking head, break a glass in a man's hand, and finally lodge itself deep inside his own flesh. Simultaneously, Freddie's mind was sent to that place where pain can no longer reach.

His last sight was of those eyes and the determination in them. He knew it was coming; no one can run forever. His last thought was, *damn, why did it have to be me?*

Chapter One

One Year Earlier

"Pimpin' is easy when you got the looks and the mouthpiece to back it up," old head Butch the barber remarked as he turned Freddie's chair toward the mirror.

Freddie Holmes looked into his own reflection, admiring his light brown complexion. He was half Dominican and it showed in his features. His father, whoever he was, had left him with naturally curly brown hair and hazel eyes that took on a greenish tint in the summer. He wore his hair close with neatly shaped sideburns and a trimmed goatee. Freddie really didn't need a haircut, but because he took pride in his good looks, he made biweekly trips to Nu Cuts Barbershop, his old friend's establishment. Butch had been cutting Freddie's hair for almost ten years, since he was eleven. So he knew exactly how he liked his hair cut.

"Unc, touch up this sideburn a little. It looks thicker than this one," Freddie said, turning his head from side to side.

"You must be goin' blind, nephew. I know what the hell I'm doin'. When you sit in my chair, I create freakin' masterpieces," Butch boasted with a chuckle. "I'm like a gotdamn Picasso in this bad boy, ḥuhhh!" Butch added with a preacher's flair, making the other patrons laugh.

"Man, just fix my joint 'fore you make me late," Freddie replied with a smirk. Butch was like an uncle to Freddie for real. Their families went back generations, even before Freddie came into existence.

Butch's second barber, Mr. Shuttleworth, a short West Indian man, stopped the cut he was doing on another brother to glance over at Freddie. "Let meh fin' out da likkle young gal yuh 'bout to tie da knot wid wear da pants and got yuh runnin' home wid your nose open," Mr. Shuttleworth joked in his native tongue as the patrons joined in with laughter.

Freddie took it in stride. "Nah, man, I got a funeral to go to."

"Oh, da wedding's today?" Mr. Shuttleworth snapped back, laughing hard. "'Cause mine damn sure was a funeral! Man!" Everybody fell out.

"Nephew," Butch said between cackles, "I ain't no gay-ass joker or nuttin', and excuse my French, Mr. Shuttleworth, but if I had your hand, I'd throw mine away. What in the hell is you gettin' married fo'?"

"Yeah, mon. All dem fine women I done seen yuh wid," Mr. Shuttleworth joined in, as he shook his head in mock disbelief. "Yuh violatin' the player's code, my youth!" Everyone in the shop just exploded in laughter.

Freddie chuckled along. "Naw, Unc, you got me twisted. See, y'all see these broads at they best. But I'm tellin' you, you ain't seen shit until they butt-ass naked bangin' at your door at two in the mornin' wit' a broken heart and a butcher knife."

"Well, I don't know about the butcher knife," Butch replied, "but a buck-naked sista can bang on my door anytime!"

"Mine too!" someone in the peanut gallery yelled out.

Freddie just shook his head at the two old coons because he knew they didn't understand. You see, he was blessed with features that spoke for themselves. And he had developed a razor-sharp game that made females Silly Putty in his hands. But he wasn't a cold-hearted individual.

He was a dog to some and a player to most; still, he wasn't cold enough to not let females' emotions affect him once he was done with them. Money, sex, in that order. Those old coons hadn't seen what Freddie could do to or get from women. Besides, they had never been desired the way Freddie often was. Now the thrill was gone and the game had become more problematic than it was worth.

"Y'all just don't understand," he stated simply.

"Understand what? Pussy? Man, the day pussy becomes a problem, I'll be the first black muthafucka in line lookin' for trouble!" the third barber, Nas, exclaimed, now joining in.

"Right behind me!" one of the regular customers added.

Then, as if on cue, the door busted open and in walked a problem. Everybody abruptly stopped laughing when they saw this big black nigga standing in the door holding this fine, thick redbone firmly by the neck.

"Cream, get off me! You hurtin' me!" the redbone begged.

"Bitch, I'ma do more than that if you don't point out this Freddie muhfucka!" the big black monster-looking stranger thundered as he shook her real hard, like a ragdoll.

Freddie tensed up at the sound of his name. Then he recognized the girl. She was a stripper he'd met, or rather ran back into, at the new gentlemen's club on Richmond Street. He'd first met her back in the day at Club Knockers in their city. He had sexed her a few times before he realized she was more of a liability than an asset. By then she had already caught feelings. And with the cat standing in the doorway, he remembered her saying that her man had been in the county jail for a few weeks, and her trick ass was out sucking the next man's dick.

"In the chair, Cream! Right there!" She pointed at Freddie with satisfaction. She'd gladly take her ass whuppin' if she could see Freddie's no-good ass take one too.

Cream shoved her aside and approached Freddie. "You know her, nigga?" Cream demanded.

Freddie silently cussed himself out for leaving his gun in the car. He eyed the Goliath in front of him, realizing he was in an awkward position. He wasn't usually defending himself.

"Come on, man, you can't be serious," Freddie replied, checking all around for the upper hand.

"Answer the question, muhfucka! Let me hear you say you fucked my wife!"

Wife? Freddie thought and looked back at the redbone. He could see her smirk through the tears. The tension was too thick to reply verbally. It was either move or get moved on, and Freddie wasn't about to choose the latter. His next move was quick and effective. He spotted clippers in Butch's hand and, with lightning-fast agility, grabbed the cord and swung the clippers as hard as he could into Cream's nose. Cream grunted and fell back, but only momentarily. As Freddie got out of the chair, Cream lunged at him, only to catch a Nike ACG boot in the nuts that folded him up. A pistol fell to the floor from Cream's waistline. Freddie caught him with a crushing left that broke the gargantuan man down, proving that he had a glass jaw.

"Bitch-ass nigga! Confrontin' me over this stankin'-ass broad!" Freddie barked as he bent down to pick up the pistol. "And, you was gonna shoot me?" Freddie grabbed a handful of Cream's cornrows and brought the steel down hard on his jaw line, making him spit out a tooth. "Don't you ever bring this shit down the west end, nigga!" Freddie yelled, punctuating every word with a blow.

The redbone was in shock. She was sure Big Cream would beat Freddie down. She jumped on Freddie's back, all nails and teeth like a wolf protecting her young. "Get off my man, motherfucka!" she bellowed.

Freddie fought to get his arm loose from her grip. "This bitch," he said, and chuckled in disgust. He grabbed a handful of weave and brought her face down hard on his knee as Butch begged him to stop. She doubled over and crumpled to the ground.

"Gotdammit, Freddie, I said stop!" Butch yelled and locked his sawed-off shotgun for emphasis. He had been calling Freddie the whole time but Freddie was in a zone.

Freddie heard the metallic clack and froze mid-motion of pummeling Cream again with the pistol. Blood was everywhere. He stood up, breathing uncontrollably. "Now, nigga, take your punk ass back to the east end," Freddie said before he spat on Cream's mangled body.

"I hate you, Freddie! You ain't shit!" the red-bone screamed with her nose bleeding.

"Neither was your rotten-ass pussy! That's why I ain't givin' you what you want now!" Freddie taunted her.

"Somebody get this brother out my shop," Butch ordered. Nas and another man helped Cream and the redbone out.

"It ain't over," Cream mumbled through lips that were already beginning to swell, but Freddie didn't hear him. He turned back to Butch as Cream was carried out.

Butch just shook his head. "On second thought, I'm glad yo' pretty ass is gettin' married."

"Just fix my muthafuckin' sideburns so I can go," Freddie spat, climbing back into the chair. "Actin' like you was gonna shoot some-damn-body." Freddie smiled.

"I was. You. I love you, but I'll kill you before I let you shut my business down, neph," Butch replied with a straight face.

Freddie knew he was capable because he was an old-school gangster, but he knew he could never harm a hair on him. "Just finish me up, unc." Freddie took another look in the full-sized barber mirror. Butch the barber shook his head as he did what he was told.

Freddie inserted his key into the door of his apartment. He glanced down at himself and at all the blood splattered over his Polo shirt. He was still mad, but the more he thought about it, the funnier it became. Cream was a grown-ass man on some high school shit, fighting over a piece of ass. Now that was a violation of the player's code. If anything, he should have shaken Freddie's hand for showing him how triflin' the woman he married really was. He was sure, in her profession, she had done a little something strange for a little change while Cream was locked up. Freddie busted out laughing at the thought, as he entered the apartment.

"Freddie?" he heard a sweet voice call out from the kitchen. "Your mother said she was gonna kill you if you . . ." His fiancée, Simone, came out of the kitchen wearing only a dress slip and stockings. Putting her earrings on, she stopped short when she saw her man covered in blood, and she quickly rushed to him.

"Freddie! Are you okay? What happened?" she asked in a quick succession, checking him for wounds. Then she noticed he was laughing. "And what's so funny?"

Freddie shook his head and kissed her lightly on the lips. "Plainfield," he replied with irony.

"What you done did, boy?" she inquired with a sigh.

"Don't sweat it, babe. This joker just had his people fucked up, yo," Freddie told her, checking his watch. "Let me take a quick shower and I'll be ready, a'ight?" He quickly stepped off to avoid any more questions. Wasn't no way he was gonna tell Simone he had to smash a brother over a piece of ass.

Freddie headed down the hallway, pulling off his Black Label jacket. He pulled his Ralph Lauren Polo shirt over his head and tossed it into the hamper. He turned on the shower and tested the temperature until it was to his liking. He got undressed, pulling off his black Nike ACG boots, Antik Denim jeans, and Movado watch.

Freddie climbed into the shower and held his head under the nozzle, letting the water cascade down his face. He watched the brown residue of dried blood slip down the drain, and thought about how easily the tables could have been turned. He could be somewhere stitched up and swollen right now.

His mind was brought back by the touch of a silky hand caressing his back. He turned around to find Simone in the shower with him, smiling into his eyes. Freddie took one look at Simone's deep, dark Foxy Brown eyes, her small but pert breasts, nipples erect, and her thick hips; and he forgot all about the fight. Freddie wrapped his arms around her waist and palmed her ass. "Now we really gonna be late," he remarked.

Simone playfully hit him then wrapped her arms around his neck. "No, we're not. I'm just checkin' on my man. You came home covered in blood, laughing, and I ain't supposed to worry?"

Freddie took one long look into Simone's eyes and knew why he was marrying her. Love was written all over her face. There was no explanation that could put her concern to rest. So he just caressed her face and gently sucked her bottom lip. Then Freddie kissed her.

"Dig, ma, I love you, okay? And ain't nothing in the world gonna take me from you, so don't worry about daddy. It's okay."

Simone gazed back trustingly and nodded. "It's just . . . It's been so crazy out there, baby. I just want you to be careful."

"Wit' all this chocolate waitin' for me, a nigga gots to be careful." Freddie grinned, making her blush. "Now, can we be a little late?" he flirted, massaging her ass and pulling her closer.

"So your mother can kill me? I don't think so," she answered, kissing him softly. "But, ah, good things come to those who wait," she promised seductively, stepping out of the shower, dripping chocolate. Simone grabbed a towel and strutted out of the bathroom knowing her man was watching. She was just happy that he was home safe.

Meanwhile, a heated Dante looked at his man Cream in disgust. *This sucka for love–ass nigga*, Dante thought as one of his top crew members, Cream, lay back on the couch with his face stitched up and his jaw wired shut. He couldn't believe his man played himself over that slut of a wife of his. Dante knew the chick was trifling because half the clique had tossed her up before Cream had married her. But this was different. Freddie had washed his man out and shit had to be handled. Dante knew what had to be done. The question was how he intended to go about it. He had options.

He had a clique of wolves on the come up who would end not only Freddie, but his entire family's lives, for the right price. After putting them in position to lock down the entire east end of town with heroin and the best weed money could buy, leaving only coke sales to the scramblers, he knew there was nothing anyone of them wouldn't jump at the chance to handle. But although it wasn't a large territory that his young boys controlled, it was a lucrative one, one he was willing to risk over Cream's matter. With that money came the opportunity to expand. Dante knew he had to protect his investment because at his command his team would do whatever it took to get paper. Seeing Cream flip over a female, and a bird at that, made Dante think. What would he do if shit got hectic and cases were caught? To be a killer in the streets was one thing, but to hold water in a storm was the test of a real gangsta. Dante planned to keep a close eye on Cream.

"Ay, yo, fam, we gonna handle this shit. But on the real, son, check yo' broad. Matter of fact, you need to check that broad out, yo. Dead ass," Dante told a wired-up Cream.

Cream nodded in agreement but, deep down, wasn't nobody gonna tell him nothing about his wife. Shorty had that snapper and she had her hooks sunk deep into Cream.

"That shit won't happen no more," Cream replied, through the wire. "Believe me." Cream was naïve enough to think an ass whuppin' every now and then was enough to turn a ho into a housewife.

"You know where this nigga rest his head?" Dante inquired.

"He from the New Prozecks, but don thik he stay dhere."

"What?"

"The New Projects," Cream repeated with saliva running down the side of his mouth.

"The New Projects? Freddie from the New Projects?" Dante asked, fighting back a laugh. "Are you serious?" The only thing Dante knew of Freddie in the streets was of him being a pretty boy, nothing remotely resembling a gangsta.

Cream nodded, relieved to be understood. Talking was painful with wires holding your grill together. Every time he winced, all he could think of was finding Freddie.

"Don't stress, my dude. That joker something light," Dante assured him. He was already contemplating how he intended to approach the newly arisen beef.

Chapter Two

What the fuck is beyond the grave? That was the thought in Slug's mind as he stood, watching the casket of his great-aunt being lowered into the ground. He had come up with his mother from Goldsboro, North Carolina, to pay respects to a woman he had never known. In the process, he would congregate with a family he hardly ever saw.

Most of his kin had stayed in various parts of New Jersey. Only Slug's mother and her brother had moved down South, where Slug was born and raised. Although his mother was from Jersey, Slug was strictly Dirty South, tried and true. He wasn't one of those Southern dudes who secretly admired dudes up North for their style or accent. He was proud to be from Webbtown, as they called it in the Dirty South.

Nothing about Jersey excited him. It stunk for one thing. The smell hit him in the face as soon as he stepped out of the car at his aunt's house. Slug looked around at all the weeping faces gathered at the grave. The only faces he knew were his mother's and his Aunt Elsie's. Some of his cousins were sho' nuff fine, which kept the service interesting, but he was searching for one face in particular: his cousin Freddie's. He hadn't seen Freddie since they were twelve, the year he stopped coming down South for the summer. And even though he and Freddie spent half of each summer fighting and the other half arguing, every winter Slug looked forward to seeing his cousin Freddie, not knowing that Freddie was in Plainfield doing the same thing. But once Freddie turned fourteen, he fell upon the game he would eat off of: females.

Freddie was born in a petite one bedroom, in an apartment of a building that sat over a corner store on Chancellor Avenue and Leslie Street in the Weequahic Way section, and lived there until his mom met a man and moved out to Plainfield. He was just five years old at the time. There, he watched as man after man came into their crib and filled his mother's head full of false hopes and dreams to get what they wanted from her: sex.

He felt helpless when it came to his mother and was affected by what he had witnessed throughout the years growing up. He had also learned something about words and the impact and influence of them. A light switch was turned on and it was then that he discovered the power of the mouthpiece.

It was out in Plainfield, in the Second Street housing projects, that Freddie perfected his craft in macking the ladies. He started to become the very same type of man he watched take advantage of his mother; but he believed he was better than them. As he got older, places like Hugo's and St. Mary's in the small city were feeding grounds for him. He started out small time with females who financed his wardrobe in exchange for the fuck or the most romantic time of their lives. Once comfortable with his new lifestyle, he advanced to females with good credit and nice cars. He became a player.

Slug, on the other hand, got introduced to the dope game. He used his stomping grounds in North Carolina as his school of hard knocks. When he took to the streets the two lost contact. But when Slug heard about the funeral, he decided to go check his fam out. Besides, it was getting hot in the Boro for him.

Slug checked his watch, realized the service was well underway, and wondered if Freddie was even coming. But a few minutes later, a money green Acura pulled up. Slug squinted against the sun, and once the driver emerged, he smiled to himself. It was Freddie. He knew that bop anywhere. He had gotten taller. He was almost as tall as Slug, who was six feet three inches. He walked around the car and opened the passenger door, helping a female out of the car. As they approached, he saw Freddie fidgeting with his tie and he laughed to himself because he knew Freddie hated ties. Whenever they had to go to church down South, Freddie's mama almost had to beat him to make him leave his tie alone. He always said it felt like a noose around his neck.

"I told you we was gonna be late, Freddie," Simone scolded him through clenched but smiling teeth.

"Shit, she ain't goin' nowhere," Freddie replied playfully.

Simone nudged him hard in the ribs. "Boy! Have you any respect for the dead?" she whispered harshly.

Freddie was about to reply until he saw the brown-skinned brother in the navy blue suit. He had to fight the urge to yell, "My nigga!" across the crowd. "Oh shit, Slug," he said and made his way over to where Slug was standing. He embraced his cousin like a long-lost sibling.

"My nigga, what da deal? I didn't know you was comin'," Freddie exclaimed, trying to be quiet; but the love in his voice resonated. Just then, his mother shot him a killer look.

"Ain't nothin', cuz. I wanted to surprise you, yo," Slug replied. "Look at you, nigga, got all tall and shit." Slug glanced over at Simone standing next to Freddie's mother. "Who dat? I hope she ain't fam," Slug teased.

"Not yet, but she will be. That's my fiancée," Freddie proudly boasted.

"Fiancée? Get the fuck outta here. You gettin' married?" Slug asked, full of surprise.

The word "married" floated to his mother's ears. She turned around and whispered, "Eric."

Slug cleared his throat.

"Yo, we better chill 'fore Aunt Ann have us in coffins," Freddie joked.

"We'll holla after the funeral."

After the funeral, the majority of the family went to Freddie's mother Elsie's house to eat. Her small two-family house off of Johnson Avenue was packed with good food and hungry people to eat it. Not to mention drinks that flowed freely, making Freddie's Uncle Jerome say, slurring, "Now, I know somebody died, but who died?"

"Great-aunt Rosa," a voice reminded him.

"Who?" Uncle Jerome stammered as he staggered.

"Great-aunt—"

"I heard what you said, but why they call her great-aunt? Old ass. She leave me any money?"

"Nah."

"Well, did she ever give me any money?"

"Probably not."

"Then, what the hell was so damn great about her?" he commented, drawing a little drunken laughter as well as a little divine displeasure.

Freddie and Slug were out on the porch catching up on old times when Simone walked out onto the porch. She stood on her tiptoes to kiss Freddie. "Here you are. I've been looking all over for you."

"Aw, shit, cuz. Let me find out shorty got a leash on you already," Slug joked, making Simone and Freddie laugh.

"No," Simone replied, "but your mother is looking for you to take pictures, and she said to put your tie on."

Freddie looked down at the mangled tie draped over his neck. "Well, tell her you can't find me."

"No, I ain't gonna lie to your mama. Just come on."

"Well, damn, can I meet your fiancée or what, cuz?" Slug asked. Simone had been busy helping out, so they still hadn't met formally.

"My bad, fam. Simone, this is my cousin Eric."

"Slug," he cut in.

"Nigga, your mama named you Eric. And, Eric, this is Simone."

"Hello, Eric."

"Slug, shorty. And I must say, if you getting married, I'm glad you picked a sho' nuff stallion. Turn around, mama, let me see what you workin' wit." Slug chuckled half jokingly.

Simone looked at Freddie with a nervous giggle, but Freddie put her at ease. "Don't pay this country-ass farmer no mind, babe." Then he turned to Slug. "A'ight, nigga, don't make me whup yo' ass out this piece," he said, faking a jab.

Slug threw up his mitts in mock defense. "Just 'cause you almost as tall as me don't mean I can't still beat yo' ass, young'un," Slug remarked.

"Still? Nigga, when?"

Simone saw that they were in their own world, so she respected her man's space. She kissed him on the cheek and said, "Don't forget your tie." Then she dipped back into the house.

"Cuz, I don't know about you, but fuck a picture. Show me what this pissant city is all about.

Where the pussy at?" Slug asked. "Or do shorty got you wearin' a screw-off dick." They both laughed.

"Nigga, if you only knew," Freddie replied. "Come on, let's roll out."

Chapter Three

Freddie cruised through downtown Plainfield in deep thought while Slug rode shotgun. He still couldn't shake the close call back at the barbershop. All he could think about was how things could have gone left and he could have been the one on the barbershop's hair-filled floor instead of Cream. Just when he thought he had closed all of his player doors, something came back to bite him on his ass. Now here it was: he had unnecessary beef over a chick he barely got $1,000 out of in money and merchandise.

He shook his head in disgust as he reflected on how low budget of a stripper Cream's chick was. He recalled the one night he posted up at Liquid Assets in South Plainfield for hours and held her down, so she wouldn't get robbed or sweated as she exited the club at the end of the evening. He watched as she went to the back room at least a half dozen times and paraded around the room trying to make her paper. Despite the wall-to-wall crowded club, he noticed how the other girls out-danced her to get major bread tossed their way. When she had told him she had made less than a G that night, he knew she wasn't about her business. She later proved to be a liability rather than an asset. She would up catching feelings for Freddie and called herself stopped dancing, thinking he would respect her more and there could possibly be something solid between them. She received a rude awakening, after Freddie cut her off like an umbilical cord. He snickered as the image of her pleading with tearful eyes for him to be her man invaded his thoughts.

"Man, what the fuck is this?" The sound of Slug's country drawl brought him back. Freddie peered over at his cousin. He chuckled as Slug skimmed through the CD cases scattered between the seats of Freddie's Acura. "D-Block, D-Block, Kay Slay, Kay Slay, Kay Slay, Jay-Z, Jay-Z, Biggie! Nigga, where the 'Pac? Face? The real shit?"

"Real? You just said it: Biggie!" Freddie answered as he drove through Newark.

"Man, fuck Biggie! 'Pac!"

"A'ight, watch yo' mouth, country-ass nigga. Up North is Biggie land, yo," Freddie replied.

"Well, do y'all got Thug Passion? Or are y'all still drinkin' Alizé?" Slug joked.

"Nigga, I'm 'bout to take you where you can get all the passion you want. You wit' Freddie, cuzzo. Lay back."

"Then let's get it crunk then."

And crunk they got. Freddie took him to the livest clubs in the Union County area and the rawest strip clubs. They even went to Plainfield to the Gentlemen's Club, even though Freddie had beef with Cream, who was from the area. But he was feeling too good to give a fuck. He hadn't seen Slug in so long. It was good to see his family and catch up on the last few years.

At the Gentlemen's Club, Freddie's name rang bells like Sunday mass so he got the VIP treatment. He broke Slug off with a private lap dance in the downstairs part of the club and a side shot of head from one of the strippers from his hood on the low, before they rolled out pissy drunk at one in the morning. Freddie was slipping in the worst way because the liquor made him forget about Cream as they walked across the street to Jay Cee's Lounge to order what Freddie felt were some of the best dinners in town. But aside from having good food and plenty of liquor, it was also a good spot to get caught slipping, and Freddie knew that. Fortunately, the last place Cream and Dante expected Freddie to be was on Richmond Street in their neck of the Crawford, so their slip made his slip irrelevant. Freddie greeted a few dudes he knew standing outside Jay Cee's and introduced Slug to his two homeboys Wajdee and Dance at the door as they entered the bar.

"Yo, son," Freddie said in between bites of greasy chicken wings, "what you into down there?"

Slug sipped his fruit punch while eyeing one of the bartenders. "You know how cuz get down. Gotta trap the scrilla. Shit hectic now though. Seem like e'rebody and they mama catchin' cases or snitchin' to come from under."

Freddie nodded. He understood because Jersey was the same way. That was one of the main reasons he stayed away from the dope game. "Damn, shorty down South thick," Slug chimed in reference to the bartender.

"That's Tawanna."

"Well, I wanna," Slug joked.

"You shot the fuck out, cuzzo."

"If you say so. But seriously, cuz, I'm tellin' you, shit is sweet down in the Dirty. I just need the right connect to get it poppin' proper," Slug added, looking at Freddie with a gleam in his eye.

"What?" Freddie asked, really questioning the look while wiping the grease off his hands. "Nigga, I ain't no connect. I don't fuck around."

"But you know who do. I'm sayin', cuz, I came to see you, true. But I also came to see what you could do for me. Put a nigga down with some peeps," Slug suggested, lighting a Newport.

Freddie did know a few heavyweights, but he didn't deal with them on a regular basis, and he didn't want to run his cousin up on a snag. But he knew of one connect who was definitely straight. Only problem was he was really trying to phase him out of his life.

"Man, wit' the right connect, I could lock the Boro down," Slug boasted. "I got a team of young'uns, and all they do is grind sun up to dinnertime. Shit, if we had a connect . . ." Slug said while blowing smoke straight up in the air and savoring the taste of chicken in his mouth.

"What happened? Caught a case?"

"Nah, cuz, a cross," Slug snarled wickedly. "I put the cross down on some bitch-ass niggas."

"And now you want me to hook you up wit' another one?" Freddie asked, thinking Slug must be crazy.

"Naw, cuz, you fam so I'll keep shit official. Just them Miami boys tried to play me, so I showed 'em how Webbtown get down."

Slug began to explain what had been going on for the last few months. Three niggas named Mo Mo, Tyrone, and Black came from Miami on the strength of their cousin Bird, who lived in the Boro. But Bird got killed a week before they were to come through with the weight. Since Bird and Slug was tight, they stepped to Slug at the wake and asked him to hold them down. He agreed.

They started him off light, with an eighth of a kilo, and it was gone in an hour. Needless to say, they were feeling Slug's grind, so they gave him another, which he did the same thing with. They then hit him off with half a brick, which Slug got rid of in three days, in straight twenties and fifties. The Miami niggas felt they had a gold mine, so they went back to Florida and came back to hit Slug off with a whole bird. In the process of moving it, one of Slug's young'uns got hit with the eighth cut up in twenties. On top of that, Slug used some of the Miami cats' money to bail him out. They grumbled, but decided to charge it to the game. But the grumbling got louder and started to get on Slug's nerves.

"Yo, Slug, this shit ain't no game. What up wit' dat paper on that big eighth?" Money growled. Slug was vexed because the nigga had jumped

out the car with a gun in his belt, purposely visible, and Slug was talking to two chicks in Green Acres at the time. He was already tired of these niggas paging him constantly, so he decided right then to dead these niggas on their paper.

"Mo Mo, chill, dog. Slug don't even get down like that. I'ma have your paper, my word. But I do need another one of them twangs and I'll grind it for free to straighten my face on what I owe." Slug tried to sound as lame as he could in order to rock the nigga to sleep.

Mo Mo's greed and his thinking that he was a real killer made him reply, "A'ight, yo. But I'm telling you, Slug, you better not fuck this up."

"I ain't man. I got you, yo, I got you," he repeated, but Mo Mo didn't know what "I got you" meant in that context. It meant "you beat." The two girls, Donesha and Li'l Monica, giggled because they knew what he meant.

"You better," Mo Mo concluded before bopping back to his Navigator like he had put his gangsta down.

An hour later, Slug had another whole bird and the better half of the last kilo they had given him. That's when he stopped returning their pages and the Miami boys heard that now he was flossing paper, their paper.

"Y'all seen Slug?" Black asked in West Haven, trying to scare up a few of Slug's young'uns. It wasn't like Slug was hiding either. He was everywhere, all the hot spots, saying shit like, "Fuck it, buy the bar out. It's on them Miami niggas!" He was straight clowning them in the club.

Girls would see Slug driving around town and joke, "You better be careful, them Miami niggas lookin' fo' you!"

"Here I go." Slug would smile. But he got tired of their threats.

So one night at Leo's Liquor House, when he heard "There go them Miami cats, Slug," he decided to take it to them. Full of Hpnotiq and Hennessy, feeling like the Incredible Hulk, he went outside with 9 mm Rugers in both hands.

"Y'all niggas lookin' for Slug? Here go Slug!" He commenced dumping shells on the Black Navigator. They tried to fire back but Slug didn't take cover; he just stood square blazing until he had shot Tyrone, giving him a permanent bag, and made Swiss cheese of Black's Navi. They finally skidded away, trying to tend to their leaking friend in need of emergency medical attention.

After that, every time Slug saw them niggas, he was headhunting. In clubs, at hotels, at the waffle place, even at red lights, until finally them niggas bowed out.

"Fuck it, Slug. Keep that shit, yo." They sent word to Slug, and just as fast as it had begun, it ended. Slug watched them niggas, but he saw the pussy had come out of them and he let it go.

That was where he was now, without a connect. Freddie sat back and listened to Slug's story, knowing he wasn't bullshitting. Slug had always been wild, that's how he got his nickname: Slugger. In his younger days, two older cats had tried to take his bike and he beat them both into a coma and landed himself in juvenile detention for eighteen months. He was thirteen.

Freddie knew Slug was serious, but he didn't want to get involved with the dope game.

"Nigga, I ain't askin' you to get down, just put me on and I'll break you off e'er month," Slug proposed.

Freddie stared out into the club. It sounded sweet, but he wasn't sure he wanted to have his name mixed up in it, period. "Dig, Slug, let me think—" He was cut off by his cell phone ringing. "Hold up," he said, answering the phone. "Yo."

"You busy?" the sultry voice inquired.

Damn. He should've known it was her. Even through the loud music he recognized her voice.

"Well?" she teased. "You must be if you ain't answerin'."

"Naw, yo." Freddie looked at Slug, who pretended not to be listening. "I'm just chillin'."

"So you pistol whippin' niggas in barbershops now?" She giggled.

Freddie chuckled and finally realized where he was. "What? You followin' me or somethin'?"

"No, but they are. I was kinda worried about you so I just called to check on you," she replied. "Where you at?"

"Jay Cee's," Freddie answered.

"You got somethin' to prove?"

"Naw."

"I can't tell. You all up in they hood, like it's sweet and them negroes is vexed wit' you."

He didn't want to say he was drunk and forgot, so he explained, "My cousin up from down South, so I wanted to show him a good time."

"Hmm hmm hmm," she hummed knowingly. "Let me guess. You took 'im to the Gentlemen's Club. Ain't you tired of them stank heffas yet? Or are you tryin' to fuck all of 'em?"

"Naw."

"Then, are you tryin' to fuck . . . me?" That was what kept Freddie open on her. She spoke her mind and pulled no punches.

"I'm sayin' . . ." Half of him wanted to say no, the half that was his heart and belonged to Simone. But his other half, which was his dick, was already rock hard.

She giggled. "Nigga, quit frontin'. We both know what you wanna say. Tell your cousin I said hi and bye. I wanna see you, boo."

"Where you at?" Freddie glanced down at his watch, seeing it was approaching 3 a.m.

"Where you think? Where I'm always waitin' for you." He didn't respond but she anticipated his state of mind. "I'll leave the door unlocked for you but, um, hurry up. I already started without you." She ended the conversation with the sound of her kiss that Freddie imagined on the head of his dick. Freddie hung up.

"Nigga, that ain't wifey, yo," Slug teased while laughing, then bellowed, "Booty call!"

Slug didn't know the half. She was the only female Freddie couldn't bring himself to cut off. She was the type of mistress every nigga wished they had: fine and a freak who asked no questions and had no expectations. Plus her paper was long. She was booty call heaven!

"Don't worry about Slug, cuz. I ain't no cock blocker. Go 'head. I'ma go back 'cross the street and try to get that bitch in the thong to welcome me to the city."

Thong? "They all got on thongs, yo."

"Exactly. Country niggas got horse dicks, nigga!" Slug laughed.

Freddie laughed with him but refused to leave Slug in the east end alone. "Alone?" Slug smirked then opened his suit coat to reveal a nine tucked into his shoulder holster. "You heard what the fuck Dr. Dre said in 'G Thang,'" he spat, believing Freddie to be familiar with the popular West Coast rap song. "I don't go nowhere without Nina." Slug added.

"Nigga, you brought that shit way up here?" Freddie asked, full of surprise.

"Shit. Rather get caught wit' it than wit'out it," Slug replied, making Freddie think about his own beef and the fact that he had left his gun in the car.

Despite Slug's protests, Freddie wouldn't leave until Slug picked out a bowlegged chick with big titties and slid into her silver BMW 325i. He jumped into his Audi Q7 SUV, eager to make his rendezvous spot.

Chapter Four

His conscience was killing him the whole ride
on Route 22 East on his way to the Robert Treat
Hotel in Newark. He knew he had a good woman
at home, but it was like his dick was driving.
He couldn't understand himself. When he was
with Simone, it was all about her and it was all
love. But once he hit the streets, it was money
and sex. And if a chick ain't have both, he wasn't
interested.

He told himself for the millionth time that
this was the last time. After this, he'd cut her off
cold. But he knew it was all a lie as he got on the
elevator and rode to the Presidential suite.

When he reached the double doors, he saw
that she had kept her word. The door was
cracked with a DO NOT DISTURB sign hanging
from the knob. He entered and closed the door
behind him. The spacious suite smelled just like
Tiffany, her favorite fragrance, and he could

hear the soft melodies of "Focus the Truth" by Floetry, her favorite song.

Freddie looked down at his feet and found her Chanel slingback heels, one after the other, lying there. As he walked, he found her open-back black Gucci dress on the floor near the plush couch and imagined how she had slithered her mahogany frame out of it. He approached the bedroom door and pushed it open to find her lying on the bed, completely naked, and touching herself like Tweet with the help of a long black vibrator.

She was ghetto thick—some might say big-boned—but she wore her weight well because she had no stomach and a small waist. It made her luscious hips curve even more into thick mahogany thighs that now were spread eagle, exposing the pink of her inner flesh to Freddie's attentive eyes. She slowly slid the sex toy in and out, taking it in as far as it would go, making her curl her beautifully pedicured toenails, then pulling it back out. She ground her hips in small, seductive circles. Her free hand massaged her large 36 Ds, pinching her nipples and placing them in her mouth, teasing them with her own tongue. The look on her gorgeous face was one of near ecstasy and sensual anticipation. It turned her on more to see Freddie standing in the door, watching her pleasure herself.

"Does it look good to you, baby?" she asked, stopping to let out a whimper and a moan. "Because it damn sure feels good to me." She slithered her right hand down in between her legs and used her pointer and middle fingers to spread her bottom lips just above her clit.

Freddie leaned against the door, enjoying the show. She lifted one of her shapely legs and arched her back, angling the dildo with her left hand, upward to hit her G-spot.

"Uhh. Say my name, Freddie," she cooed. She licked her lips seductively as the sex toy slid inside of her.

"Gina," he snarled.

"Say it like, ohhh, you want this pussy." She closed her eyes and bit down on her luscious lip.

"Gina," he repeated. "But how can I want what's already mine?" He smirked, knowing it was.

Gina smiled back and sat up on her knees, putting the play toy aside. "Come show me it's yours then." She parted her legs like the Red Sea.

Freddie could see the flames burning in her lustful eyes and he smiled. He knew he was the one who had lit the fire in them. He crossed the room and slid in between Gina's legs. He wrapped his arms around her waist then leaned in to kiss her. But she turned her face away abruptly.

"No. I don't feel like being kissed tonight. I just wanna fuck," she told him as she unbuckled his pants and slid her hand inside, grabbing his dick. She pulled his pants down, and at the same time she laid eyes on his manhood and cooed, "Damn, I missed you, daddy." She slid it into her warm mouth, wrapping her full, juicy lips around the shaft, licking along the whole length. Then she took his nuts one at a time into her mouth.

"Because he is the truth," Floetry played in the background.

"I wanna play a game," Gina whispered seductively.

Freddie was still feeling the sensation of her tongue on his sack. "What kind of game?" His interest was piqued. Nothing ever surprised him when it came to her, and he always benefitted from it, which was why he was eager to know what she had in mind.

She replied with a smile and turned around doggie style, bending over the bed and cocking one knee up on it. She reached between her legs and grabbed Freddie's dick, rubbing it against her clit, then stuck only the head in and tightened her muscles around him. Freddie reached to grab her ass but she abruptly stopped him.

"Uh-uh, you can't touch me and you can't move," she ordered softly, slowly taking more of him inside of her. Freddie thought it would be easy until she took his whole dick and began to long stroke herself, spreading her pussy lips with her fingers. His hands began to tremble trying to keep from palming her pretty, voluptuous ass and ramming himself deep inside of her, but Gina was in control and she intended to keep it that way.

"Can you take this pussy, daddy? Ooh, can . . . can you?" She spoke in spurts between moans. She placed both her feet on the floor and grabbed her ankles, grinding Freddie until he couldn't take it anymore.

The sensation of a woman's body to a man's hand is underestimated, until he's deprived of it. He cuffed her thighs in desperation making her gasp and giggle as he took control.

"I knew you couldn't handle this pussy, damn."

As strong of a dude as he would have liked to believe himself to be, Freddie couldn't take it any longer. He switched his hands to Gina's hips and gripped them tightly. He thrust his own hips in rapid succession, causing her ass cheeks to clap like applause was in order. Gina let out cries of ecstasy until she damn near lost her voice. It was if she could feel Freddie's dick up inside of her intestines. She got off on what she called pleasurable pain.

"Let me be daddy's freak! If I can't be daddy's girl, let me be daddy's freak!" she groaned.

"You are daddy's freak," Freddie replied.

"You promise?"

"Definitely," he grunted as he pumped his full length as deep as it could go.

"Ugh! Make your freak cum. Freddie, make me." Gina shuddered and her knees got weak. Her body felt as if it were going through an out-of-body experience.

"Oh, fuck!" she cried out.

Her legs began to shake as she curled her pretty toes. Her muscles spazzed as she tried to gain control over them. She stretched out on her stomach with Freddie still inside her. She continued to have multiple orgasms as he switched up his stroke. Gina squeezed her ass cheeks and released them as Freddie delivered short, strong pumps inside of her love box.

"Ooh, yes," she growled.

Freddie slipped his thumb in her brown eye as he bit into the right side of her neck. He brushed her hair to the side to gain better access to her spot. Gina's body cringed as a thousand volts jolted through her, when Freddie's tongue hit her earlobe. She knew he knew that was the one place that would drive her wild. She began to rotate her hips, forcing Freddie's dick deeper inside of her. Freddie could feel her pussy getting wetter. He removed his thumb and rose up. Gina started throwing her ass back at him like she was half snake. That was all it took. Freddie could feel the tidal wave building up. He tried to match Gina's strokes but he couldn't hold it anymore. He released his soul deep inside of her right before he collapsed on top of her.

"Damn, baby, what you do to me?" she asked more of herself than of him.

"Whatever you want me to," he responded, and kissed her between the shoulder blades, causing a shiver to run along her spine.

"Don't do that or that young girl won't ever see you again," she joked to hide the tear rolling down her cheek. "Get up and get on your stomach. Let me massage you."

Freddie rolled over, pants still around his ankles, and turned onto his stomach. Gina sat on his ass and began to massage his shoulders. She could tell he was tense.

"So you gonna tell me what happened?"

Freddie shrugged slightly, feeling the massage. "Some chicken-head stripper and her man caught feelin's. That dude Cream."

"Yeah, I know Cream. He one of Tay's people." Gina sighed. "You want me to get somebody to holla at 'im?"

Freddie knew what Gina meant by her question because her family was heavy in the game all over Jersey, as deep as Atlantic City. The Peterson clan was well known and well respected. None of the women in the family worked unless they wanted to, or they had their own business. Gina, herself, had never worked a day in her life, but she lived a lavish life. Her only official source of income was a foreign car lot in Montclair, New Jersey, which she hardly ever visited and was run by two Jews in her name. The business had been a gift from her uncle, Lou Peterson, who doted on her. All she had to do was say the word and Dante and his whole clique would be marked for death. But Freddie's manhood wouldn't allow him to let a woman handle his beef.

"Holla for what? Fuck them jokers. I can handle me, yo," he boasted.

"I knew you was gonna say some ol' fly bullshit like that." Gina climbed off his back and pushed him onto his side. "Freddie, listen to me. These niggas is not playin' wit' you. Yeah, it's stupid, but since when you known niggas wit' guns for hearts to think smart? What you gonna do when Tay and them come for you?" she asked with clear concern.

Freddie rose up on his elbows, agitated because his young mind thought she was questioning his manhood. "Yo, you talkin' to me like I'm some coward or something! Fuck you mean what I'ma do? I'ma do me! Niggas bleed just like me!" he spat.

"Thank you, Biggie Smalls," Gina remarked sarcastically, rolling her eyes to the ceiling. She framed his face with her hands, admiring his beauty and loving his warmth but loathing his youthful ego. "Did I say you were a coward, Freddie? Did I? What? You think being a man is so-called 'doin' you'? Baby . . . My sweet, sweet baby. The measure of a man is not this," she said, grabbing his dick, "or how bad he can be. It's this," she said, tapping his forehead. "I know you got it in you, Freddie. You smarter than that. Don't let these people drag you down. Think. I see so much in you. That's why I . . ." She stopped short, hoping he didn't know what she'd started to say, but he did.

"You what?"

Gina palmed her head, then ran her hand through her microbraids and waved him off.

"Just . . . go home, Freddie. Do you, like you said. Go on home to your little girlfriend and do you. Shit, I'm a grown-ass woman. I ain't got time for all this high school bullshit," she stated, fighting to sound strong and not let any tears flow.

"A'ight, yo," was all he replied and got up, pulling up his pants.

Once he was dressed, he looked at Gina who had her back to him, looking out the window. He knew what she was feeling and, he couldn't front, he was glad she felt that way about him. Gina was a jewel and he was glad she was his jewel, even if it was only on the low.

"Can I have a kiss before I go?" Freddie teased.

"I thought I told you I ain't wanna be kissed tonight," she answered.

He checked the time on his phone and smirked. "Technically, it's not night anymore." He paused. "It's almost five."

"Still no." She rolled her eyes.

"Please," he begged with a smile.

"No."

He crept up on the bed and tried to kiss her, but she turned away.

"Oh, you gonna kiss me!" he demanded, tickling her along her sides, knowing that drove her crazy.

She laughed until she stuttered, "Freddie, stop! I'll kiss you! I'll kiss you!"

"A'ight then," he said triumphantly.

He slithered his tongue in her mouth, which she caught firmly between her teeth.

"I'll bite it off if you tickle me one more time," she warned playfully.

"Zoo gaa a winna!" His words came out as gibberish.

"I got a winner?" she decoded Freddie's words.

"Yeah!" he confessed.

She released his tongue, caressed it with her own, then broke the kiss and looked him in the eyes. "Then act like one." It was moments like these she cherished.

Freddie held her gaze. "I'll call you," he said as he backpedaled toward the room's door. He turned around and then exited the room.

"And I don't care what you say. I'ma take care of that for you!" she yelled after him. After she didn't get a reply and heard the door close, she breathed a sigh of relief, glad she had made her point.

Driving home, Freddie thought about the knowledge Gina had dropped on him about the measure of a man. She had seen right through him and she knew his pride was defi-

nitely running away with his reason. He had
fixed his mind to go to war; whatever happened,
happened. And for what? If he was faced with
a "kill or be killed" situation, Freddie wouldn't
hesitate to kill. But then what? He wasn't tryin'
to see prison for a murder rap. Then there was
the flipside: if Cream killed him.

He shook off that thought. Kill him over a
piece of pussy they both knew was no good?
With all this pussy in the world, Freddie wasn't
tryin' to die over no piece, regardless of who it
was. *So, yeah, let Gina's fam squash the beef.* He
had nothing to prove and niggas knew he wasn't
no sucka, so fuck it, he figured, and get on with
life.

Thinking of the situation and Gina's support
drew him that much closer to her, even though
he tried repeatedly to convince himself that
there wasn't anything to their relationship and
that he could cut her off at will, like a chain
smoker who claimed he could quit anytime he
wanted. Cats knew cigarettes were killing them,
but that puff . . .

Gina was like that puff to him. She was what
he craved after every meal, and his meal was
Simone. Just thinking of his fiancée and watching the sunrise made his heart sink. Of course he
had an alibi: Slug. They had hung out all night.

But if he claimed he loved her, why was it so easy to lie to her over and over again? Who was he fooling: her or himself? These were the thoughts running through Freddie's mind.

Chapter Five

Freddie pulled up to his and Simone's one-bedroom apartment in North Plainfield. He quietly turned the key. The plan was to enter his crib unnoticed and jump into the shower, then slide into bed next to a sleeping Simone like he had done so many times before. But what he smelled made his guilt turn into sickness: pancakes and turkey sausage. He could clearly hear the sizzle of the sausage as the buttery smell of pancakes wafted through the air. "Damn," he cursed to himself under his breath. He knew there was no way he was going to be able to bypass one of his favorite breakfast meals without Simone becoming suspicious.

"Hey, baby. I'm in the kitchen," she called out sweetly.

All he could think about was the song "It's a Thin Line Between Love and Hate."

"Are you hungry, honey? Did you eat yet?" Freddie was bombarded with this as soon as he walked into the kitchen. He found Simone at the stove in one of his COWBOYS VS. EVERYBODY T-shirts. He felt like shit to see the smile she flashed him as he quickly kissed her. He prayed and hoped Gina's fragrance wasn't clinging to his clothes.

"Where's Slug?" she asked, looking over his shoulder.

"I, uh, dropped him off at Mama's. He ain't wanna cock block a brotha," he flirted, only because a lie is best swallowed with laughter, and Simone did laugh.

"I thought y'all would be hungry so I fixed y'all some pancakes," she said, gesturing to a stack of eight golden brown cakes next to the stove as she worked on the ninth.

He gently pushed her shoulder-length hair away from her face and caressed her cheek. "Damn, girl. Will you marry me?" He smiled.

Simone held up her left hand and wiggled the two carats on her finger. "I'm sorry, I'm already engaged."

"I hope that joker appreciate what he got."

She blushed. "I think he does."

"Yeah?" he asked, inching closer for her kiss.

"Yeah," she replied and met him halfway for his.

Simone was his heart, and not once did he regret asking her to marry him. He pulled her close to him and pressed his body up against hers, running his hands up her shirt and tickling her nipples. She could feel herself going there, so she floated back to say, "I hope I didn't slave over this hot stove for nothin'." She smiled.

"Oh, yeah, the pancakes. I almost forgot," Freddie replied. "Damn, let me get my plate." He reached up in the cupboard, took out a plate, and set it on the table. Then he poured syrup all over the plate.

"What are you doing?" Simone asked, thinking he forgot the pancakes.

"Getting ready to eat," he replied, picking her up as he lifted the T-shirt to reveal that she was pantyless. Then he sat her in the sticky syrup.

"Freddie!" she screamed, tickled, trying to squirm out of the plate. "You got me all sticky!"

"Not yet." He grinned, laying her back across the table as he rubbed her inner thighs until they were coated with syrup.

"Freddie," she purred, "This is craz—"

The feeling of his tongue tracing along her walls caught her words in her throat. He gently rubbed her clit with his thumb until it stood perky; then he began to suck on it and Simone grabbed the back of his head, trying to direct his tongue while running her fingers through his short, curly hair.

"Ooh, I love you, Freddie. I love youuuu," she moaned, allowing Freddie's tongue to dance and flicker inside of her garden.

He cocked her legs higher and licked along the whole length of her lips until he reached that sensitive spot near her asshole, making her gasp for air.

"Don't stop, baby, don't stop," she begged, and he didn't, licking, nibbling, and sucking her until she felt it in her stomach.

"Don't ever leave me, Freddie, please don't. I love you sooo much," she groaned passionately, rotating her hips to the rhythm of his tongue. "Right there, Freddie, right . . . Wait, wait," she cried out in ecstasy as her love juices flowed out, mingling with the syrup, and her whole body shook and spasmed.

He tickled her along her thigh, making her giggle. "Freddie, I'ma kill you if I'm stuck to this plate. Nasty-ass self. And mark this plate 'cause I ain't never eating out of it!"

"Freddie! Ay, yo, Freddie! Wake yo' ass up, nigga! This Slug!" Freddie had answered the phone in a daze. It seemed like he had just gone to sleep when Simone was shaking him and handing him the phone.

"Slug?" he croaked. "What time is it?"

"I don't know, like ten-somethin'. Shit, time to get up. Come get me, nigga!" Slug yelled into the phone in his usual hyper tone.

"Come get you from where?" Freddie asked, slowly coming around.

"I'm downtown Plainfield, yo. Went on a little shoppin' spree. Now I need a ride 'cause I don't know how to get to your crib."

Freddie wanted to tell him to take a cab but he was up now. *Fuck it.* He checked his watch: 10:11. "A'ight, yo, gimme about half an hour. Meet me in front of the music and book store in an hour."

"I don't know where the fuck that's at. You gotta gimme a name or address or somethin'"

"It's called Muzik N Motion & Real Edutainment Books. You can't miss it, next to a jewelry store called Bong's."

"Oh, shit, I was just down that way. I brought me this platinum chain and medallion from the Asian joker, said he knew you."

"Yeah, that's my man Bong. Good dude. But yeah, right next door."

"A'ight, I'll be there."

"One."

"One."

Freddie rolled out of bed still dressed in his suit. He was so tired he had just crashed. He got up and took off his clothes to take a shower. Then he got dressed in a Black Label shirt and jacket and a pair of Red Monkey jeans, finishing it off with a pair of all-black high-top Pradas before grabbing his keys and heading out the door.

Chapter Six

The early afternoon traffic was light as Freddie made his way downtown, pumping a mixtape CD from a young, local upcoming artist by the name of Base. The artist's father was from his projects so he had copped a copy of the I'm Almost There independent mixtape. What started out as mere support ended up becoming some of his most favorite music to listen to in rotation with Big Sean, Future, J-Cole, and Kendrick Lamar. The lyrics—*I roll me a blunt and I sit and I meditate. So many snakes in the grass, I don't walk I just levitate*—echoed through the speakers as he whipped Simone's Acura through Plainfield's Front Street like only Jersey dudes could. He was in and out of lanes while timing yellow lights. He got downtown ten minutes to one, made a right onto Park Avenue, then a left on Second Street, until he reached the parking lot behind downtown. He fed the empty meter, thinking about the meter maids who lived for writing tickets in that particular area. He had gotten caught a few times, hopping out of his whip and running into a store for a fresh fitted or pair of kicks. If he didn't know any better, he would have sworn that they hid behind cars watching and waiting for shoppers like him.

Freddie cut through the music and book store in search of Slug. He was not in the mood to be searching around downtown, so he hoped Slug would be where he'd told him they'd meet. As he walked through Muzik N Motion & Real Edutainment Books, he picked up the latest DJ Don Juan CD and J. M. Benjamin's last two books, *My Manz and 'Em*, which had the housing projects where Freddie was from on the cover, and *Ride or Die Chick*. Freddie had always supported the local author, who was actually the owner of the establishment and happened to be from his hood. On many nights, rather mornings, he had spilled out of the owner's after-hour parties he threw from two to seven a.m., with someone sexy and curvaceous to take back to his awaiting hotel room's bed.

Glad to see Slug at the proper place, Freddie greeted him.

"What the deal, cuz?" Slug said, giving him a pound. "Let me cop this *Best of 2Pac* so we'll have somethin' to ride to."

"Yeah, okay, nigga." He protested. "Picture you rollin' in my shit bumpin' that shit," Freddie joked.

"Cuz, you trippin'. And if you ever come to the South, don't say that shit too loud, unless you want a problem," Slug warned. "Niggas don't play when it come to Pac."

Freddie paid him no mind. Slug shook his head at his cousin's nonchalant demeanor. He chalked it up as a Northern thing.

"I'll be right back." He ran into the store and paid for the CD, then gathered up his bags.

"It's on the Miami boys, huh?" Freddie joked again once he'd returned, referring to all the bags and sneaker boxes.

"Naw, yo. It's on that stripper broad," Slug smoothly replied. "Shorty got that paper, yo. She damn near had a G in tips."

Freddie stopped walking. "Come on, Slug. Don't tell me you did some petty shit like that."

"Shit, they do it to us! Soon as that chick fell out, I hit her ass up, grabbed a cab, and told *papi* to drop me off down here!"

Freddie couldn't help but laugh. And Slug was right: females in the game were good for hitting a brotha's pockets and creeping out the back door. Freddie laughed it off.

"Hold up, let me go see my man Bong. He 'posed to be makin' me this new piece in white gold. Then we out."

Chapter Seven

Cream stood inside Dante's brother Mannie's bodega on Fifth and Richmond Street impatiently. He couldn't stand Mannie. Mannie thought that just because he was the boss's brother, he was boss too. Cream only tolerated his ass on the strength of Tay. "Ay, Mannie! Nigga, is you ready yet?"

Mannie ignored him and continued to talk on his cell. Cream sighed heavily and turned to look out the door. He was tired and his wired jaw ached, but he had to run Mannie around to make the pickups down on Sixth Street. He glanced up the street just out of boredom and his eyes caught the gleam of a green Acura RL. He looked again because his heart leaped and pounded in his chest. It was Freddie's car!

"Hell yeah! Yeah! Ay, yo, Mannie!" Cream exclaimed, pulling his burner out and shaking Mannie's shoulder.

Mannie looked up, agitated. "Nigga, can't you see I'm on the phone? And fuck you doin' wit' a pistol out in my spot?"

"It's that bitch-ass nicca, Freddie!" Cream barked. "I see his car, yo! I'ma lay his ass down right now!"

Mannie knew about the situation and laughed on the inside because he too had fucked Cream's wife, and was still fucking her whenever the opportunity arose. But he knew Tay wanted an example made out of this nigga Freddie. Word got around the streets how their squad rolled, so it was on.

"I'll call you back," Mannie said into the phone and hung up. "Where?"

"Up the block," Cream informed him, cocking his four pound.

"A'ight, yo. We gonna lay his ass. And when he sees your face . . ." Mannie let his words drift off because Cream already knew the outcome.

Freddie and Slug rounded the corner of short Third Street and Richmond, on their way back to the car. The two had gone into Jay Cee's and thrown back a couple of shots of Henny and Coronas, seeing as how Freddie had to see his man Wajdee for a minute, who worked at the spot. He knew he was pressing his luck coming back into enemy territory, but having his cousin in the area and knowing how his cousin got down had him a little carefree. Freddie chirped his alarm as they approached, and Slug went around to the passenger side.

By this time, Mannie and Cream had made their way up the block and were a short distance away from the street Freddie was parked on, locked and loaded. Had Freddie, or Slug for that matter, glanced to their left, they may have noticed Mannie and Cream.

"There he go!" Cream pointed out, making his move.

Freddie inserted the key into the car door and looked up, about to answer Slug's last question, when he saw a familiar face emerge from across the street. *Cream*. They were already swinging out the door and raising the steel to clap.

"Slug!"

Slug took one look at Freddie's face and knew there was no time to ask what, how, or where. His ghetto instincts kicked in and he knew the problem was behind him. As he reached for his pistol, dropping his bags, he dove over the hood of the car just as the passenger window exploded from the gun blast.

"Freddie!" Slug hollered, hoping Freddie hadn't gotten hit too.

"I'm good!" Freddie said, pinned against the door, nervously trying to get in the car. Slug used the hood as cover and fired back at Cream and Mannie, who were crouched down behind an old Buick.

Slug only had one and a half clips gone before Freddie got the door open and reached under the driver's seat. His hand fell on Cream's nine. He grabbed and cocked it, and came up firing. Short Third and Richmond Streets erupted in gunfire, screams, and a stampede of pedestrians running for cover.

Mannie's clip gave out. "Yo, Cream, let's be out! Five-o comin'!"

Cream heard the sirens but his focus was on Freddie. He kept firing and watched Mannie, out of his peripheral, make a dash. Freddie leaped up with a barrage of bullets, two of which found Mannie in the back of the head. Mannie met with death before he hit the pavement.

"Mannie!" Cream screamed. He wanted to keep it hot but sirens were too close, so he headed back into the hat shop looking for the back door. Slug saw him run and duck, and he tried to cut him down but missed. All of a sudden, a cop car skidded around the corner.

"Slug, let's go!" Freddie ordered, and Slug was right behind him.

One of the cops jumped out too soon and yelled, "Freeze!" But Freddie turned around and let off his last three shots, catching the cop in the chest, sending him flying back against the open car door.

Freddie's whole life flashed before his eyes. He had acted on reflex, out of fear and panic. He was making his escape and the police were the last obstacle, so he fired. Boom. Boom. Boom. His sporadic shots ripped into the cop he'd shot at.

He tried to turn his momentum from back-pedaling to forward speed as he crossed the street, but his timing was off and an old Caddy skidded to a halt, landing him on top of the hood. The car hadn't run into him so much as he had run into it. The impact wasn't enough to hurt him, but it was enough force to jar the gun from his hand, making it clatter yards away.

He wanted to go back for it, but Slug hollered, "Freddie, fuck you doin'? C'mon!"

More police were on the way. There was no time to go back for the gun. Freddie ran past Slug and took the lead. It was if his feet were moving faster than the rest of his body. Sirens wailed in the air as they fled. Freddie reached the old, abandoned ex–Knockers strip club and dipped to the side of the haunted house–looking building.

Police swarmed the area and quickly gained control, finding out how many gunmen there were and that they were on foot. The manhunt was on.

His heart banged up against his chest as he tried to catch his breath. The thought of knowing that the police station was literally right around the corner from their temporary hideout did not sit well with him.

"Yo, we gotta bounce from here," Freddie announced once he had regained control of his breathing. He stuck his head out to the main street and looked both ways. Once he had established the coast was clear, he darted out.

Minutes later, they were making their way up the Plainfield train station's steps. Freddie figured his best bet was to take the train tracks all the way down to his projects. Escaping the Plainfield police dragnet out of downtown wasn't a problem; escaping the twisted fate he saw ahead of him was.

"You a'ight, cuz? You ain't hit, is you?" Slug queried as they walked the tracks, looking at the blood and torn fabric on the shoulder of Freddie's sweatshirt.

"Naw, that's from the car, yo," Freddie replied. He was huffing and puffing real hard as if he were asthmatic. His adrenaline was pumping so hard he still couldn't feel the wound.

"Cuz, what the fuck just happened? Who was—"

Freddie waved him off. "Later, yo. Son, I shot a cop."

That made both men shudder because they both knew what it meant. Killing Mannie was one thing, but shooting a police officer? And if he died, if he wasn't dead already . . .

"I ain't goin' to no fuckin' prison, yo," Freddie vowed. He didn't want to die or go out guns blazing, and prison wasn't an option either.

"Fuck you gonna do?" Slug asked.

The question was like a crossroads. The answer would determine his destiny. There was no way he could stay in Plainfield or New Jersey period, for that matter. The decision had already crossed his mind in midflight, and it loomed before him like the promised land.

"Yo, I gotta blow Jerze, cuzzo. I'm goin' down South wit' you," Freddie spat.

Slug nodded solemnly. "I was thinkin' the same thing. Seem like the only thing to do, cuz. What about Simone?" Slug then asked.

"Shit! Fuck!" Freddie grabbed hold of his head with both hands. The sound of her name stirred panic in his stomach. Not because of love, but fear. The Acura he had left at the scene of the crime was in her name. He knew it was just a matter of time before they traced it back to her and headed to his apartment. If he did not get her out before the police showed up, the spot would be too hot to get her and his stash out at all, he concluded. It was all he had.

Freddie checked for his cell, but it was gone, lost in the shuffle. He had to get to a phone. He was already thinking of the safest and closest pay phone to or in his hood to use.

The New Projects was oddly quiet, thought Freddie as he peered through the trees on the tracks that made it almost impossible to see from where he and Slug stood.

"Follow me," he told Slug as he made a mad dash down the train track's rock path that led to West Second Street. He wasted no time running up in building 524.

"Stay here," he directed to his cousin.

"Where you goin'?" Slug wasn't feeling being cooped up in the project hallway building. He had known enough stories about them to know they didn't take too kindly to outsiders being in their hood. It was one thing for Freddie to be with him, but another to be solo and out of pocket.

"I gotta hit up baby girl," Freddie replied. "You got some change?"

Slug handed him two quarters. "Yo, hurry up back, cuz. I ain't feelin' this shit," Slug let him know.

"No doubt." He turned back around and crept out of a building, headed toward the corner's payphone. He knew it was a big risk. *What other options do I have?*

He had walked to the corner payphones countless times, but at that moment it seemed as if he'd never reach the corner, which was only half a block away. He inserted the coins and dialed the house number so fast he misdialed and had to dial again. In the distance he could hear sirens.

"Hello?" Simone picked up on the third ring.

"Simone, listen to me and don't ask questions. Empty the safe and stuff a bag full of clothes. Not much, just what you can fit in my blue duffle bag, A'ight? Get out of the house now, you hear me? Now! Take a cab to JFK; not Newark Airport. JFK. Now! I'll meet you there!" Freddie talked so fast, she hardly understood him.

"Freddie, slow down! What did—"

"The money and you. Meet me at JFK, a'ight? JFK, now!" he repeated, this short, firm order clarifying the first, more detailed one.

"Okay, baby. Are you okay?" She sounded close to tears.

"I will be when I see you at JFK. I love you." He hung up before she could respond. In record-breaking time, he made it safely back to building 524.

Slug was right where he had left him. The look on his face let Freddie know he wasn't cool with what had just went down.

"Yo, cuz, my bad. I needed to reach out to Simone and let her know what the deal was." He apologized to Slug sincerely.

Slug nodded. "I ain't trippin'. I woulda done the same thing." He leaned in and gave Freddie a pound hand-shake and a hug.

"Appreciate it," Freddie said, relieved. Right now, Slug was all he had, besides Simone.

"Cuz, I need you to go back to my mother's house. Tell her what happened, a'ight?" He broke their embrace. "We need to split up. Cab it up to Rock Avenue, or call her to scoop you up, cool?" he explained.

Slug looked around. He didn't know Plainfield from a can of paint, but he did know how to evade the law, and splitting up was always a good option. "Don't worry about me, cuz. Just be safe. I'm good," Slug assured him, giving him another pound and a hug. They split up like two shadows in midday, fading from the waning sun.

Chapter Eight

Back at the scene of the crime, the police had Richmond Street roped off at all four corners. People milled around, gossiping and straining their necks in an attempt to satisfy their voyeuristic thirst for bloodshed and violence. Mannie's corpse lay on the sidewalk under a bloody sheet, and the officer had been rushed to the hospital where he lay in critical condition. Detective Francis Wilson and his partner, Detective Andre Crawford, surveyed the scene with experienced eyes.

"You got a name on the body yet?" Wilson asked casually. He was a fifteen-year vet on the force and murder was his daily business. The younger Crawford was just getting his feet wet, so he was more gung-ho.

He flipped open his trusty notepad and read, "Manuel Mincey, aka Mannie; twenty-two-year-old black male with a list of priors. Drug charges mostly, and some assaults."

Wilson nodded knowingly. "Now that you've read the official report, let's get down to what solves the crime. Are you familiar with Mannie?"

His partner was clueless.

"He has a brother, Dante, who they call Tay. He and his crew come from Sixth Street. They have been making quite a name for themselves lately. Remember the double murder on Third and Prescott about two weeks ago?"

"Yes: two black males, sixteen and twenty-four, names—" Crawford ran off like a computer, but Wilson cut him off.

"No need. I was there. That was Tay's work. Heroin beef. Remember the dead girl we found in the Dumpster in the Fourth Street housing projects?"

"Yes."

"Tay again." Wilson looked at Mannie's corpse. "Whoever did it made us lucky this time. Once we run the prints and the identification on that Acura, we'll have all the answers we need to wrap up this case."

"We already did," Crawford announced proudly, glad to finally know something Wilson didn't. "The car is registered to—"

"Let me guess," Wilson cut him off dryly. "It's registered to a female, correct?"

Crawford's pride deflated like a balloon. Wilson could tell by his expression that he was right. "Then we don't know jack shit. These hoodlums always register their vehicles in their mama's, baby mama's, girlfriend's, or crackheads' names. Finding out who really owns the car is where our answers lie."

At that point, a uniformed officer ran up carrying a plastic bag. When he was close enough, Wilson was able to see what was in it and his heart leaped.

"Detective Wilson! We found this in the street," the officer reported, handing Wilson the gun.

Wilson smiled. "The next best thing to a scripture from heaven: a smoking gun!"

An enraged Dante had Cream pinned against the wall by the collar, nostrils flaring, eyes tearing. "He killed my brother? You let that nigga kill my fuckin' brother?"

Cream was almost a foot taller than Dante and outweighed him by almost fifty pounds, but he didn't resist because he knew that Dante's rage was really pain and grief. Besides, Dante was a bull. He stood five feet six inches and had a stature like a short linebacker. He didn't work out and it showed in his gut, but he was naturally strong and had the heart to take on anybody.

"What could I do, Tay? I ain't let 'em do nothin'," Cream tried to reason; but Dante was beyond reason.

Dante released Cream from his grip and spat, "Then, nigga, you should be in the street lyin' beside him!" Dante paced the floor. The rest of the crew was silent, like real killers. They didn't talk much and they only moved on Tay's word.

"Tell me again. Tell me again, slow," Tay snarled, eyeing Cream squarely.

"We was at Mannie's store when I saw Freddie's car. I told Mannie, I told him, 'Let's follow him and find out where he lives.' But you know Mannie, son. You know his heart, God bless the dead. He said, 'Naw, fuck dat, we hittin' the nigga right where he stand.'" Cream lied 'cause there was no way he was telling Tay it was his idea. There was no telling how Tay would react.

Dante watched Cream closely, listening to every word. A wise man knows when a scared man is lying, but not a hysterical one. All Tay could see was blood: his brother's, and soon Freddie's.

"Fuck e'ything! Fuck money, fuck bitches, and fuck Plainfield! Until I got this nigga beggin' me to kill him, on his knees in front of me, no one eats, no one sleeps! Period! You say he from the New? Them niggas bleed. Fuck them bitch-ass project niggas, I don't give a fuck! They can get it too! Find this nigga!" Dante had declared war.

Chapter Nine

"Thank you, Gary. I'm standing outside the Gentlemen's Club in Plainfield, New Jersey, on the corner of East Third Street and Richmond Street. An early morning shootout has left one man dead and a police officer in critical condition," the female reporter spoke into a camera and informed the inquiring public. A picture of the officer flashed on the screen.

"Officer Paul Williamson was shot once in the chest, answering the call of what police believe to be a drug-related incident. The man killed has been identified as one Manuel Mincey. Mincey died on the scene. The police haven't made any arrests, but they did recover a gun that they believe to be the murder weapon. We'll have more as this story continues to unfold."

Gina sat in the bedroom of her Bound Brook, New Jersey, townhouse in utter disbelief. As soon as she saw that the shooting had happened in Plainfield, she had a bad premonition. All she could think of was Freddie dead, in a pool of blood. When she heard the name of the dead man, her heart began to beat closer to normal. But when she saw the green Acura, with its doors open and police around it, she experienced a whole new set of fears.

"Freddie," she groaned as if she was in physical pain. "Freddie, what have you gotten yourself into?"

There wasn't anything she could do now. She knew Mannie, and she knew Mannie was Tay's brother. There would be no talking to Tay, and her family wouldn't go for an all-out war over a nigga she was fucking. Freddie was on his own. All she could do was sit, wait, and say a silent prayer for his safety.

"Freddie, baby, where are you?"

At about the same time, Simone was standing in the middle of JFK thinking the same thing. Throngs of people moved all around her and she looked back and forth constantly, hoping to see Freddie's face coming toward her. She felt like a small child lost in the mall. Freddie's call was so urgent and his tone so intense that she couldn't help but fear the worst. She loved her fiancé and she trusted her man. She knew he was in the street doing God knows what because he always had money; he paid all the bills and pampered her like a queen. But she never asked questions about what it was he actually did. He never got arrested or into any serious beefs in the street, so she just went to school preparing for a career as an accountant and took care of her man.

But now, standing in the middle of an international airport with only a handful of clothes and $5,500, her heart told her their lives were about to drastically change. *"Get out of the house now,"* she remembered him telling her, as if the house was on fire or about to be raided by the police, or—

"Simone Jackson, Simone Jackson. Paging Simone Jackson. Please meet your brother in the waiting area of Terminal C."

She heard her name on the paging system and exhaled, knowing "her brother" was Freddie. She picked up the duffle bag, looked around, located the directions for Terminal C, and quickly headed off in its direction.

When she spotted Freddie, she wanted to run to him but restrained herself until she reached him. The first thing she noticed was his torn shirt and bloodstained shoulder, which he was desperately trying to conceal. Her mind went back to the last time he'd shown up bloody and she automatically made the connection.

"Freddie, what—"

He silenced her with a breathtaking hug, like he was a drowning man suddenly being saved. It had been a hard trip back to New York for him, but once a car thief always a car thief. He crept from back street to back street, making it all the way to Pennsylvania Avenue before he spotted an '88 Cutlass Supreme. Being without a screwdriver or snatch bar, he had no choice but to bust out the little side window and hotwire the ignition. It was like riding a bike: you never forgot.

He jumped on the highway and headed for New York, and it seemed that every few miles, he passed a trooper or a trooper passed him. One glance at the window and the jig was up. His asshole stayed tight all the way to JFK. All he could think of was Simone and never seeing her again. He thought about how his lying ways had put him in a position to lose everything. He vowed that if he made it to her, and she was waiting for him, he would change for good.

Now, holding her in his arms, he felt renewed. "Ssshhhh, boo. Everything's gonna be all right. But we gotta get out of town right away," he told her, and then held her at arm's length.

Her eyes shone like crystal because of the tears of confusion. "Out of town? Why, Freddie? Where? Why are you bleeding?" These were the questions she felt she had a right to know.

"Please, boo, trust me. I promise I'll tell you. Right now, I need a change of clothes and we need two tickets to Raleigh, North Carolina, a'ight? Can you handle that while I get out of this shirt?"

She nodded and Freddie kissed her softly. "I love you, Simone." He pulled the duffel bag to him and began to rifle through it. Her clothes and his were haphazardly thrown together. He rummaged through the bag until he found a white and blue Rocawear hoodie. He dashed off to the bathroom to change.

While he was gone, Simone bought two tickets for Greensboro, North Carolina, because there were no flights leaving for Raleigh. The flight wasn't scheduled to leave for almost two hours. She prayed that wouldn't be a problem.

When Freddie returned and she broke the news, he sighed, resigned. "It's all we got," he replied.

"Freddie, please. Have I ever questioned you before? Baby, I need to know what's going on. You're acting like . . . like somebody's after you," she stressed, grabbing her head.

Freddie looked at his watch. With two hours to spare, there was no reason not to tell her. Besides, as much as he loved her, if she decided to leave him, it was best that she didn't know where he was going.

"Okay, yo. Let's get something to eat and we'll talk."

Simone looked down at her engagement ring, knowing it would never mean the same thing again. She and Freddie sat in a small airport coffee shop as he explained what had led up to the present situation. He was completely honest with her, but every sentence seemed to slap her love and trust in the face. She listened as Freddie explained about the stripper, and how Cream had confronted him in the barbershop. That was where the blood had come from the morning of the funeral. He explained how he had gone downtown to get Slug. That was when the shootout jumped off and he killed Mannie and shot a cop. She knew the Acura was in her name, and that the police would want to question her now. The whole thing made her look at Freddie in a whole new light.

Simone told herself that she should've known. Freddie was gorgeous. Anytime he came around, all her friends changed their attitudes and fought for his attention. She felt like she should have known just from the way they'd met, with his smooth approach and his demeanor, that he was a dog.

***

Simone was working in a flower shop when Freddie walked in one day. Just looking at the nigga's soft green eyes and juicy lips made her panties wet, but she played it off and kept it professional. He had ordered a dozen yellow roses and a teddy bear when she said, "Hmm. Expensive. She must be pretty special, huh?"

"I hope she will be."

Her heart dropped. She was hoping they were for his mother, but his answer confirmed her suspicion: he had a girl.

She cleared her throat and asked, "And what would you like on the card?"

"Put, 'I hope to see you again real soon. 555-2345. Freddie.'" He smiled and made her stomach do a dance.

She processed the order and handed him the flowers, but to her surprise he handed them back. She thought something was wrong.

"Naw, everything's fine . . . if you'll accept my gift."

She was hooked. And from that day on, her feet never touched the ground. Now this. She felt like she had been slammed face first back into reality.

"Freddie, what do you expect me to say? You . . . you call me and tell me to pack up. For what? I don't know. Where? I don't know. But silly me, I'm runnin' around like crazy because I trusted you, Freddie. And now you tell me it's all because of some . . . bitch you couldn't keep your dick out of!" She sniffed up the tears, exasperated. "You know what? I—"

Freddie reached across the table and touched her hand, but she flinched and slowly withdrew, unable to look him in the face.

"Simone, yo, I know I fucked up, but—"

"Do you, Freddie? Did you fuck up because you fucked up or because you got caught fuckin' up? Huh? What are you sorry for?" Her voice elevated an octave, causing a few heads to turn around and tune in.

Freddie gave them a hard ghetto grill to reestablish their privacy and then turned back to Simone. "Ma, I know I'm askin' a lot of you. And right now, you don't have any reason to believe what I say but, Simone, I love you. And I promise to spend the rest of my life makin' it up to you. I need you. If I didn't, I woulda just left without you, disappeared. But where could I go without you by my side?" He reached across the table again and took her hand in his. This time she didn't pull away. "Simone, I promise, boo. It'll never happen again."

"You promise, Freddie?" she asked incredulously. "Why would you expect me to believe that?"

"Because I ain't never promised that before."

She held her ring finger up in his face. "Oh, no? Well, what is this supposed to mean?" she challenged.

"When I gave that to you, I didn't know what having a wife really meant: the woman I come home to, have babies and grow old with. But now, I know it means much more, and I hate that it took this for me to realize it. But now I know. I know it means the woman you share your life with, not just your bed or your roof. And I pledge to you, on my soul, to give you just that, boo: my life, and nothing less."

She wanted so badly to believe him. Her heart yearned to trust his soothing voice and emerald eyes, but she couldn't find a reason she should. Except for the love she couldn't live without.

Freddie took her left hand and gently slid the ring off her finger, and it felt like her soul was being ripped out of her body.

"No, Freddie. I believe—"

He gently placed a finger on her lips and rubbed them with his thumb. "The ring could never mean the same. Every time you see it, what would it represent? I want our love to be pure, flawless, like a true diamond. As soon as I can, I'ma get you another one to symbolize the struggle we went through to reach the understanding we now share. You're my winner, baby. And if I die before I ever stand at the altar, God knows I've already pledged my heart to you forever."

Every word was like a healing balm to her spirit. "I love you, Freddie. Please, don't hurt me, okay?" The tears made her look like an innocent child he only wanted to protect. He pulled her from her chair and into his lap. She hugged him tightly.

"Now boarding for Greensboro, North Carolina. Gate forty-seven," the PA announced.

Freddie looked into Simone's eyes and asked, "So is this good-bye or will you come with me and share my life?"

She clung to him, afraid of the word "good-bye." "I wanna be with you, Freddie. I wanna be with you."

Her words were music to his ears.

Chapter Ten

Slug stood in his Aunt Elsie's living room silently. He didn't know what she and his mother, Caroline Ann, known to the family as Ann, would say. They both sat quietly. All you could hear was the ticking of the clock. He had told them all he knew, which wasn't much. All he knew was that they had started shooting and that he and Freddie had clapped back, a nigga dropped and a cop got hit, and now Freddie was on his way down South.

Elsie was no stranger to the streets. Freddie's absentee father was a high roller back in the early eighties: a Dominican player with long paper and a sweet dick. Elsie was young and naïve, got sucked in, ended up pregnant, and Freddie Sr. disappeared. She wouldn't acknowledge his desertion at first, even naming Freddie after him to let all them jealous bitches know who had borne his seed. But after a few months of seeing him everywhere and still being ignored, she finally got the message.

As Freddie grew up, she saw some of his father's womanizing traits in him and tried to beat them out of him, but to no avail. Elsie knew her son wasn't a murderer, just the victim of harsh circumstances.

"Well, one thing's for sure. You can't run forever," she remarked.

"Naw, but he can run for now," Slug replied.

"What does he want me to do?" Elsie asked, ready to troop out for her only child.

"He knows they'll be comin' around questioning," Slug explained, "so he—"

"I know all that, Eric, believe me. I know how to handle police. I mean, what does he want me to do? Does he need any money? I ain't got much, but Lord knows he can get my last."

Slug appreciated his aunt's devotion to her son. "Naw, Auntie, he'll be okay. I'll take care of baby boy," he assured her.

"How?" Ann questioned. "Slug, he in enough trouble already to be messin' 'round wit' you." Slug's mother was fully aware of her son's notorious reputation.

"Ma, I ain't mean it like that. I meant . . . get him a job or something," he lied.

"A job? Boy, how you gonna get him a job and you ain't never worked a day in yo' life?" Ann inquired.

"Besides, with the police lookin' for him, ain't no way he can work a regular job," Elsie added, shaking her head. "What is my baby gonna do? I should go see a lawyer."

"Good idea, Elsie," Ann commended her. "Try to work some good out of this. I mean, the way you explained it, Eric, it was self-defense."

Their dispositions brightened considerably. Slug didn't have the heart to bring them back to reality. Freddie had shot a cop. There wasn't any self-defense for that.

"Yes, the Lord works in mysterious ways," Ann said.

Slug turned to his mother. "Ma, I'm 'posed to meet Freddie in the Boro, and I don't want him down there too long without me. Just let me gather my things and I'll be ready." He reached for his mother's arm. *I just hope Goldsboro will be ready for me and him*, was his current thought as he helped his mother stand to her feet.

Chapter Eleven

Freddie and Simone emerged from the Piedmont Triad International Airport in Greensboro just as the sun had taken on an orange tint. They had both been in their own world, flying high above the real one. Simone thought about the decision she'd made. She didn't regret it because wherever Freddie was, she wanted to be. But she realized all she had sacrificed to do so. Because the car was in her name, she knew that if she got a job it would just be a matter of time before the police came looking for her. And even though she had nothing to do with the shootout, it would bring heat to Freddie. The same thing with school; this hurt the most. She only had a few months to go before she would have been a certified public accountant. Now, all of that was gone, at least for the time being.

Freddie spent the flight wondering what he would do once he reached Goldsboro. He had never worked a nine-to-five a day in his life, and he was willing to square up but he couldn't.

Everything was being set up to involve him in some type of criminal enterprise. But Freddie wasn't a hustler; he was a player. All he knew was macking women; that was how he ate, how he paid bills, how he pampered Simone with everything, even the two-carat engagement ring. Still another reason to get rid of it. Simone never knew that the steak she ate, the clothes she wore, and the roof that sheltered her all came out of other women's pocketbooks. But now that he had committed himself to Simone, what would or could he do to support her?

Simone looked out over the airport parking lot and yawned. "Boo, I'm exhausted. Let's just get a room instead of going straight to Goldsboro, okay?"

Freddie looked at her and felt it was a good point. He needed to give Slug a chance to get there first. "Yeah, no doubt, ma. That's a good idea." He placed his arm around her waist and led her to one of the waiting cabs.

"Welcome to Greensboro," the cabbie drawled. "How was the flight?"

Freddie was a little taken aback by the man's Southern hospitality. In Jersey, you were lucky if a cabbie didn't say, "Where the fuck you goin'?"

"Uh, it was cool. Thanks for askin'," Freddie replied.

"Where to?" the cabbie asked as he pulled off.

"You know any motels you could suggest?" Freddie asked.

"Top of the line, nice, flea bitten, or damn near condemned?" The cabbie chuckled.

"Nice."

"Comin' right up."

The cabbie drove them to the Red Roof Inn on High Point Road. "This good enough? Real nice prices, real nice people."

Simone giggled because he sounded like a commercial.

"Thanks, yo," Freddie said, handing him a twenty. "Keep the change."

The meter only read eight dollars and thirty cents. "Well, I thank ya kindly. Y'all enjoy your stay in Greensboro."

Freddie and Simone climbed out of the cab with Freddie carrying the duffle bag. "Real nice prices, real nice people," Freddie mocked, imitating a country accent.

Simone hit him. "Stop, Freddie, he was nice!" She giggled. "But that did sound like a commercial."

They went in and Freddie copped a single room for three nights. Their room was on the second level. They entered the room and turned on the light because the sun had already set. The room was immaculate and had a peach bedspread, matching curtains, and off-white walls. It was a little stuffy because it had been a warm spring day in North Carolina, so Freddie turned on the air conditioner. He tossed the duffle bag onto the bed and Simone lay across it on her back. "Ohhh, that feels good."

Freddie clicked on the TV and flipped through a few stations, caught the news, and left it there, just in case. "You hungry?" Freddie asked.

"A little. But for real for real, I just wanna take a bath and go to sleep," she said, stretching her arms over her head.

"Well, I'm about to starve, yo."

Simone was rummaging through the large duffle bag, pulling out clothes randomly. She had only managed to pack three sets of clothes for Freddie and four for herself, along with a few pairs of shoes, sneakers, and boots.

"Damn. I hope I packed some panties." She giggled, still pulling stuff out. She found a few pair of Freddie's boxers and a couple of bras. She shrugged. "I guess I'll just have to get some tomorrow."

"Dig, I'ma go get somethin' to eat," Freddie informed her.

"Okay."

Freddie left the room. Simone had just pulled off her sweatshirt when she noticed that the TV had a radio on it as well. She fiddled with the remote until she figured out how to turn off the TV and turn on the radio. She turned the digital dial until she heard Avant's "Read Your Mind" on 104.3.

Simone took off her low-rider jeans, panties, and bra before entering the bathroom completely naked. She opened up the taps and sat on the toilet seat to watch the tub fill with steaming water and bubbles from the complimentary bubble bath she'd poured in. When the tub was full and the bubble level to her liking, she put her hair up in a ponytail and tested the water with the tips of her toes. *Perfect*.

Simone slid into the warm water like she would slide under a quilt on a cold and stormy winter night. She let the water cradle her, rocking her ever so gently whenever she moved around. She held up her left hand and looked at the light spot the ring had left on her chocolate complexion. She thought about calling her mother but didn't want to do it from the motel phone. She promised herself she'd call in the morning. What to say, she hadn't figured out yet. She couldn't picture herself saying, "Hey, Ma, me and Freddie on the run from the police. I'll try to stay in touch."

She laughed to herself to keep from crying because the whole situation was madness. She lathered up and washed her body to the sounds of Sade, Maxwell, India Arie, and Mary J. before she got out to dry off. As she toweled her back, she heard one of her songs by Jaheim fill the air. She opened the door to go turn it up but found the room completely dark except for several flickering candles strategically placed around the room. Freddie was straddling the sole chair in the room backward, his chest against the back of it. Simone stopped in front of the light, right outside the bathroom, where the sink and a large mirror were.

"Stay right there, boo. Just let me look at you."

Freddie's eyes devoured his woman from head to toe, from her silky Indian mane to her slanted brown eyes, sculpted cheekbones, African nose, and full, pouty lips. His eyes traveled along her slender neck, which curved into small feminine shoulders. The cool air from the AC made her pretty pink nipples stick out almost a full half inch. It was like she could feel his eyes kissing her all over, because as he looked lower, her heart rate increased, her breathing shortened, and her wetness began to lubricate her thighs.

Freddie continued his visual nibbling. As Keith Sweat began to sing, so did he, but in that melodic octave that always made Simone melt.

Freddie began to chime the lyrics. He got up and walked over to her. He continued chanting the words to the popular '80s track as he took her hand in his and kissed it.

"Damn, you beautiful, Simone." He gently turned her around to face her own reflection in the mirror. "See what I see," he whispered, running a tantalizing finger down her spine, making her jump slightly and bite her trembling bottom lip. She watched and felt his hands cup both of her breasts, pulling and teasing her nipples as he sang softly in her ear. Each syllable pronounced sent chills throughout her entire body, moistening her inner thighs.

Simone squirmed. Her chest raised as she placed her hands on top of his. She gripped them tightly as he massaged her breasts. She relaxed her chocolate body against him.

Freddie kept eye contact with her through the mirror. He slid their hands down to her belly. She watched them go lower and lower. Her eyes took on a panther-like glow, letting Freddie know his sensuality had taken her as he'd intended it to. He continued with his serenade as he ran his finger along her pussy lips, inserting two up to the knuckle inside her.

She gasped.

"I . . . won't."

Simone was so creamy she milked his fingers as Freddie licked along her spine. He used his free hand to slowly push her forward, bending her over the sink.

"Freddie, I want to feel you inside me soooooo bad," she purred.

Freddie came out of his pants and slid inside her tightness, slowly, taking his time until he was all the way inside. "Look how beautiful love makes you look, boo. Look at what love looks like in your eyes," Freddie urged, long dicking her into losing control.

Simone kept steady eye contact with herself, getting more and more turned on by the expressions on her face, as she watched her own ecstasy. Freddie gripped her around the waist and ground her hard, making her eyes roll up in the back of her head.

"Freddie, don't stop. Don't ever stop loving me, baby."

"You're so beautiful to me, Simone. So beautiful," Freddie replied. "Kiss yourself, ma." Simone kissed her own reflection on the lips as if it were her long-lost twin.

"I'm beautiful," she moaned, reaching back to pull Freddie to her as she felt the quiver in her stomach build into a rumble.

"Freddie, I can feel it. I can feel . . ."

Freddie knew his woman well enough to hold himself until he felt her walls flare and tighten, timing his release to match hers. The intensity of the moment damn near made Simone lose her mind.

"Freddie, I'll kill you. I'll kill . . . you," she stuttered, too low for Freddie to hear. And he was too unconscious to care to understand.

Chapter Twelve

It had been a week since Mannie's murder and Tay had already sent a message to the hustlers around the New Projects. He sent a team through to wet up the buildings of 116 in the back on Elmwood, 528, across from the infamous 524 building, in the front on Second Street, 532 in the middle, and 544 near the corner. Every day a different crew of shooters darted through the money-getting housing projects and lit the block up like Independence Day. No one was hit because no one was meant to be, but the message was loud and clear, too loud for Power to ignore.

Power was from building 528, but he repped his stomping grounds to the fullest. He and his manz and 'em controlled the front, after the feds had come through and swept the housing projects he was born and raised in. Before him, it was his sandbox homies, Malik, Cheddar, Pete and Doub who ran the two West Second Street buildings. They were legendary for their hustles, but his methods required force. He played the role of enforcer, and he played his role well. He had outlasted many of his contemporaries, who were either dead or doing fed bids, so dudes from his city respected his longevity, Tay included. But this wasn't about respect; it was about revenge, which was why Power decided to go see Tay before things really got out of hand.

He pulled up in his classic burgundy Jaguar XJR with a beige butter-soft leather interior. Power was beyond the need to floss. He didn't have oversized tires or spinning rims like the young cats. The Jag was still as it was off the showroom floor.

There was a little league baseball game being played in Silas Field Park. He decided this was a good place to have the meeting. He didn't believe Tay was that stupid or gung-ho that he'd do something dumb like talk slick and provoke or force Power's head, but still he came with his manz, Bash, who was also a known gunman in the town, as an extra precaution. They climbed the half-full stone bleachers and took a seat behind cheering parents and siblings. He looked around and spotted a young cat profiling along the wall.

"Yo, *akh*, lemme holla at you."

The young boy recognized Power's face but didn't know his name. He just knew he had paper and pushed a sick Jag. He bopped over, trying to look cooler than he was.

"What up, OG?" the boy asked, addressing Power by the term reserved for elders.

Power pulled out a wad of money and peeled off a Benjamin. "Do me a favor, li'l bruh. Go tell Tay Power said holla at him, and tell him where I'm at, a'ight?"

The boy recognized the name instantly. In his mind, according to the streets, Power was one of the legends from the Queen City. Had it been anyone else, he woulda kept the hundred and dipped, but since Power was who he was, there was nothing to talk about.

"If I can find 'im," the boy replied.

"Yeah, you can find 'im. Hurry up for me."

The boy hurried off as the batter on the field got a hit that landed in left field, almost rolling to the fence. The crowd erupted with cheers.

"That's my baby!"

"Run, T, run!"

"Safe!" the umpire declared as the runner slid into third base.

Power laughed. "Good hit!" he yelled and clapped. He turned to Bashir. "You see this, beloved? You see these pretty black mamas cheering for their man-children? Everything we do, we do for this," Power explained, gesturing with his hand. "Niggas forget that. They forget and lose focus. But this is why we do what we do."

Bashir nodded knowingly.

Out of the corner of Power's hawk-like vision, he saw Tay enter the park, followed by the boy and another cat, looking like he didn't wanna talk. His ice grill stood out to Power above all. He glanced over at Bashir, who also now had a mean mug plastered across his face. It was apparent that he too noticed the facial expression of the dude who was with Tay.

"Bash, let me talk to Tay alone. But be on point. You know how these east end niggas can get," he stated.

"Bruh, you sure?" Bashir did not like Power's plan one bit, but no matter the case, he had to respect it. Still, he wanted to be sure.

Power let out a light chuckle. "Yeah, I'm positive," he said, patting the butt of his .40-cal. tucked under his Polo collared shirt as he took a quick look from left to right to see if anyone was paying him any mind.

"Say less."

Bash stood up and descended the bleachers. When Tay saw Bashir coming down, he immediately understood. He tapped his hitter and gestured for him to do the same thing. Tay climbed the bleachers. Power extended his arm and greeted him with a handshake.

"Power. What the deal, my G?" Tay greeted him, a little out of breath. "How you livin'?"

Power chuckled and patted Tay's protruding belly. "Not as good as you, fam."

Tay smiled as they sat down on the top row of the bleachers.

"Let me ask you something. You ever come out here and watch these games?" Power abruptly asked.

"For what?" Tay was visibly perplexed.

Inside, Power shook his head because Dante was a living example of the point he was making to Bash about losing focus. "You ever read Akbar's book *Death of the Game?*"

Baseball games, books; Tay didn't know what Power was getting at, but he wished he'd get to it. "Naw, P, I don't read much. Sorry," Tay replied sarcastically.

Power detected the sarcasm in his voice. "I only asked because he said snitches killed the game. And the reason niggas snitch is because they lose focus. What we do, we don't make money just to make money. We make money to provide for our family, for our people, and if niggas was in the game for that, wouldn't be nothin' to snitch about or nobody to snitch on, because they'd know this is all we got."

Dante's young, greedy mind couldn't grasp the totality of what Power was saying. All he knew was mo' money, mo' murder. "I feel you, P," he said, but Power knew he didn't. "I feel you. It's about family."

Power just let it go. "That's why I understood why you did what you did, and it's why I wanted to talk to you, face to face, on some real G shit." He paused and shook his head before he continued. "My li'l homie Freddie, bruh, he not even about that life like that," he admitted.

"You ain't gotta tell me that," Tay spat. "I know the nigga marshmallow." He took a jab at Freddie to see how Power would react.

"Soft or not," Power began, "ya manz Cream forced his hand and he did what any cat would do in his shoes. He from the projects, *akhi*, so at minimum he seen some gangsta shit up close and personal," Power ended, shooting a jab back himself, letting him know there was nothing soft about his hood or his homies. He may not have agreed with or condoned Freddie's methods or actions, but being a New Projects nigga, he didn't expect anything less.

"Yo, so what you tryin'a say?" Tay let out a gust of hot air in frustration. He was growing tired of the conversation. As far as he was concerned, first blood was drawn and he had no intentions until he spilled some of his own. The question was, whose blood?

Power picked up on the fact that although what he was saying made sense, Tay wasn't really feeling everything he was saying. He tried a different approach. "Yo, you got my word, none of my people got nothin' to do wit' it. Everybody want this shit to be dead. You know war and cash don't mix and motherfuckas tryin'a eat, feed their families. True, he a New Project head, born and raised; but he ain't no shooter or trapper. He a playboy. You know all the real ones, my dude. Tizz, Money, Chet, Pete and Squirm, Doma, Buie, Krush and 'em," Power began to sound off, doing a quick roll call of his hood. "And you know my young boys who hug the block: Wheels, Nider, and my li'l folks from 116, Macho and 'em. Bottom line, dude ain't no hustler or no gangsta either. He a player."

"So you sayin' your hood ain't claim him or ride for him? Well, who is? Where his mother rest?" Tay wanted to know. His blood began to slowly boil. "Fuck gonna be held accountable for my brother? I need some answers, if you expect me to keep shit to a bare minimum," Tay pointed out.

Power knew Tay had totally missed his point. He looked him dead in the eye. "Nah, that's not what I'm sayin', bruh. What I'm sayin' is niggas choosing gettin' paper over catchin' frivolous bodies. But, as far as what you asked me, I don't know none of that. But even if I did, I wouldn't tell you. Point blank!"

Tay started to protest but Power continued.

"Now dig. I'm not gonna pretend to know how you feel 'cause I ain't never lost nobody as close to me as you have, but my word on everything, I'll do whatever I can to help you resolve this issue. Hell, if I could I'd murder the nigga myself and bring you the body. But we both know that's not gonna happen. So, I'm askin' you—no, I'm beggin' you—please don't bring that gangsta shit to me and mine no more, because I don't need that and neither do you, on some real G shit." Power kept his tone steady, but Dante knew what he meant.

"My brother was my heart, P, and I'ma do whatever I gotta do so his death not in vain. But I respect the fact that you came to holla at me. I appreciate it."

Die in vain? Power thought. *No matter what you do*, akh, *you can't change the fact that he died in vain. Look what he died for.* Power sighed. He had tried, but he was sure he hadn't fully gotten through to Tay. He extended his hand. Tay gripped it firmly. "Anytime, bruh. Anytime. And do me a favor. Try 'n' make a game or two this summer. Trust me. It'll help you focus."

Dante stood up. "I'll try, fam," Tay replied nonchalantly.

But Power knew he wouldn't. He doubted he even heard him. He knew the only thing on Tay's mind right now was revenge, and it had Freddie's name written all over it.

Chapter Thirteen

Don't let yourself get attached to anything you are not willing to walk out in thirty seconds flat if you feel the heat around the corner.

Detective Wilson couldn't help but think, as he looked around Freddie's apartment, about the line from his favorite movie, *Heat*, that Robert De Niro had quoted. As soon as they'd identified the prints, they swooped down on his spot like a hoard of badged vultures, certified to pick the carcass. Wilson and several officers searched the apartment top to bottom, and from what they could see, their man had definitely left in a hurry. Big-screen TV, DVD, stereo with stacks of CDs were all intact. In fact, besides the few drawers that were pulled out and a few hangers that were strewn about, most of the clothes were still there.

"So, see, she went with him," Wilson commented to himself, but Crawford had walked in behind him.

"Who? The Jackson woman?"

"Who else," Wilson stated rhetorically, strolling around the room and stopping at the dresser. The only drawer open was full of Freddie's boxers. "He must've called and told her to meet him because she did the packing."

"How do you know?"

"The two loaded pistols we found in the hall closet. If it was him, he wouldn't have left those." Wilson turned to Crawford. "Andre, are you familiar with women's clothing?" He smiled.

"What do you mean 'familiar'?" Crawford asked, ready to take offense because the older man had a sick sense of humor.

"I'm not askin' you if you got a thong on, kid. You're young and hip, I suppose. Do you know the styles?" Wilson shook his head and ran his fingers through his dirty blond and gray hair.

"I guess. I never really thought—"

"Step over here."

They both walked over to the closet and looked at Simone's dresses, outfits, and shoes. "Look closely and tell me what's missing: summer clothing, winter clothes, what?"

Crawford surveyed the Prada, DKNY, Gucci, Chanel, BAPE, and Baby Phat hanging in a rainbow of colors, fabrics, and styles.

Wilson continued, "Chances are, he headed down South. I don't know a black man in New Jersey who doesn't have family down South. But where? Atlanta, South Carolina, North Carolina? We call it fugitive country." Wilson winked. "Every cat on the run usually ends up in one of those three places."

"Why not Baltimore or DC? That's predominantly African Americans down there in them parts," Crawford inquired.

Wilson shook it off. "Migration patterns. You'd be surprised how much like birds we are. We fly south in the winter." He smiled. "And a man usually runs to a comfort zone."

Wilson closed the closet. "Keep a close eye on the Jackson woman's credit cards. From the looks of that wardrobe, she's definitely a power shopper. Chances are they won't use 'em, if he's smart. But everybody slips up sooner or later, even the smart ones," Wilson ended as he jotted a note to himself on his handheld notepad.

Chapter Fourteen

After spending a few days in the motel in Greensboro, Freddie came out to see Slug leaning against the bowling ball–painted Caddy, sparkling. When they got in, Simone sat in the back seat. She was unused to the bearings. She looked at the TV screen in the rear and her eyes opened wide. She blushed when she saw that a porno was playing. She nudged Freddie's knee with hers and motioned to the screen.

Freddie looked up and saw the screen. "Yo, Slug. Fuck you into, dog?"

Slug looked into the rearview mirror to see what Freddie was talking about and chuckled. "My bad, dog. Long night." He switched off the TV, pumped 'Pac, and began the three-hour trek to Goldsboro.

Goldsboro hadn't changed much since the last time Freddie saw it. It was still a small, sleepy town, despite the new businesses and buildings.

They rode into town in Slug's tricked-out Cadillac Brougham, and it was definitely that. It was a navy blue '85 model, sporting twenty-six-inch hundred-spike Daytons. Slug had the back doors modified to open like suicide doors. He had also taken the back seat and reset it, facing it toward the rear of the car. It gave the inside a limo feel. The TV was mounted in the middle of the back of the car. The system was ear splitting, and he pumped nothing but 'Pac.

"You in the dirty Dirty, cuz," Slug drawled. "We don't push Acs, we push Yacks, nigga," he boasted.

Once they arrived, Slug explained, "Yo, cuz, I had to move on short notice, so I did the best I could on the apartment."

When Freddie saw his new layup, he understood Slug's explanation. It was a two-story apartment building, diagonally across from the Piggly Wiggly supermarket on Leslie Street. It sat in the heart of Webbtown, the black ghetto of the Boro. Freddie remembered the building because it had been many things over the years. It had been a liquor house, a crack house, and a ho house several times over. Now, it was owned by a closet smoker who didn't ask questions, especially of Slug, and who wanted his money in cash only, under the table. Perfect for Freddie,

Slug explained. But, looking at it, that didn't make him feel any better.

It was run-down and rusty on the outside, and dingy and roach-infested inside. It looked like the previous occupants had moved out as quickly as Freddie had left his apartment. Most of their broken-down furniture remained, including a dirty-ass brown couch that was sunk to the floor, a three-legged kitchen table, and several soiled mattresses in each of the two bedrooms. The only good thing was that the apartment was definitely spacious with cathedral ceilings. Years earlier, it had been a prestigious office building. But as the area became more and more ghetto, the building did too.

Simone was taken aback by the apartment as well, but she looked at it with a woman's eye. With a good house cleaning and delousing, the place had potential. The hardwood floors were covered with drug-related debris and soot, but she imagined them shined up and waxed. It wasn't the best, but it was all they had.

"Ay, yo, we'll get some heads to get all this shit out, then we'll go on and lace this shit out," Slug proposed.

"Lace?" Freddie echoed. "A nigga ain't holding no lace paper, yo."

Slug smiled. "Nigga, gimme a G and I'll bring you all the luxuries of home, plus a muhfuckin' computer," Slug told him.

Freddie was sold. He gave him the money.

"A'ight, yo. I'll be back wit' the heads," Slug told him and left.

An hour later, Slug was commanding a small army of several heads: lift this, pull that, bring this, drop that, scrub, nigga, scrub. By nightfall, they had the joint cleared out and as clean as they could get it. When crackheads worked, they did work. Slug paid them and they left.

"What up wit' the furniture?" Freddie asked.

"Tomorrow, no later than five." Slug grinned mischievously. "But tonight, it's my turn to show you around, nigga."

Freddie looked at Simone. "You wit' it?"

"In this?" she answered, referring to her soiled outfit. She had already worn everything she had brought and they hadn't been to a Laundromat.

"Naw, boo, I'm takin' you shoppin'. Matter of fact, we goin' shoppin'," Freddie offered, taking her by the waist.

"Freddie," she whined cautiously, as if to say, "we're on a budget."

"Nothin' major, yo. Just a little sumptin' to let niggas know how Freddie do and how he got the baddest chocolate *mami* in town." He smiled and she couldn't resist.

Freddie then turned to Slug and smiled. "Let's go to the mall." He tossed his arm around his cousin's neck.

They didn't stay long at the mall, but the time they were there put a dent in their kitty. Freddie was used to the best, and giving Simone the best also was no exception. No matter how much it cost him. As they say, old habits are hard to break.

They went back to Slug's apartment in Jefferson Court to get dressed. Freddie looked at himself in Slug's full-length mirror. He had copped a few pairs of Coogi and Red Monkey jeans. He threw on a black pair of jeans, a pair of black on white and red Jordan 9s, an Ed Hardy hoodie, and a solid black Yankees fitted. He smoothed his curls and inspected the trim up Slug had given him very closely. Freddie was picky about who cut his hair, but he couldn't front; Slug had done a good job with just a razor and a comb.

"Razors give you a sharper line than clippers, nigga. Just chill. I got this," Slug assured him.

Simone came out of the bathroom looking irresistibly delicious in a pair of curve-hugging Seven blue jeans and a multicolored blouse that fastened at her belly button with two metallic Zs, exposing her cleavage in a dagger-like V.

"Boo, look at this, yo," Freddie said, pointing to his goatee. "Does it look even to you?" he asked his lady.

Simone inspected the trim and gave her approval. "Yeah, baby, Slug did a good job."

"You sure?" Freddie asked with skepticism in his tone. He had never been cut with a razor, let alone by an unlicensed barber. Even on the run, he was still conscious of his physical appearance.

"Yeah, she sure, ol' pretty-ass nigga." Slug chuckled.

"Fuck you, cuz!" Freddie shot back. "Babe, seriously, how it look?" he asked Simone again.

"Baby, it's fine, I'm positive," she reassured him. "But what I'm not so sure about is spending all this money. You sure you don't think we should take some of this stuff back?"

Freddie took her by the hands to reassure her. "Dig, boo, regardless of our situation, we ain't gonna stop livin', you hear me? I want you to be happy, and I want you to look good bein' happy, so whatever I gotta do, it's done, feel me?"

She wrapped her arms around his neck, "You make me happy, Freddie. I understand what you're sayin' and I appreciate it, really. But, boo, I'll wear Payless shoes and eat beans out of a can if that's what it'll take to stay together."

She touched Freddie down deep with her words, and all he could do was kiss her as a reply. "I love you, girl." He added a hug. "Now let's forget about everything except havin' a good time. Bada boom?"

"Bada bing!" She smiled, completing their way of saying, "Understand? Understood."

Simone turned to walk out the door. Freddie couldn't help but admire her perfectly heart-shaped ass. "Damn, boo, you gonna make me hurt one of these country niggas behind them jeans."

"Shut up, boy." She blushed. "It's yours."

"Yeah? Well, walk nasty like it's mine." He slid behind her and gripped both cheeks with the palms of his hands. "Matter fact, save mine for later." He kissed her on the back of her neck, then spun her around. "I'm glad you decided to come with me. I won't make you regret it." He then planted his lips against hers and delivered a deep kiss.

Simone pulled back, breaking their lip lock. "So am I." She flashed him a smile. "And"—she paused and inhaled—"I hope not." She exhaled as she stared into his eyes.

Slug watched the scene. It was something straight out of a Lifetime movie, he thought.

This nicca pussy whipped to the tenth power. He chuckled to himself. "Cuz, sorry to break this up but we gotta make moves," Slug reminded him.

Freddie looked over Simone's shoulder and nodded. "Babe, gotta make some runs with Slug to learn the lay of the land."

It was Simone who now nodded. "Okay, be careful, baby."

Freddie could see her eyes misting up. "Hey." He cupped her chin. "Don't I always?"

Simone grimaced. She tried not to roll her eyes but a half of a roll managed to escape.

As soon as he said it, the words had tasted like shit coming out of his mouth. Up until now, he had been careful, but that had changed. And because it had, they were now in the South in unfamiliar territory, hiding. "I will," Freddie retracted, giving Simone one last kiss before he followed Slug out the door.

Chapter Fifteen

"Kiki, come get this li'l muhfucka 'fore I kill 'im!" Slug yelled, sitting on the couch.

Slug had come to pick up Kiki from her apartment in Green Acres. Kiki was his girl, his love-hate ghetto relationship. Her three-year-old son was kicking Slug in the leg, and Slug was fed up with it.

"You better leave my baby alone!" Kiki screamed back from the bedroom. "Chris! Come here, boy!"

"No!" the little brat yelled.

"I'ma kick yo' ass," Slug told him, really wishing he could.

"I'ma kick yo' ass," Chris replied, and kicked Slug again.

Slug shoved him, not hard but hard enough, and Chris screamed, "Mama, he hit me! I'ma tell my daddy!" He ran to his mother for safety because he could tell Slug was mad.

"Fuck yo' punk-ass daddy! Tell that nigga suck my dick!" Slug yelled back.

Kiki came into the living room carrying Chris on a curvaceous hip. She was dressed like the average hood rat: tight spandex dress and open-toed heels from the Shoe Barn, extension braids dyed at the tips and pinned up in a bun. But she was still a real cutie. She was a redbone with light brown eyes and was bowlegged as hell. Her only flaw was a chipped tooth that she got while fighting, which she loved to do, especially with Slug.

"Boy, I know you ain't put your hands on my baby! He ain't none of your chile!" Kiki said, rolling her neck.

"I know he ain't," Slug said, cracking the top on a bottle of E&J. "Dat's why I'ma beat his ass he keep fuckin' wit' me."

Kiki rolled her eyes at Slug and kissed Chris. "Don't worry, boo. He just mean," she said. She shot Slug a look.

"I'ma tell my daddy." Chris played the moment through crocodile tears.

"No, no, don't tell your daddy," Kiki quickly stated. Neither she nor Slug wanted to see her baby daddy fucked up behind something so petty.

"Shit, let him tell him. I'll tell his bitch ass," Slug boasted, serious as a heart attack. "Girl, just bring yo' ass on 'fore I leave you."

"Let me take Chris next door and I'll be ready, ol' mannish ass," Kiki huffed and left to take Chris to her mother's.

Slug shook his head. It was a damn shame when daughter, mother, and grandmother all lived in the projects. It was like blacks were trapped in a game they didn't know was being played. He stood up and left, locking the door behind him.

"Okay, Ma, damn, I heard you!" Kiki said as she slammed the door angrily. Slug was already outside. "You ready?" she snapped and stormed past him to the car. "Bitch make me sick. But let it be the third and she got her nose all up my ass," she mumbled to herself.

Slug chuckled.

"Fuck you laughin' at, Slug? It ain't funny!"

"Man, shut yo' ass up and get in the damn car," Slug replied smoothly.

Freddie and Simone sat in the back seat giggling to themselves, listening to the lovers' quarrel. Kiki opened the front door and the inside light came on. Then she ducked her head down because she damn near drooled. But it happened so quick, no one noticed except Simone. She had just nutted on herself at the sight of Freddie.

"Hey," she said, surprised.

Slug closed his door. "That's my cousin, Freddie, and his wifey, Simone. Y'all, this Kiki."

"Hello," Simone said politely.

Kiki flashed a forced smile.

"What da deal, ma?" Freddie greeted her. His accent tickled Kiki's ears.

"So where we goin'?" Kiki asked, cutting her eye at Freddie in the dark car.

"Pop Bogan's," Slug replied.

Pop Bogan's was the ghetto hangout for the ballers in the Boro. It was a club/ restaurant / pool hall. Only the livest came through because the wannabes got clowned, and Slug was definitely among the live crew of his city.

The spot was flooded when they arrived, as he had expected. "I'm about to show you how we do it down here, cuzzo." He flung his arm around Freddie's neck as a bouncer ushered them inside.

Freddie cut his eyes over at his cousin. "Whatever you say, cuz." He really didn't care one way or another; his mind was elsewhere. For him, it was no vacation or party mode. Had it not been for the altercation he had gotten sucked into back home, he knew he wouldn't even be in the South at all. He looked back at Simone, who walked along side Kiki, trailing behind him and Slug.

"You good?" he mouthed.

Simone read his lips. She smiled and nodded. That put Freddie a little at ease.

"Girl, bring yo' slow ass on." Slug stopped abruptly and turned, directing his words to his shorty.

"Don't rush me!" Kiki rolled her eyes. "And don't be trying to play me out here either," she added as she looked around. She saw a few haters in the long-ass line snicker while waiting to get in. "You gon' fuck around and get one of these bitches fucked up out here thinkin' they can talk to me like," she spat, never taking her eyes off of the three girls.

"Man, just come on. Fuck dem hoes." Slug hooked her by the arm.

His words made her smile as she now rolled her eyes at the hoes Slug was referring to.

Freddie followed suit and drew Simone closer to him, as the two joined in a light laughter.

Although he had been in the state when he was a young buck, he knew it was going to take some getting used to the South again, especially since he had Simone with him. He figured tonight would be as good a time as any.

Chapter Sixteen

Slug pulled his Caddy into the parking lot between a candy apple '64 and a Benz G wagon. Freddie glanced out the window at all the sick whips and niggas blingin'. He promised himself he'd step his game up. Doing what? He didn't know. But he was too used to ballin' to be out-shined by these country niggas.

Once he stepped inside, though, the tables turned and he outshined them all. Trick Daddy's "Thug Holiday" blared in the background, and everyone was doing their own thing. But when Freddie came through, he got the eye of damn near every female and the grill of mad hating-ass niggas.

"Who that? Ginuwine?" he heard one girl inquire to the crowd of lovelies surrounding her.

"Shit, Ginuwine wish he looked that fine!" he caught another reply.

Seeing as how Simone was in the building, he kept a stone face out of respect, but on the inside, he laughed, feeling himself. Simone had never seen the reaction women had over him up close and personal but he was used to it.

Kiki was so not feeling Simone at the moment, the way she was holding on to Freddie's arm, head held high. Simone had niggas sweatin' her on the DL, but since she was with Freddie, and Freddie was with Slug, they checked their tongues.

The four of them caught a corner booth and slid in, keeping the girls next to each other in the middle. It wasn't long before a flood of familiar faces Freddie hadn't seen in years came through. Amp, Cee Jay, and Scoob all came to welcome Freddie back. Freddie could tell they were all doing well and that they hadn't changed a bit. Scoob was still sneaky and treacherous, Amp was blingin', and he could tell Cee Jay was playing, but not as hard as him.

The females itched to come check out the new face, but they saw Simone sitting next to Kiki, and they didn't know if she was Kiki's people. None of them really wanted problems with Kiki, so they just slithered by, asses out and eyes dancing, trying to send Freddie all kinds of messages. Simone didn't miss a beat. She watched them with one eye and Freddie with the other. She had forgiven her man but she hadn't forgotten. Freddie appeared to be taking it all in stride, laughing with the fellas and eating from the shrimp platter they had ordered.

The only female Simone didn't see was to her left: Kiki.

But Slug saw her. He wasn't sure at first, because every time he looked at Kiki to see if she was watching Freddie, she'd slyly look away. It was a cat and mouse game until Slug finally caught her looking at him and plucked her hard in the face.

"A'ight. Don't get fucked up in here," Slug warned her. He was feeling some type of way a little behind the fact that Freddie was getting so much attention, especially from Kiki. It reminded him of how the Miami boys commanded attention when they used to pop up in not only the spot they were in now, but in one of the hot spots he caught them in. He was no hater; he just didn't take too kindly to out-of-towners coming in and soaking up the shine time. Since Freddie was his cousin, he shook it off; he was an exception.

"Boy!" Kiki exclaimed, and mushed Slug in the head just as hard.

Slug responded by plucking her again, harder than the first time, and she lunged at him with her nails.

Simone didn't know what was going on, so she leaned away to keep from getting hit.

"Yo, Slug! Slug! Fuck you doin'? Watch Simone!" Freddie demanded.

Meanwhile, Slug was laughing and pulling Kiki's weave, trying to keep her hands from his throat. "Don't worry, cuz, this broad crazy. All she wanna do is fuck and fight."

"Don't hit me no more, Slug," she growled, hitting him in the chest.

Slug locked his backhand back. "A'ight now, I'm through playin'. I'ma smack the shit out of you now."

"Move then," Kiki replied, pushing his hip with hers. "Move so I can go to the bathroom."

Slug, amused, slid out of the way. Kiki turned to Simone. "You wanna come, girl?" she offered politely.

Simone nodded and slid out of the booth behind Kiki. As the two walked away, Slug slid closer to Freddie and popped a shrimp in his mouth.

"Nigga, y'all on some Ike and Tina shit, for real," Freddie remarked.

Slug chuckled. "Me and Kiki got a crazy understanding. She the only broad I trust. There's been many a day a nigga was shootin' bad and she gave me her last to grind. She just like it rough," Slug explained.

Freddie nodded.

"But, yo," Slug continued, lighting a Newport, "now that you here, what's the next move? The way these chickens sweatin' you, you need to mack these hoes." Slug said it with a subtle hint of bitter sarcasm, which Freddie missed. Freddie was in his own world. From the moment he stepped into the place, he felt like a former crack addict in a smokehouse. Every female's lustful gaze made Freddie think of the paper she represented. He was fien'ing to crack but he wanted with all his heart to keep it real with Simone.

"Nah, yo. Simone proved she'd ride or die when she came wit' me. Shorty gave up a lot for me and I gotta respect that."

Slug took a swig of E&J. "No doubt, no doubt. But you gotta eat. You gotta feed that pretty li'l thang. And believe me, love don't pay no bills."

He had a point there.

"Remember what we talked about up top? 'Bout the connect?" Slug reminded him. "What the deal wit' dat?"

It sounded like the move to make, but the only person Freddie knew and could trust was Gina, and he was trying to leave all that behind. He looked at Slug. "Dog, I can't trust none of them cats in my situation, yo," Freddie lied. "I'd just be askin' for trouble."

"Well, dig, cuz. Whatever whatever, you know I'm wit' you," Slug said and gave Freddie dap. "You play Cee-lo?"

"No doubt."

"Feel lucky?"

"Shit, it ain't but one way to find out."

Meanwhile, in the ladies' room, Kiki was trying to pick Simone's brain. "So how long y'all gonna be down here?"

Simone touched up her lipstick in the mirror and shrugged off the question. "I'm not really sure. Probably not long."

Kiki saw that Simone was being evasive and selective with her information, so she changed the subject. "I love that top, girl. I ain't never seen an Azzure like that. Where you cop that?"

"Thank you," Simone said, smoothing the material. "Just somethin' I had."

The lies you tell, Kiki thought. They sold those at the mall. Something wasn't quite right about her and Freddie, Kiki's nosiness told her. Either Freddie was fine but broke, or he had it and was keeping a low profile. She knew if he was fucking with Slug, family or not, sooner or later if he didn't have paper he would.

Just then, two girls who had been eying Freddie walked into the bathroom. They looked Simone up and down and rolled their eyes as they passed. Simone was about to say something but Kiki stopped her.

"Girl, don't even sweat these no-good bitches. They just hatin' 'cause your man is fine and, believe me, in a town small as the Boro, that's a problem. But don't sweat it. I got your back," Kiki said.

But all Simone could think about was Kiki's own reaction to Freddie. *With friends like that*, she thought as she conjured up a smile.

On the way over to the Cee-lo game, somebody called out, "Freddie! Freddie Holmes! I know that ain't you!" It was a deep, sultry, feminine voice.

He turned around and automatically had to do a double take. She was double-dipped chocolate, a shade darker than Simone, with baby doll eyes and deep-set dimples. She was killin' 'em in her peach and white DKNY velour suit and matching, customized Air Ones. Her jewels sparkled even brighter because of her dark skin tone and she was cutting across the room with the kind of walk that made a nigga hard just watching.

"Tina? Tina Jones?" Freddie echoed, a moment before he was smothered by a full-body hug and subtle grind.

She stepped back and looked him up and down. "How you gonna come home and not make Tina a priority? I thought we was better than that."

Freddie had done his own visual evaluation on her as well, but on the low. He didn't know where Simone was. He looked from his left to his right before he fully engaged in conversation with Tina. His survey was quick but effective. She had developed nicely in all the right places, he noticed. Her breasts protruded out perfect enough to be used as someone's drink holder, while her hips prevented others from getting too close if they stood next to her. Her thick thighs looked like she had on football pads, not to mention the baby knuckles poking out of her V, between her inner thighs. She definitely did not look like the petite country girl he remembered.

Tina had been his summer girlfriend when he was twelve and she was thirteen. It was little kid puppy love. Besides a few tongueless kisses and games of "catch a girl, get a girl," which sent him home with tents in his Fruit of the Looms, it was innocent. Back then, Tina was long legged, skinny, and taller than him. But now she was Trina thick, Luke dancer thick, and a whole head shorter than him.

Tina saw that Freddie had eyed her figure, so she whirled around to slap his eyes full of ass and stood with her hands on her hips. "Yeah, nigga, it's me. All growed up and out." She laughed, exposing his weakness: a platinum tongue ring. Her lip gloss popped with each syllable that exited her mouth. Freddie's dick jumped at the fullness of them. He could already envision them wrapped around him.

"I see that," was all Freddie could get out.

Slug was definitely not feeling this. He had been trying to fuck Tina, but since she was fucking that Miami nigga, she wouldn't let him smash.

"So what up, Freddie? Slug know where I live, but I bet you ain't even ask," she remarked, mock pouting.

Before Freddie could answer, Simone and Kiki came out of the bathroom and quickly approached. Simone thought all this competition was quickly getting played out but she held her composure. "Hey, baby," she cooed, wrapping her arms around Freddie's neck and giving him a quick kiss. "Did you miss me?"

"No doubt," Freddie stuttered, tearing his eyes away from Tina and focusing on Simone.

Simone fronted at first like Tina wasn't standing there, then acknowledged her presence. "Oh, hello, I ain't even see you. Were y'all talkin'?" Simone asked innocently, but her eyes staked claim.

Tina wanted to say something fly, but Freddie cut in. "Simone, this is Tina, an old childhood friend. Tina, this is Simone, my fiancée."

Simone's facial expression was bland. "Oh, you're from Plainfield?"

Tina giggled. "Naw! I'm from da Dirty, born and raised," she chimed.

A confused look appeared across Simone's face.

"Long story, babe," Freddie intervened.

Tina rolled her eyes but Simone didn't catch it. "Humph, congratulations," she shot at Simone like a subtle accusation.

"I know." Simone smiled.

Freddie saw where this was going. "So what up, boo? You ready to bounce? I'm tired as a muthafucka."

"Tired?" Slug repeated. "I thought . . ." He motioned toward the Cee-lo game but Freddie shot him a loaded glance.

"Sure, baby," Simone replied, letting him off the hook. For now.

He turned to Tina. "Yo, Tina, on the real, it was good seein' you, ma." He could see the lust in her eyes the moment he turned and faced her.

She shot him a full frontal gaze that she made sure Simone caught, licking her lips, exposing his weakness. "It was good seein' you too, Freddie. Real good." She put emphasis on her last words.

Tina then sashayed off and faded into the crowd. Freddie had to fight not to watch her juicy ass jiggle. The entire ride home, Freddie couldn't stop thinking about how thick Tina had gotten. Big girls were not his thing, but Tina made him curious about a BBW. He had always heard that everything was bigger and better when it came to plus-size chicks. He wondered if that applied to Tina. He was sure he was bound to run into her again.

Later that evening, Simone lay in bed wide awake, staring up at the ceiling. She too could not shake the encounter at the club. She didn't want to be petty or be a pain, but something about the girl just seemed to rub her the wrong way. She rolled over on her side and propped herself up with her left hand, while shaking Freddie with her right.

"Huh?" Freddie jumped out of his sleep. For the first few seconds he didn't know where he was. It wasn't until he saw Simone's beautiful face that he realized he was only having a nightmare. Grateful she had woken him out of it he asked, "Why are you still up, bae?"

"Who was she?" Simone ignored his question.

"What?" Freddie looked at her oddly. He had no clue what she was talking about.

"Who was she? At the club?" she repeated, being a little more specific. She was convinced he knew exactly who she was talking about.

"Who?" Freddie answered her question with a question, trying to play dumb.

Simone propped herself up on her elbow some more and looked at him with the "Nigga, don't play wit' me" face. But Freddie knew that if he had come right out and started talking about Tina, she would think Tina was on his mind, which she obviously was.

"I'm serious. Who was that disrespectful-ass girl at the club, Freddie?" she insisted.

"Disrespectful? What she do?" Now Freddie began to play the tapes back in his head.

"Just answer the question, Freddie."

"Tina?" he asked, or rather, confirmed.

"You used to be wit' her, didn't you?" Simone stated.

Freddie sucked his teeth nonchalantly. "If you call two li'l twelve-year-olds bein' together, then yeah."

"Did you do it to her?" Simone asked directly.

Freddie laughed. "Do it to her? You sound like you twelve or somethin'."

"Oh, you want the grown version?" Simone found no humor in his statement. "Did you fuck her, huh, Freddie?" she asked, irked.

"No, I didn't do it to her. I didn't fuck her either. I told you, we was twelve. Damn," he cursed. He hated being accused of something he didn't do, even though it wasn't like he wasn't trying to fuck her at twelve.

Simone sat up and wrapped her arms around her knees. "Freddie, I'm not going to compete for you. I love you with all my heart, but I don't like feeling like everywhere we go or everything we do I have to compete, because every time I turn around, somebody somewhere is plottin' to take what I got. It's too much. . . ."

Her words drifted off in frustration. Freddie sat up to cradle and comfort her. "Come on, ma. You ain't never got to compete for me. What did I do tonight to make you feel like that?" he wanted to know; but deep down inside he already knew.

"It wasn't you, Freddie. I just saw all those girls looking and—"

Freddie kissed her on the neck. "Simone, look at me." He put his finger up under her chin and guided her face in his direction. She turned her head and looked into his eyes.

"Just like I can't stop niggas from lookin' at you, I can't stop females from lookin' at me," he began to explain. "But I can control how I handle it. So I ask you again, did I do anything tonight to make you feel like you ain't the only one for me?"

She searched his eyes for a moment and found nothing but sincerity. "You didn't do anything."

"And I won't. I promise, babe." His tone was sincere. "After all we've been through, I'd be a fool to give up the best thing that ever happened to me," he assured her.

"She was pretty, though." Simone smirked, referring to the girl back at the club.

"You're prettier," he replied.

"No, I'm beautiful, remember?" she reminded him.

Chapter Seventeen

Slug kept his word. The next day, a U-Haul truck full of furnishings was delivered by a couple of crackheads who were running ghetto moves on Rent-America, flipping apartments. He had paid the extra to put everything together for them. Simone opened the apartment door and took a step back to take it all in. It looked just like a photo straight out of IKEA.

"Welcome home," Freddie, said giving her a glimmer of hope. He led her inside the house and helped her get comfortable by taking her coat and giving her permission to take off her shoes. "Follow me."

Slug had hooked them up. As if hypnotized, Simone didn't say a word and followed Freddie up the stairs, down the hall, and into his bedroom.

"Have a seat on the bed," Freddie said as he went into the bathroom. He came out with five candles and a lighter that he had grabbed from the dollar store earlier. He set the five candles on top of his dresser. He lit them one by one then turned off the lights in his room.

Simone looked around the room as if the lights had gone off by themselves. Her ears suddenly heard the sound of one of her favorite male R&B groups, coincidentally one of her favorite songs. She looked at Freddie, now shirtless, standing by the radio with the remote in his hand.

"What's going on?"

Freddie grooved toward her, snapping his fingers with each step he took. He placed his finger over her lips and grabbed her hands to lift her from the bed. She allowed herself to follow. He wrapped his hands around her hips and locked his fingers together so that she could not pull away from him. She responded by throwing her hands around his neck, turned on by the fact that he wanted to slow dance in the middle of his room.

Freddie!" she protested.

"Dance with me, baby." He smiled.

Simone couldn't resist his charming grin. She stepped into his embrace. They swayed back and forth, silently, and let their eyes do all the talking.

Simone instinctively laid her head on his bare chest and stared down at his abs. She inhaled his masculine scent and ran her hands down his back. Just as the music changed to the next track, she kissed his chest. She looked up at Freddie immediately afterward, as if she had done something wrong.

"Everything's going to be okay, isn't it?" she asked in a low whisper.

"I promise," was the soft reply she had received. Then Freddie whisked her into his arms and carried her over to the bed. Without asking, all in one motion, he unfastened Simone's jeans and began lowering them.

"Freddie," Simone said, shy and bubbly. "Didn't Slug say he'd be back in thirty minutes?" she reminded him as she inched away.

"That's more than enough time." He flashed the same smile he had just revealed moments ago.

Simone let out a light chuckle. She wanted to feel his full lips kissing every part of her body and his firm, large hands gripping her thighs as they made love. It amazed her that she was moments away from getting that desire. It caused her heart to beat faster.

"You sure?" she cooed, running her hand along the side of his face. Her fingers outlined the shape of his lips, as she examined the passionate look on his face. "I'm just nervous."

It was Freddie's turn to chuckle. He ran his hands along the curves of her legs until they were resting on her arm. "Nothin' to worry about. I got you. You trust me, right?" he asked.

Simone nodded. "With all of my being," Simone answered, staring around his face. Anywhere but into his eyes. But the moment she did, her eyes told it all and Freddie seen every ounce of it.

He ran his fingers through her curly hair. "You really want this?"

Simone nodded silently. Then, their eyes met again. She was lost in them, every emotion in her body being released. His smoldering looks were overwhelming her.

He swept her off her feet and laid her onto the bed. He went in for the kill and kissed her strongly. Their kiss led to hands touching every part of the other's body. They stripped each other of their remaining clothes, both ready for what was going to take place in the next moments. Simone prepared herself to give Freddie what she knew he wanted, and receive what she needed. With all that was going on, she could use a stress reliever.

Freddie let her sweet scent be his guide as he traveled down to the moist center between her legs. He gently kissed her inner thighs until he was face to face with her prized possession.

He ran his tongue across her more sensitive area, causing her legs to quiver. A sensual gasp escaped from her mouth, turning Freddie on. He gripped her thighs as he continued to taste her. His tongue explored her sex while his lips sucked on her clit.

"Ooooooooooooooooooh, Freeeeeeeeddddie," Simone moaned. She tried to push his head from between her legs but he wouldn't budge. Her legs shook uncontrollably when she felt her first orgasm, a sensation she had not felt in a long time. "Aaaaaahweeee."

Freddie pulled away from her and licked his lips. Round two. He grabbed his now rock-hard dick ready to take Simone's body to the next level. He opened her legs wider. He leaned over to the nightstand, opened the drawer, and pulled out one of the Magnums. He stared at her as he slid it on. She flashed a half of a smile.

He leaned down and kissed her as he placed his hand between Simone's legs. He massaged her clit with two fingers while slipping one inside of her. His manhood stiffened even more. He knew she was ready and so was he.

Simone's body tensed up when Freddie entered her. "Please, Freddie. Go slow, go slow," she whispered in his ear.

"I got you," he replied. He paused, just to absorb the moment. She felt incredible. She was a place that he never wanted to leave. He had waited for this moment a long time too. He wanted to make it pleasurable for her and worth it. He wanted Simone to know that she wasn't a quick bang he had been waiting to score. She was his future wife, and so he would sex her as such. He was not into giving oral but there was no doubt in his mind that he was going to make Simone an exception. She was different and he wanted her to know that.

He slowly slipped deeper inside her wet center. Tender from her tight hole being reopened, Simone bit her bottom lip and took the pain, and the pleasure that followed.

"You good?" he asked her as he continued his slow grind.

"Yes," she moaned in ecstasy, her nails clawing into his back.

It turned him on so much that with each light scratch to his back he thrust harder inside her. Simone's legs quivered with the onset of a second orgasm. She let out a loud moan and let her juices ooze onto Freddie. Even through the condom, Freddie could feel her sex muscles contracting. Unable to hold on any longer, Freddie pulled out, snatched the condom off, and released himself onto her inner thighs. She watched, breathing heavily, as his cream spilled onto her leg. She reached out for him, grabbed hold of his dick, and began stroking it, to be sure that every ounce of his juices was released. Freddie tried to resist. His dick was still sensitive and her touched was weakening him. His body collapsed on top of hers. He himself was also winded. Simone cuddled him in her arms and planted a kiss on his forehead.

"I love you, Freddie Holmes," she whispered.

"I love you back, ma. I needed that," he replied.

Freddie found the strength to get up and go into the bathroom to grab them each a wet towel. He returned and wiped his juices off Simone's legs and her own from between hers. With the other towel, he wiped himself clean and returned the two towels to the bathroom.

"Did you want to shower?" he asked her.

When he didn't hear a response, he looked into the room to see why. The sight of her resting on the plush bed caused a huge grin to appear across his face. Rather than take a shower, he climbed onto the bed and nestled up under Simone. She scooted her voluptuous, round bottom back to him, and reached for his arm. Freddie pulled her in closer until they became one as the two drifted off into a dream world.

Chapter Eighteen

For the next few weeks, Freddie and Simone were inseparable. They spent the type of quality time together they hadn't spent in months. They went to the movies and out to dinner, or just took long walks, then watched bootleg DVDs on their jacked wide screen.

Freddie continued to spend the little money they had until it dwindled down into a no-win situation. He had to cop a half ounce and start his nickel-and-dime hustle with Slug as his mentor. Slug schooled him on the ins and outs of the dope game. They set up shop in the Old Projects and Freddie stayed true to his grind. His problem was his spending habits. As soon as he made it, he spent it, determined to look like a thousand dollars even if he really couldn't afford to. Freddie didn't slack on Simone either. He kept her dipped, hair and nails done.

Simone and Kiki became running partners if not close friends. Kiki turned her on to the best hairdresser in town, Nina Simone. And Simone still got sly looks and snide comments thrown her way. Not only because Freddie was her man, and no female had been able to violate that, but because of her gear. Freddie did what he could, keeping her in new shit, but his paper was too short to elevate her to diva status. But Simone didn't mind. The way things were going with Freddie and her, she'd wear rags and sweep floors to keep their love strong. She did try to get Freddie to stack paper instead of always spending it.

She pulled up in the '90 Accord Freddie had copped for $1,500. It wasn't much but it got them around. Freddie was in front of the white store shooting dice when she pulled up. He jogged over to the car, leaned through the window, and gave her a kiss.

"Freddie, I'm going to pay the bills," she informed him.

He knew the monthly tab usually came to about $700. He gave her a grand. "Take that other three hundred and go to the jeweler and pay on my watch for me, boo."

"Freddie," she whined. They had been through all this before. "What about food? Hello? I need to go shopping, too," she reminded him.

"Oh, I got that. This head owe me like two and some change. I'ma get it off they welfare card," he replied.

"But still, Freddie. You know you don't need to be out here in the first place. Please, boo, we need to put somethin' up, you know?"

He gave her a shut up kiss. "After I cop my watch, okay? I gotta go. I'm killin' these niggas!" He jogged back to the dice game and Simone pulled off.

Freddie's conversation with Slug became redundant. He constantly heard, "Cuz, I'm tellin' you, this li'l nickel and dime ain't shit. We need a connect." But for Freddie that was out. He was failing to see the bigger picture; that was, until the whole frame changed.

Freddie was out in front of the white store, waiting for Mandrell to come through and sell him an ounce. He was listening to a club mix in his CD Walkman, so he didn't even hear the jump-outs skid up and hop out on him.

The big, burly redneck and his even bigger black partner walked up on him and said, "Don't make us chase you; we get ugly when we're out of breath."

Freddie's heart froze. This was his first run-in with the police since he had heard, "Freeze," and fired, which was what landed him in the situation now confronting him. Fortunately, it was nighttime and he was wearing a fitted Yankees cap. But the fact remained that if he went to jail, it was a wrap. He didn't have any drugs on him and his gun was twenty-five feet away, under the bushes. All he had was $1,500 in his pocket. He tried to play it calm.

"Run? For what, yo? I'm chillin', waitin' on a cab," Freddie replied.

The cops picked up his Northern accent so they automatically assumed he was a drug dealer. "Oh, you one of them New Yawk boys, huh? I been seein' you a lot lately. What's your name, boy?" the wannabe black officer asked, stepping toward Freddie.

Freddie weighed his options. They were too close for him to run. If he did and got caught, it was jail for sure. But if he stayed and sweated it out, maybe he could get away. "Antoine Jackson, Officer."

"Jackson, huh?" the redneck asked, frisking his pockets. "You got any drugs or guns we need to know about?"

"No, sir," Freddie answered, his hands raised.

"Any outstanding warrants?" he questioned.

"No, no, sir."

"Oh! What's this?" the redneck said triumphantly, taking the wad of money from Freddie's pocket. He whistled. "Jackpot!"

If Freddie was gonna run, that would have been the time, but he hesitated, and his window of opportunity closed as quickly as it had opened.

The redneck officer handed the money to his partner, who counted it and said sarcastically, "Boy, it's over a thousand dollars here. What you doin' carryin' this kind of cash in a neighborhood like this?"

The redneck frisked Freddie again. "Take off your shoes, boy."

Freddie obliged without hesitation and they found nothing.

"Well, Mr. Jackson, unless you have some kind of check stub, we're gonna have to confiscate this legal tender here," the redneck drawled.

"Come on, yo," Freddie whined. "After I cash my check, what I look like keepin' the stub?"

"Where you work?"

"In Raleigh," Freddie shot back quickly. Too quick for the redneck's taste.

"Where in Raleigh?" the redneck drilled.

"Vs Everybody. It's a clothing store," he lied. The store was really in Florence, South Carolina, but it was the first thing that came to Freddie's mind. The store was actually owned by one of his homies from back home who had migrated to South Carolina and opened up a customized clothing store.

"Well, unless you got that stub . . ." the red-neck continued.

Freddie sighed. "Man, fuck it. I ain't got it, yo. So do what you gotta do." He was sick to be losing all he had, but he'd be sicker if they tried to run him in. He was ready to get it over with.

"Just like I thought. You gave up too easy, New Yawk." The redneck smiled. "Looka here, if I drive through here and see you again, for any reason, I won't be so understanding. You got me?"

Freddie nodded.

"You got me?" the redneck repeated, firmer than before.

"Yeah, I got you." His head shook up and down rapidly.

The redneck flashed him a big smile, held his money up, and replied, "You have a nice night, ya hear? Come on, Willie."

The two officers walked away and got into their car. Freddie's knees damn near went out. He was that close to making a break for his pistol because jail wasn't an option. When they drove away, reality set in.

He was dead broke and it was past the first of the month. Freddie walked the few blocks to the crib not knowing what to do. He could easily get money for the bills from Slug, or Mandrell could front him a pack, but he had been fingered. Now the jump-out boys knew his face, and he couldn't afford to get hit wit' murder one just because he got caught pitching.

Before he knew it, he was home and walking into the living room. Simone was making his favorite: lasagna. He could smell it, but his stomach was too sick to eat. He walked into the kitchen to a bubbly Simone. She was singing and cooking, and she turned around when he came in.

"Hey, boo!" she said like she hadn't seen him in days instead of hours. She kissed him passionately, but when he didn't return the fire, she looked him in the eyes. "Freddie, what's wrong?"

He sat down heavily at the kitchen table. "The fuckin' police, yo."

At the sound of the word "police," Simone's heart skipped a beat. "Where? What happened?" She was heading for panic mode. Now was not the time for her man to go to jail. She was prepared to run to the ends of the earth before she'd let Freddie get caught. "Do we have to leave?"

"Naw, yo. The muthafuckas just took my money! All my shit!" he exclaimed angrily. He was so mad he might've cried.

Simone kneeled down in front of him. "Baby, it could've been worse. We can get the money back. Besides"—she winked—"I got a little some-thin' put up."

Freddie looked into her smile like a new day had dawned.

"I told you and I told you to save, so I just took my own advice. Instead of getting my hair done, I just did it myself," she said, shrugging.

He pulled her up onto his lap and hugged her tight, "Damn, you my heart, girl."

"But, Freddie," she said, pulling back from the hug, "you can't go back out there. Now they know your face."

He had surmised as much, but he wasn't prepared for what Simone said next.

"Let me go."

He couldn't believe his ears. He looked up into her eyes and they were dead serious. "What?"

"I said, let me go. Let me go out there. Nobody'll bother me because they'll know I work for you and Slug. And you can be somewhere close by but out of sight."

Damn. She a ride or die chick for real. "Naw, ma. I can't let you do that," Freddie said, head hanging.

Simone put her hand under his chin and lifted it. "Well, I can't let you go back out there," and she was serious. Then she took a deep breath.

"They say when it rains it pours, right? Well, right now it's stormin'." She tried to smile to lighten the mood.

"No doubt," he agreed.

"No, I mean . . ." She stood up and walked to the stove, then turned back to Freddie. "Freddie, I got somethin' to tell you."

He looked her in the face and didn't need to hear any more; he already knew. Freddie hopped out of his chair, joyfully. "Say word!" All the Jersey in him came out then.

Simone had been trying to figure out how to tell him all day. She didn't know how he would take it because she didn't know how she felt about it, so she planned a special evening and cooked a big dinner to break the news. Simone nodded slowly.

"Hell, yeah!" Freddie exclaimed proudly and picked Simone up, spinning her around. "I'ma be a daddy!" He picked her up again and kissed her like he was trying to eat her up. After a moment she spoke up.

"But, Freddie, with the way things are, do you think—"

He cut her off, firmly but sweetly. "Don't even think it, boo. I told you, regardless, we ain't gonna let nothin' stop us from living. And a baby? Yo, that's what living is all about!" He held her tight, squeezing the tears out of her eyes. "I want you to have my son, Simone. Nothing in the world will make me happier."

She had needed to hear her man say just that. There was no way she wanted to have an abortion, and she didn't know what she would have done if he had suggested it. But hearing him say what he said gave her the strength to be happy.

"Thank you, Freddie," she whispered through tears of joy. "You don't know how much it means to me to hear you say that."

He looked into her eyes. "You just take care of my little man. Let daddy worry about the rest."

"Okay, daddy," she cooed like a woman in love.

Chapter Nineteen

Freddie told Slug about the police incident and he agreed with Simone. "Yo, cuz, Timmons and Jake ain't no joke. Word up, if they said it, they meant it, and you can't afford that shit."

But Slug agreed for his own reason. He thought that now Freddie would finally try to hit up a connect. Freddie had other plans. He rode out to the mall. He didn't know exactly what he was going to do but he knew what he was going for. He was dressed to kill, casual in a pair of beige Polo slacks, a black, beige, and brown Polo button-up, and a pair of black Clarks. He was wearing Pleasures for men and had his short curls groomed and shining. He finished off his outfit with a pair of oval Polo frames that gave him a studious and intelligent air.

As he cruised through the mall, looking for a victim, he tried to tell himself that this was going to be a one-time thing, just to get him over the hump. But like an alcoholic deciding to have just one drink, he knew what he was doing was dangerous.

Smiling and flirting, holding doors open and warmly greeting each female's face made him think of Simone, and the guilt weighed heavily on his back. He thought of their unborn child growing in her womb and the promise he'd made to be true. Still, he tried to convince himself that this was for her, that he was only looking for a woman to seduce and juice for their growing family. He finally found one at the perfume counter in Belk. She was a white woman with blond hair who looked as if she might be in her early forties. He peeped the ring confirming that she was married, and he eyed the platinum Visa confirming that she was also paid.

"Excuse me," Freddie said, approaching the counter, "I noticed that you just purchased White Diamonds by Liz Taylor. I love that fragrance." He smiled.

The woman looked up into his green eyes and smiled back. "Oh, it's not for me. It's a birthday gift for my sister," she responded.

"What a coincidence, it's my mother's birthday." Freddie chuckled. "But the problem is, she hates White Diamonds. So, um, I was wondering"—he began to lick his lips and made the woman watch his tongue—"if maybe you could help me pick out a nice fragrance for her."

The lady giggled. "Oh, I don't know. I'm really not an expert or anything. I just know what I like."

"But you have such good taste," Freddie said. He gently placed his hand on hers and felt a slight tremble run up her arm. "Please."

"Well . . ." She thought about it. "Maybe just for a minute."

Freddie eyed her closely from head to toe. She was dressed conservatively, but everything she wore was expensive. Her silk blouse clung to her ample bosom and her skirt hugged her petite waist. She stood about five feet three inches but her heels made her taller.

"What about this?" she asked, showing him a bottle of Sung by Alfred Sung. She sprayed a little into the air.

"I can't tell, uh . . . I'm sorry, I didn't even ask your name."

"Cynthia."

"I'm Freddie, and I think I could decide better if you sprayed it here." Freddie took the bottle and sprayed a little on the inside of her wrist. Then he gently lifted her arm to his nose, making sure his lips brushed across her flesh ever so gently. He could hear the faint sigh in her throat.

"No, that's a little racy for Mama. That's more of an evening out on the town." Freddie picked up a bottle of J-Lo. "What about this?"

Cynthia looked at the bottle. "J-Lo. I've never heard of that."

"No?" Freddie fronted like he was surprised. "J-Lo is short for Jennifer Lopez. She's a very beautiful Latina singer/actress who is known to be very hot, very sensual. In fact, if I may . . ." He raised the bottle and sprayed a little on her neck, making her eyelids flutter. "May I?" Freddie flashed a charismatic smile.

Cynthia could only nod.

He leaned in close to her ear so his words could be felt. "Now this reminds me of red: red roses, red wine, red satin sheets, and sexy red toenails in sexy red six-inch stilettos."

Cynthia's pink erect nipples pressed against the silk of her blouse like a child pressing his or her face to the glass of a candy store, licking his or her lips.

Freddie pulled away and shrugged. "Definitely not a mommy fragrance. Maybe I should just get her a wok," he joked and Cynthia giggled.

"Thank you so much for your time, Cynthia." He shook her hand, running a finger across her palm and causing her to reflexively grip his hand as the sensation ran up her spine.

"No . . . no problem, umm, Freddie," she replied, slightly hoarse.

"How can I make it up to you?" He was still holding her hand.

"Oh, there's no—"

He gently cut her off. "No, there is, because it would break my heart to see you walk away."

It was a wrap. It didn't take much to convince the well-off, lonely housewife to drive around the corner and meet Freddie at the Irish Inn, a seedy, secluded motel that fit Cynthia's fantasy of taboo.

Once inside the room, Freddie wasted no time putting his mack down on the squareness of Cynthia's naiveté. He pinned her against the door, snatching her skirt up to her hips, pushing past her panties, and shoving three fingers inside her warm pinkness.

"Is this how you want it, huh? You want that thug shit, don't you?" Freddie woofed and Cynthia was loving it.

"Oh, yes! Yes!" She tried to kiss him but he turned away.

"I got something for you to kiss," he told her, snatching his manhood out of his pants and pushing her down on her knees. He slid the whole length into her mouth, pumping in and out, sexing her face.

"Damn! You a nasty bitch, ain't you? Ain't you?" Freddie accosted her. The only reply was the gagging in her throat. He didn't even try to hold back. He came in her mouth and watched it spill out and run down her chin. He lifted her off her knees, took her to the bed, and pushed her down onto it.

"What are you gonna do to me, Freddie?" Cynthia panted, unbuttoning her blouse and exposing her pale, white breasts and pink nipples.

"Did I tell you to speak?"

"No," Cynthia stuttered in mortal fear, but she was getting more turned on by the minute by the huge black dick that was in her face.

Freddie slid on a condom, cocked her legs back until her knees damn near touched her shoulders, and entered her with the force of a jackhammer. The pain and pleasure made Cynthia scream out and cum instantly, clawing Freddie's shirt. She broke a nail.

"Oh, my God!" she squealed, trying to squirm away from the incessant pounding. She felt herself coming a second time. "Oh, Freddie, not again!" she moaned as her juices flowed, soaking the bed beneath her ass.

Freddie abruptly pulled out and stood back.

"Fr . . . Freddie, why did you stop?" she huffed.

"You want this dick? Crawl to it. Crawl to this dick," he commanded, and she slid off the bed onto the floor on all fours as Freddie backed away gradually.

"Oh, please, Freddie. Come—"

"Crawl yo' pink ass to this dick!" Freddie repeated emphatically until his back was against the wall between the bed and the bathroom. She was all over him like a woman possessed, dragging him down to the floor and squatting on top of him. She rode him furiously, taking all of him inside of her. Freddie sat back and watched her go crazy, smiling.

"Don't cum in the condom, Freddie. Cum in my mouth again, cum in—"

She felt him building up and hopped off his dick. She snatched the rubber off and let it explode all over her face. She licked her lips as if it were whipped cream.

After they showered together and redressed, Freddie closed the deal.

"Freddie, I can't give you my home number, but this is my cell number. Will you use it, please?" Cynthia asked, wrapping her arms and one leg around him.

"I can't. I don't know, ma. You see . . ." He sighed. "I feel so embarrassed telling you this."

"What?" she asked with a concern born of lust.

"I may have to leave town."

"No!" She gasped.

"I got, like, this gambling habit, and I owe a few guys a lot of money. They've been all over me and if I don't pay soon . . ." Freddie shook his head then kissed her forehead. "So if I never see you again, Cynthia, I'll—"

"But, Freddie, how much do you owe them?"

He should have been an actor. Denzel didn't have a better method. "I don't know, like, three Gs."

"Gs?" she asked, confused.

"I'm sorry, three thousand. Three thousand dollars," he replied in sheer defeat.

"Freddie, that's a lot of money." Her eyes widened. "And besides, we just met," she pointed out.

"I know, I know. And believe me, I hate even coming at you like this. Now you see why I have to leave."

All she had to hear was the word "leave." She couldn't imagine losing the lover of a lifetime. "I . . . I can give it to you."

Freddie looked at her and had to hide his laughter. "Cynthia, I hardly know you. I can't."

"But if you leave, I'll never be able to get to know you."

"Oh, Cynthia!" he exclaimed, hugging her and smirking behind her back. "Thank you so much, sooo much! I promise I'll pay you back as soon as I can!"

"Pay me back now," she said, and pushed him back toward the bed, fire burning in her eyes. She felt that her husband's money had never been so well spent.

Early That Next Morning

Freddie lay in the waterbed next to Simone, staring at himself in the overhead mirror. *Nigga, you ain't shit*, he thought. He had brought the three Gs home and told Simone he had won it gambling, a boldfaced lie that just rolled off his tongue like ice water. Once again, he had broken his promise to Simone. She lay snuggled up under him, safe and content.

Freddie felt like he had done what he had to do. If he wasn't shit, so be it, but the bills were paid, their stomachs were full, and both of them had new outfits. Freddie thought of Cynthia. He could see that she would get crazy the more he sexed her and played mind games with her. Her hormones had been bottled up too long, and now that they had been released, shit could get out of control.

But if not her, who? he wondered, knowing he wouldn't stop until he found a worthy candidate. It would take months to build his stable up like he had back in New Jersey, and Goldsboro was entirely too small for that type of mack. Naw, he had to keep his circle small, real small. *One. Gina.* If he was gonna play, Gina killed two birds with one nut. It was time to give Slug the connect he'd been begging for. Why not? He couldn't resist who he was, what he was. He loved Simone, but he loved himself at the same time. Only time would tell who he loved more.

Freddie swung his feet out of bed. Simone instantly missed his warmth and stirred. "Go back to sleep, boo," he said, and she did. He threw on his pants and a T-shirt, and slid his bare feet into a pair of construction Timbs. He left the apartment and crossed the deserted street to the phone booth in front of Piggly Wiggly. He dialed the number he knew by heart. The phone rang, and rang again, and again, and again.

"Freddie, this better not be you," Gina's sleepy voice warned when she picked up the phone.

He wasn't surprised that she knew it was him. Whether it was the caller ID or the late hour, Gina was always on point. "Yeah, ma. This me," Freddie confirmed.

"Well?"

"Well, what?"

"Nigga, what you want? I ain't heard from you in damn near three fuckin' months! I didn't know if you were dead, alive, where your ass was at, if you were okay . . ." She caught her breath, glad to hear from him and, at the same time, releasing three months' worth of stress and frustration. "So I know you want something, callin' here three in the mornin'. What? You had to wait until that little bitch went to sleep?" she barked. She had never called Simone a bitch before, so he knew she was heated. "What do you want, Freddie?" she demanded.

"I just called to see how you were doin', yo." He tried to sound casual.

Gina laughed in his face. "Nigga, fuck you for thinkin' I'm some lame-ass trick! Matter of fact, good—"

"A'ight, a'ight, Gina. I don't want anything. I need to see you."

There was silence.

"Gina? You hear me, ma?" he asked, his heart sinking thinking Gina was too through with him.

"I heard you. Just gimme one reason why I shouldn't hang up in your face."

This time he was silent.

"Uh-huh, just what I thought," Gina declared. "You know you ain't shit, don't you, Freddie?"

"I am what I am."

"What you are is a no-good little boy wit' some good community dick. And if I decide to see you, it's because I know it's killin' you to know that there's somebody who knows you for who you truly are, who you can't fool, who you ain't slicker than." She laughed. Freddie couldn't do anything but accept the painful truth.

"I'll call you when I get to Raleigh," she said, then abruptly hung up.

Chapter Twenty

Freddie sat in the Blue Note bar tossing back top shelf Rémy while contemplating his next move. He was still gloating about the fact that soon he would be seeing Gina. She was one of the few things he had missed about being back up North. When he was out ripping and running in the streets, seeing her name randomly appear across his phone's screen was always a highlight and reward for how hard he really played. Gina was something special he knew. She was the only one who ever made him question or doubt how solid his love really was for Simone. She was the type of woman who would make any man want to do better. He knew he had to at least appear to be on top of his game when Gina came down. The last thing he wanted her to see was him looking like he had fallen off. She had seen him one way and one way only: fresh to death at all times. Out of all the times in the world, when he had gone to Slug for some extra cash to set it out for her, he had discovered that Slug had already flipped what they had hustled up throughout the week. Financially, his options were limited. He actually only had one option. Against his better judgment, he pulled out his phone and texted Cynthia. Her immediate response and answer caused a huge smile to appear on his mug.

An hour after she'd received the text, Cynthia pulled across the street from the place Freddie had texted her the address to and parked. Although she was from the area, she had never before been in the particular part of the city where the local bar was located. She sat nervously in her silver Mercedes-Benz truck, waiting for Freddie to come out as she peered out of all mirrors. Every time she saw a black face walk passed her SUV, her heart skipped a beat. Just when she thought she couldn't take it anymore, out came Freddie. She watched as he slightly staggered out of the hole-in-the-wall establishment.

Freddie looked around. Once he spotted the Benz, he flashed a smile and held up his hand. Cynthia flicked the big beams to confirm what he had already known. It didn't take a genius to figure out that she didn't belong in the area. It wasn't until Freddie had reached her truck that Cynthia unlocked the doors. Freddie laughed on the inside as he climbed in.

"Hey, beautiful," Freddie semi slurred. He could tell by her grimace that she both smelled the liquor on his breath and knew he was intoxicated. But he didn't care. After all, he was in charge, he believed. "Pull off," he instructed.

"Where to?" she asked with hesitancy.

"Wherever." He leaned over and grabbed her inner thigh firmly.

His hand sent a thousand volts through Cynthia's body. She was instantly turned on. She started to head straight to where he had first managed to get her open in under twenty-four hours, but decided on another destination.

He inhaled the scent of her cucumber-infused perfume. A tipsy Freddie smiled at nothing in particular. Cynthia noticed. "Are you okay?" she asked. "I mean, what's your deal?" she added.

Freddie chuckled. "What do mean what's my deal?"

"You're drunk, apparently," she pointed out. "Are sure you don't want to get together another time?" she asked, even though that's not what she really wanted. She realized although Freddie did something to her body, she knew nothing about him. The last thing she wanted was to wind up dealing with a replica of her alcoholic husband. Her thought was ended by the sound of Freddie's voice. "Excuse me?"

"You heard me. Turn around and take me back to where you picked me up at," he repeated. Her words had sobered Freddie up just enough to put her in her place.

"Why? What's wrong?" She was confused.

"Because it's apparent this ain't what you want!" he boomed. "I don't have time for these games you wanna play. It's either you want this dick or you don't." His words sounded like something straight out of a pimp guide. "Maybe another time, another place," he then said instead.

"Noooo! Please, baby," Cynthia pleaded. "I didn't mean anything by it. I was only concerned," she lied. "I do want you. I wish I could have you inside of me every night," she confessed.

The four double shots of 1738 he had thrown back had him feeling a little more than nice. "I'm cookin'," he said to himself, shaking his head.

Cynthia pulled into the driveway of her and her husband's five-bedroom, two car–garage home. She hit the garage switch over her visor and drove in. Her husband was out of town on business and she knew her bed would be perfect for her young boy toy.

Freddie had sobered a little bit in the car, but he was still far gone. She led him inside and up the stairs to the master bedroom and got him undressed. She then removed her clothes.

"I'm about to get in the shower. You joining me right?" she asked seductively.

"That's what you want?"

"I wouldn't have asked if I didn't," Cynthia replied, slipping out of her Victoria's Secret thong.

A broad smile appeared across Freddie's face. He watched as her petite waist, protruding hips, and voluptuous bottom all swayed rhythmically together as she made her way to the bathroom.

"You comin' or what?" she looked back and asked.

"Make me come," Freddie teased.

"Follow me and I will!" she shot back, devilishly.

Cynthia was already lathering her body with the body wash by the time Freddie made his way into the see-through walk-in shower. He stepped inside and slid behind her.

"Here, let me help," he said in a smooth baritone voice, taking the scrub sponge out of her hands.

He began to run the sponge in a circular motion on her back. Cynthia grabbed a handful of her blond hair and moved it out of the way. With his free hand, Freddie reached in front of her and cupped her left breast. While his right hand trailed down her back with the sponge, his left hand massaged upward until it found Cynthia's erect nipple. Cynthia head rotated from side to side from his touch. By now, Freddie's hand had made its way in between Cynthia's ass cheeks. He slid the sponge up and down her crack then placed the sponge up under the water to rinse it off. He then spun Cynthia around and lathered the sponge again. Water cascaded down her breast, onto her midsection, and then finally disappeared between her inner thighs. Freddie leaned in and planted a kiss behind her ear, then on the side of her neck, followed by her collarbone. His kisses turned into his tongue trailing from her blade to her breast until he reached her nipple. Freddie took her nipple into his mouth and gently bit into it. This move caused Cynthia to purr like a kitten. She placed her hands on top of Freddie's head, lightly pushing him off her. At that moment, she wanted him to bite her somewhere else. Freddie released her nipple and began bathing the front part of Cynthia's body. He made Ss over her breasts until he reached between her legs. By now, Cynthia was on fire and there was only one hose that could put it out. She reached for Freddie's dick, but he pulled back.

"I'm not done yet," he whispered just enough for her to hear. He knew how turned on Cynthia got whenever he took control. He parted her legs with the sponge and began to massage Cynthia's clit with it. She moaned and ground her hips while belly dancing to the rhythm of Freddie's touch. The sponge was sending an electrifying sensation throughout her body, making her yearn for the real thing. Just when she thought she couldn't take it anymore, Freddie removed the sponge and rinsed it out for a second time. He placed Cynthia under the water while he aided it in clearing her body of the soap residue. Convinced the suds were washed away, all in one motion, Freddie spun Cynthia back around until she faced the shower's wall.

"This what'chu been waitin' for?" He pressed his weight up against her and whispered in her ear.

"Yes, give it to me, daddy! Fuck me!" Cynthia exclaimed.

Her words were what Freddie needed to amp him up. His dick stood at attention immediately.

Freddie pushed Cynthia up against the wall and bent her over. "Umph," she let out as she grabbed hold of the soap shelf. Freddie had wasted no time sliding his rock hard inside her aggressively.

"Yeah, take this pussy," Cynthia looked back and said.

"Shut up," Freddie shot back with a strong thrust and smack on Cynthia's ass.

The combination of water, flesh, and grunts could be heard as Freddie delivered long, hard pumps into Cynthia's sex box. "You like this dick?" Freddie called out in between pumps.

"No, I love this dick!" Cynthia corrected him. "Don't stop, don't ever stop! Fuck me harder, daddy!" she chimed.

Freddie grabbed a fistful of her hair for balance and granted her wish.

"Ooh, shit! Yes! Yes! Yeeesss!" Cynthia screamed as she felt herself cumming. She started throwing her ass back at Freddie who was riding her like she was a bronco and he was a professional cowboy. He had now clamped his hands around her waist.

"Come for mama, daddy! Make that big dick cum for me," she cheered him on. Freddie could feel himself building up. His pumps became rabbit-like. Just as he was about to reach his peak, Cynthia announced, "Oh, daddy, I'm about to cum again. Cum with me!" And then, as if on cue, Freddie's sexual volcano erupted to match Cynthia's own explosion. His body tensed up and his legs buckled but he held firm.

"Fuck!" he yelled out as he pulled out of Cynthia. Before he could get a chance to release his juices down the drain, Cynthia had taken him into her mouth and swallowed every ounce of him. Freddie grabbed hold of her head and slow pumped her face until he was limp. Cynthia looked up at him with a devilish grin on her face.

"Now," she began, "I can go to bed." She stepped out of the shower and left Freddie alone.

Freddie rinsed off once more. He cut the water off and grabbed a towel from the rack. He quietly dried off before lying down next to Cynthia. He needed to sleep off everything he was graced with that night. Cynthia's arms were wrapped around his waist. He instantly changed sleeping positions so she couldn't spoon with him.

Freddie's inner thoughts were tormenting him with the odd feeling of guilt. He started to think that screwing around with Cynthia was another means of hustling, his way of hustling. It never failed, though: after he did some unfaithful shit, Simone always popped up in his mind.

***

What I gotta feel bad for? Freddie tried to convince himself that he was doing what he was doing for him and his fiancée. The $2,500 Cynthia had promised him for tonight would come in handy for him and Simone. With that in mind, Freddie slipped out of bed and called Slug. Thirty minutes later, he was back on their side of town and it was back to business as usual.

Chapter Twenty-one

Four days later, Freddie drove the forty-five minutes from Goldsboro to Raleigh. It took him a few wrong turns before he found the high-rise Radisson Hotel downtown. It fit Gina's style to a T; it was high class, trendy, and urban. The glass elevator floated up smoothly with a view of the large sparkling water fountain down on the lobby floor. Gina's suite was located on the top floor.

Freddie was dipped in a brown, beige, and white linen outfit and a pair of brown and beige mid Gucci loafers. He had to admit to himself that he was nervous. With Gina, he never knew what to expect. She knew he was in a bind. And although he knew in his heart that she would look out, he knew she'd make him sweat it out, one way or the other.

Freddie got off the elevator, walked the hallway to her room, took a deep breath, then knocked on the door. He didn't have long to wait before Gina opened the door.

"Hello, Freddie," she said evenly, showing little emotion.

Freddie looked her up and down admiringly. Her dress was an auburn brown Versace with spaghetti straps. It had diamond-shaped cuts in the fabric on both sides that exposed the smooth mahogany tone of her firm hips. Her shoes, a pair of crystal-beaded mules with a modest heel, matched her dress. She didn't look thirty-seven; she looked twenty-seven. Her natural hair, straightened and silky, framed her face in an asymmetrical cut.

"How you, ma?" Freddie asked. "Damn, you look good."

He tried to kiss her but she turned away and replied, "I know. Let me get my purse and I'll be ready to go." She walked over to the nightstand and grabbed her small clutch bag.

"Ready? Where we goin'?" Freddie asked.

"Oh, you ain't know? You takin' me to dinner, a show, and whatever else I can think of. Just like you do Simone. You done spent enough of my money on her; now it's time for you to spend some of her money on me," she said as she glided by him and out the door, leaving him no choice but to follow.

When they reached the parking lot, she frowned and asked, "What is that?" She was referring to Freddie's Accord.

"My car," he replied, now feeling a little self-conscious about the late-model hooptie.

"Humph, we'll take mine," she said and tossed him the keys. Two rows away sat a platinum CLK 320 gleaming under the street lamp with milk-colored interior. Freddie opened the door for Gina, closed it, then walked around to the driver's side. She unlocked his door and he got in. As soon as he started the car, the sounds of Colonel Abrams blared through the speakers. The club song took him back to Jersey as he put the car in drive and whipped out onto the main road like a typical "up north" driver.

Gina wasn't playin'; Freddie was definitely taking her out. They went to a modern dance exhibition at the Durham Arts Theatre, then to a small and very exclusive jazz club, tucked away on the outskirts of Cary. Then they hit the high-class restaurant Zakia Blue's in Raleigh. Freddie's little stash was shrinking by the hour.

They walked in and were escorted to a cozy corner table overlooking the Raleigh skyline. Once they were seated, it wasn't long before a waitress approached and cheerfully took their order.

"Yes, we'll have the shrimp cocktail appetizer, then the grilled salmon and salad, and crème brûlée for dessert, with coffee."

"Very good. And to drink?"

Gina smiled at Freddie. "Freddie, what do you suggest?"

Freddie could see it in her pores: she was loving draining his pockets. "Water," he replied sarcastically.

Gina giggled. "He's so silly. We'll have the best red wine you have in the house. It goes well with fish."

"Very good," the waitress repeated, then left them to themselves. Gina had spent the entire evening evading his attempts to talk business, but Freddie thought the time had come to cut to the chase.

"So what's goin' on up top?"

"Later," Gina answered, quickly sipping her water. "Right now I wanna know if you enjoyed the show." She smiled at him over her glass.

"Them niggas dance like faggots," he stated flatly.

Gina laughed. "I should've known you'd say that. I think it was sexy. You should learn how to dance like that."

"Yeah, psss, picture that."

"I am!"

The food arrived promptly and the waitress departed.

"Look, I know you're enjoying yourself, draggin' me all around town and drainin' a nigga's pockets, but you can at least tell me if the cop died, yo. That shit is driving me crazy. The other cat don't matter, but the cop . . ." Freddie dropped his sentence.

"No. He didn't die. Now can I enjoy my dinner?" Gina asked, cutting into her grilled salmon, taking a bite and trying to feed Freddie, too.

The look on her face made Freddie smile, then chuckle and accept the bite. "Ay, yo, word up, you somethin' else!"

"Naw, you just can't figure me out like you want to, that's all." She smirked, tasting her salad.

"What's to figure out? I thought you said we knew each other for who we truly are."

"No, I said I know you for who you truly are. I didn't say anything about you knowing me. Eat your salmon, Freddie." Gina sipped her wine, then asked, "So, when's the wedding?"

Freddie shrugged his shoulders and continued to dress his salad.

"Can I come?" she smiled deviously. Freddie just looked at her like, "Stop playin'," but she continued. "You should have a summer wedding. I love summer weddings. Have you set a date yet?"

"Naw."

"I know you're not having second thoughts, are you?"

Freddie wiped his mouth. "We'll probably just wait until after the baby is born." He grinned.

He could've slapped her in the face and it wouldn't have hurt as much. Freddie knew Gina couldn't have kids. He knew it was a cold way of letting her know, but if she wanted to play games, he decided not to play fair.

Gina averted her gaze, unable to meet his eyes. "That's . . . that's nice. I'm happy for you."

Now it was Freddie's turn to control the flow of conversation. He laughed in her face. "No, you ain't, so why is you lyin'? I can see it in your face. But it's all good. Just know you ain't the only one who can play games."

"Games? You think I'm playin' games wit' you, Freddie? You think I drove five hundred miles to play a fuckin' game?" she hissed, struggling to keep her voice low.

"Oh, what you call all this dinner and dance?" He mocked her voice: "'How'd you enjoy the show?' Smilin' and shit, knowing you breakin' a nigga pockets. That ain't no game?" Freddie asked, matching her intensity.

"Nigga, you owe me at least this. After all the bullshit you put me through? You can't even take me to a funky li'l show and a dinner? When have you ever taken me on a date, Freddie, huh? When? Where? But as soon as your black ass is in a bind, who do you call? And you gotta have a stank-ass attitude? That's why I'm actin' like this! 'Cause you actin' like that!"

Shorty was right. He had never taken her out. It was either a hotel rendezvous or one of her spots: sex, maybe takeout and a movie. But he thought she was cool with their arrangement.

"Dig, yo, I'm just sayin', I—"

She cut him off. "You said it, baby, and I hear you loud and clear." She sipped her wine, wiped her mouth, and placed the napkin on her half-eaten plate, signaling that she was finished. "You wanna get down to business? Okay, let's do business."

Back at the hotel, Gina settled into the plush leather table chair that sat near the foot of the bed where Freddie sat. She crossed her thick, beautiful legs, dangling her mule off her right foot.

"Okay. Dante has a ten thousand dollar contract on your head. It's really an open one, but Ak Kabir really the only cat on it. You know how Ak do, but nobody knows where you are, so you straight. And like I said, the cop didn't die and he's out of the hospital, so it's definitely hot, but not as hot as shit could be if he had died."

Freddie let it all sink in. He knew who Ak Kabir was: a straight murderer, dead ass. Dante was bad enough, but Ak Kabir? Going back to Jersey for any reason was out. But he was relieved that the cop had lived. It was still attempted murder, but that was damn sure better than murder one.

"You think there's any way I can beat it?" Freddie inquired hopefully.

"Mannie? With a good lawyer, yeah. Don't nobody care about another dead nigga. But the cop? Even wit' a good lawyer you can't beat that. And even if you could, what about Dante and Ak? Either you come back ready to go all out, or stay yo' ass down here and hope them niggas catch cases or somethin'."

"I need money for that," Freddie announced, glad to finally get to the point.

She looked at him like, "And?"

"I got a spot in Goldsboro, matter of fact a few spots. But I need a connect. Wit' the right connect I could sew shit up," Freddie explained, sounding a lot like Slug.

"A connect?" Gina smirked. "All the country pussy down here and you gonna risk gettin' trapped in some federal shit selling drugs? Fuckin' wit' cats you don't even know?"

"It ain't gonna be me. My cousin is gonna handle everything," he answered.

"Your cousin who?"

"Slug."

"Slug?" She giggled. "And I'm supposed to get you a connect for some nigga named Slug?"

Freddie waved her off. "Naw, ma. He ain't some nigga; he family."

Gina looked at Freddie for a minute before telling him what she had already decided. "I already knew what you wanted so I talked to my uncle. Straight up, he doesn't want to fuck wit' you. He doesn't know you, you're on the run, and you're desperate. So he ain't doin' it for you; he's doin' it for me. So these are my rules." She paused to make sure she had his attention. "I don't want to meet Slug, Thug, or whoever else you got on your team; that's your problem. When we meet, you come alone every time. You violate that, your ass is cut off, point blank. Understood?"

He nodded to confirm.

"Second, I'm only comin' once a month. Not twice, once. Whatever you say bring, I'll bring, but not over five at a time."

"Five? Gina, we can kill five in a week! You know how much money we can make in the Boro?" Freddie was ready to get rich or die trying, 50 style.

"I'm not doing this for the money, Freddie," she stated.

"Then what are you doin' it for?" he flirted, hoping he could change her mind. But she ignored the question.

"And I'm chargin' you fifteen a brick."

Freddie wasn't that familiar with cocaine in large amounts, so he didn't know the blessing he was getting. "Fifteen? Is that good?" he asked, partially oblivious to the whole drug game.

She laughed out loud. "Damn, Freddie! How you gonna be a drug dealer if you don't know what it's worth? Just ask Slug."

He took that to mean she was looking out on the price. "I appreciate this, Gina."

"I take that to mean you accept my rules, my way."

He eyed her delicious thighs. "It's an offer I can't refuse." He smirked, licking his lips.

Chapter Twenty-two

Freddie woke up the next morning with Gina shaking him vigorously. "Get up," she ordered.

He blinked himself awake. The sun had barely risen but Gina was already fully dressed in a PINK sweat suit with her hair pulled up in a ponytail. "Come on, Freddie. I need you to drive me to the airport."

Freddie sat up. He had slept in his clothes. "Airport? I thought you drove down here."

Gina smiled like she knew something he didn't. "You ask too many questions. Just get up and brush your teeth before you make me miss my flight."

Gina seemed to have an entirely different attitude from the night before. Last night, she had been cold and distant, businesslike. She even got in the bed wearing a pair of oversized pajamas with footies, totally closing herself off from Freddie, telling him, "You're welcome to stay, but you ain't gettin' no pussy." He was too tired to argue and just cradled her.

But now she seemed lighter, her expression open and flirtatious. This always kept Freddie open on Gina because he could never figure her out. She seemed to always be one step ahead of him, and that one step kept him chasing.

He got up and went into the bathroom to use the complimentary hotel toothbrush. After getting himself together, he picked up Gina's small carry-on case and garment bag. Gina threw on her Versace sunglasses and they were out.

They drove to Raleigh-Durham International in Gina's CLK. She massaged the back of Freddie's neck singing along to her Jill Scott CD. When they got to the airport, Gina looked at Freddie and said, "I'ma leave the car wit' you because I am not feelin' that bucket of yours. Leave it to rot."

Freddie was like a kid on Christmas morning. *A brand new CLK 430*. He looked at the car in a completely new light: his.

"And," Gina added, looking at her watch casually, "in the lining of the trunk is a little something to get on. After that, straight paper."

Freddie's game had nothing on Gina's expertise and experience. Once again, she had come through like a trooper. He leaned over and kissed her like he really meant it. Gina felt herself slipping into a zone too explicit for an airport parking lot in broad daylight, so she pulled away.

"Stop, you gonna make me miss my flight," she said, checking her lipstick in the mirror.

"We can make up for last night," Freddie suggested.

She pecked him on the lips and replied, "Next time. I have some things I really need to take care of."

Freddie took the key out of the ignition and they got out to enter the terminal. Once inside, the announcement for Gina's flight echoed through the terminal. When they reached the gate, Gina threw her arms around Freddie's neck and kissed him like she hadn't eaten in days and he was her first meal.

"Oh, so you gonna tease me and just leave me wit' a hard dick, huh?" Freddie chuckled.

She sucked his bottom lip and looked into his eyes. "Just givin' you a little something to think about."

"So when you comin' back?"

"When you call."

"That's business. I'm talkin' 'bout when you comin' back?" Freddie emphasized, letting her know her kiss had made her point.

Her eyes became searching and serious. "You asked me why I'm doing this, remember?"

"I remember."

"I'm doing this because I love you, Freddie. I love you and don't say it back because you don't love me back. But I'm cool with that. I'll be here for you until I get you out of my system or you realize where you need to be. Until then, I'll do whatever I can for you. All I ask is that you don't forget who takes care of you, Freddie. Don't ever forget that. Ever."

"I won't."

"Promise me. Promise me you'll never use my love against me!" Gina needed to hear him say it.

For the first time since he had known Gina, she let her vulnerability show, and it touched him in ways he didn't understand. "I promise, ma," he repeated solemnly.

She searched his eyes for a hint of deception, and whether she saw any she didn't let on. She just kissed him hard and hugged him tight. "Call me," she whispered as she backed away.

He watched her walk away, not looking back, head held high as she disappeared from sight. He looked at the keys to the Benz in his hand, felt Gina's kiss still lingering on his lips, and wondered what he had promised and if he really could hold true to it.

***

I promised worse, he thought as his mind shifted elsewhere. This was cause for a celebration. He smiled as he whipped along I-40 feeling like the motherfuckin' man. The Benz purred like a kitten but raced like a cheetah. It was a far cry from the clanks and clunks of the Accord he left in the hotel parking lot to rot, just like Gina had told him to do. He gripped the steering wheel in a gangsta lean, feeling like the Freddie he knew himself to be. Not the scrambling, block-hustling nigga he had been forced to become, but the player he was born to be.

Gina had held him down. Whatever was in the trunk, he knew it was his jump off, and he didn't plan to look back. As he pulled up to a light in Smithfield, heads turned and admired his profile with praise and envy. This was the life he was meant to live. He was tired of pulling up to a light or taking Simone to the movies surrounded by sick whips and having to get out of the bucket, niggas smirking because their shit was still spinnin' while his shit was still rattling, threatening to leave him right there in the middle of the road. *Now it's time to show these country jokers a true playa for real.* Freddie's ego emerged.

***

He opened the door to his and Simone's apartment to find her sitting on the couch with her arms folded across her breasts. "Where have you been all night, Freddie?" she inquired with quiet intensity.

He wasn't used to Simone questioning him, but he knew it was justified because he hadn't called all night. Besides, he had a surprise, which was also his alibi. He kneeled down in front of her and took her hands in his, then kissed her on the cheek. "Don't be like that, boo. I made you a promise and I'ma keep it, okay? Your man been out makin' shit happen for the three of us," he explained, and caressed her stomach through her T-shirt. "Come outside. I got somethin' to show you." He gently lifted a skeptical Simone to her feet and walked her to the door.

"Naw, naw, wait. We gotta do this right. Close your eyes."

Simone looked at him with building anticipation. "Freddie, what are you up to?"

"Just trust me. Close your eyes."

Simone closed her eyes, but Freddie covered them with his hands anyway. "I got 'em closed," she whined, her skepticism about his whereabouts melting away.

"Naw, yo, I know you. You might peek." He chuckled.

He helped Simone out the door and down the steps, then stopped a few feet from the Benz. "Once upon a time, there was a beautiful little girl named Simone and her dime-ass man, Frederick Von Da Bomb," he joked, making her laugh before continuing. "They loved each other very much, but times got rough, and everything got dark. That's why your eyes are closed," he added, and parted his fingers just a tad to let the sunshine in. "But there's light at the end of every tunnel, and the dark past gave way to a bright future."

Freddie moved his hands. Simone gazed at the CLK in awe, slack-jawed. She gasped. "Freddie, where did you get—"

He kissed her to silence her. "I made a few calls and talked to some cats who owed me a favor. It's on, ma. No more huggin' the block and no more run-down-ass shacks. I told you we wouldn't stop livin' just because of our situation. Your man kept his word, like he always will."

Simone felt her stomach leap even though it was too early for the baby to be kicking, and threw her arms around Freddie's neck, feeling guilty for thinking what she'd been thinking about his whereabouts. "Oh, Freddie! I'm sorry I doubted you. I just didn't hear from you, and I didn't know what to think. I love you, baby!"

Freddie allowed Simone to cover his face with kisses and tears of relief. She started jumping around like a little girl. "I wanna drive!"

"You wanna drive?"

"Yeah, c'mon!"

He held the keys above her head but moved them when she reached for them. "What you gonna give me?" he asked mischievously.

Her eyes danced flirtatiously. "Come with me and find out," she teased, taking him by the hand and damn near dragging him to the car.

Chapter Twenty-three

"Nigga, what bank you done robbed, and why you ain't come get me?" Slug probed half jokingly when Freddie pulled up to Kiki's apartment building. Slug had been sitting on the porch in his bed shorts smoking his wake-up Newport. His pockets were thirsty and he was thinking about going back to his stick-up bag when he saw the bright, shiny platinum Benz pull into the parking lot. He had never seen this car around before, and since it had Jersey plates, he thought it was another crew of out-of-town boys trying to trap off some of his sweet country paper.

Slug didn't know it was Freddie until he got out grinning from ear to ear like the cat that swallowed the canary. Freddie left the door open and 50 Cent's "In Da Club" flooded the parking lot. Freddie approached the porch with an exaggerated pimp and chanted, "What up, blood, what up, cuz, what up, Slug, what up, gangsta?"

That's when Slug asked the question about what bank he'd robbed, to which Freddie replied, "Tony's."

"Who?"

Freddie lifted his Knicks throwback to reveal the kilo of cocaine stuck in his waistline next to his pearl-handled nine. He quoted a line from the classic movie *Scarface*, when Al Pacino aka Tony Montana burst out of his office with the assault weapon. His Spanish accent flowed naturally due to his half-Latin bloodline as he mimicked the talented actor.

Slug's eyes got big as plates. He flicked the cigarette aside and stood up. "Connect?"

"Connected. You ready to get this paper?"

"Cuz, I been ready."

Inside, Freddie explained the situation to Slug, leaving out the who and sticking only to the what: the details of the agreement. Slug had broken out the mayonnaise jar, wasting no time in rocking up a few ounces to test its potency. The results made him smile. He lit a cigarette and sat down across from Freddie at the kitchen table.

"Fuck meetin' the connect. I don't want them to know me either. But that five a month shit . . ." Slug shook his head. "Fuck? Them niggas don't want no paper?"

"This is just the beginning," Freddie assured him. "Once they see what we can do, them cats'll come through."

"But that eighteen . . ." Slug drawled.

Freddie had added three Gs to the real price. He figured an extra three in his pocket each month wouldn't hurt, but he hoped he hadn't gone too high. "What? That's good, ain't it?"

Slug looked at him in amazement. "Good? Nigga, you don't know?"

Freddie shrugged. "I told you I ain't fuck wit' coke like that. That's why movin' the shit is all on you and we splittin' it fifty-fifty. Gangsta?"

"Gangsta!" Slug echoed and gave his cousin dap. "Shit, that eighteen is a blessing! Cats 'round here chargin' eighteen or better. We could kill 'em just in weight, but if we ain't gettin' but five a month, we might as well grind this shit and stretch it out."

"We?" Freddie asked as if Slug was speaking French.

"I got you, cuz. *We* meanin' any young'uns and such. You just keep this shit hot and I'ma show you how to trap off this paper."

"Now that's wassup."

And trap it they did. All across the Boro, Slug's young'uns were stopping cats' paper with that hard white yayo. They were pitching chunks compared to other hustlers' pieces. Hate filled their hearts, but fear kept them in check, because they all knew how Slug was about his paper. But Slug played fair. He had young'uns in every spot that was bubbling, but he called his team in every night at eight-thirty to give the other hustlers the late-night rush and a chance to get their paper up. It wasn't only fair; it was smart, because Slug knew that some cats wouldn't mind diming him out to the police.

Even the Miami boys came through to cop a deal. Slug cut them some slack because he felt like he owed them at least that and, besides, they turned out to be all right cats. They just had their people fucked up. Now that was straight real recognized real.

Slug flew through that package and stayed on Freddie about the five a month limit. Freddie, in turn, continued to try to convince Gina. He took a lesson from her first visit, and this time had an evening planned. He took her to Atlantic Beach to enjoy the scenery, walk barefoot along the beach, and take a moonlight cruise on the Atlantic. She wouldn't relent, but along with the two he copped, she threw him a third.

Slug and Freddie were grinding their way to a lock on the Boro, even expanding to the small surrounding towns of Fremont and La Grange.

And while they were making the money, Kiki and Simone were spending their share. No more did Simone hear the stifled giggles or get the condescending looks. Now, whenever she pulled up in Freddie's Benz, the bitches turned green. Nina Simone still did her hair and whenever she was there, she could see the other chicks studying her shoes, wishing they were in them.

The newfound wealth and Freddie's periodic absences no longer weighed as heavily on Simone. Her stomach was growing and her skin was glowing with the love of pregnancy. Freddie pampered her with all the luxuries she could want, along with the little things. He was thoughtful enough not to forget.

They spent many an evening with Freddie massaging her feet and spoon-feeding her Chinese takeout or Italian food, or listening to soft, mellow music while she read poems to him from one of her old school books from a literature class she had taken.

Her total trust for Freddie was slowly returning. She attributed her swollen condition to the fact that Freddie had truly realized where the love was, and she felt secure in his vow to devote his life to her. She knew her man was fine, and with the paper he was checking, she knew females would try their luck. She had seen it herself, over and over.

One night at the club, Simone decided to test Freddie. She saw the chick scoping him subtly all night, but she was constantly by his side. She kissed him on the cheek. "I'll be right back. I gotta go pee," she lied. Freddie helped her out of the chair and then sat back down. But Simone didn't stay in the bathroom. She doubled back and watched Freddie from a distance. The girl finally saw her opportunity to advance and approached Freddie. Simone was too far away and the club was too loud for her to hear what was being said, but she knew her man's body language well enough to read the disinterest he displayed. It wasn't long before the girl walked off and Simone returned to the table triumphantly. She draped herself around Freddie's neck. When she caught the girl's eye this time, she winked and smiled, making the girl roll her eyes and turn away.

Simone no longer mentally questioned the overnight trips and the smells of perfume she didn't even own on Freddie. They say love is blind, which was why as Simone's heart and belly blossomed, her eyes fluttered shut.

Chapter Twenty-four

Slug loved the way Kiki rode his dick: the way she worked her inner muscles, gripping and pulsing on the upstroke, then relaxing as he penetrated her to her deepest depths on the downstroke; the way her pretty, yellow titties jiggled in front of his face, peppered with soft red freckles, nipples like elevator buttons. Her grinding hips curled his toes and made him fight to hold back his nut with every 360 degrees she made.

He watched her face contort with different expressions of ecstasy, and all he could think about was how real she had always kept it with him. She was ghetto as hell, but she had always been there for him. When he was broke, she gave him her whole AFDC check to flip. Whenever he hit county jail, she bailed him out if she could, and if she couldn't, she held him down. He never heard a word about her creeping on him, so even if she had, she respected him enough not to let it get out.

Now that he was on, he hadn't forgotten any of it. She was the only chick he laced. Whoever else he might be fucking only got dick and a donut, meaning zero. Quiet as it was kept, Slug was grudge fucking all the gold diggers who wouldn't give him the time of day before but who were sweating him now. He dogged them with a capital D. He was making them bitches feel it and he was lovin' it. But he kept it all the way live with Kiki, putting her on with all that fly shit she liked: Dolce & Gabbana, Prada, Versace, and other big-name designs. He and li'l Chris even got along better, once they got a better understanding of each other.

"Look, li'l nigga. Now I'ma take you up in this toy store, but if you keep tryin' to play me I ain't gettin' you shit else," Slug informed him outside of KB Toys in the mall.

"I'ma be good," Chris vowed.

"And you gonna stop cursin' so fuckin' . . . I mean, so much?" Slug added.

Chris nodded his head vigorously.

"A'ight, c'mon." He took little man inside and laced him lovely.

Even Kiki noticed the way Slug had begun to step up and raise Chris. "Thank you, boo," she told him one day, giving him a big, nasty, wet kiss on the cheek as they started having sex.

"Go 'head wit' that. I ain't tryin' to hear that shit," Slug replied, but he really was.

"Ohhh, Slug, I can feel it, baby! Ooooh, oooh, oooh!" she squealed, clinching up. "Slug, don't move. Don't . . ." Her body shuddered from the force of their simultaneous orgasms and she collapsed on top of him, sucking on his neck. "Tell me you love me, Slug."

"Naw."

She sat up and looked at him. "What you mean 'naw'?"

"'Cause you already know, shit. I just said it awhile ago," he answered.

"No. You said you loved this pussy. I said say you love me," she repeated and sat back on his semi-erect manhood, hard.

"Ay, yo, check this out," Slug began, trying to find his words.

"Say it!" Kiki demanded through clenched teeth. "Right now!"

"Hold up, I'm tryin' to tell you something if you'll shut the fuck up and let me talk."

"Well, if it ain't 'I love you,' I ain't tryin' to hear it," Kiki said with an attitude and unstraddled him, lying down with her back to him.

Slug ignored her attitude and continued. "Ay, yo, on the real, I ain't no romantic type muhfucka or nothin', right, but dead ass, you kept it gangsta when a nigga was fucked up and I respect that. But . . ."

Kiki looked over her shoulder. "But what?"

"Now that a nigga gettin' a little paper and I can afford to throw back, yo, I don't feel like that's enough."

Kiki didn't understand what he was getting at so she turned to face him. "Slug, what is you talkin' 'bout?"

Slug looked her in the eyes wondering if thugs were supposed to feel butterflies. "Marry a nigga," he said quickly.

Kiki rose up on the palm of her hand, trembling. "M . . . marry you?"

Slug couldn't read her reaction, so he got defensive. "Hell yeah! Fuck you say it like that for? And you better not say no or I'ma beat yo' ass," he said, trying to mask his nervousness with testosterone.

"Oooh, my baby does love me!" Kiki squealed like she was cumming again and threw herself all over Slug. "Yes! Yes! Yes!" She punctuated each yes with a kiss.

"I'm sayin', nothin' fancy. Just go down to the courthouse tomorrow, and just do it. Fuck all that other shit, yo. Be my wife, official." Slug made the demand sound as romantic as he could, gangster style. And Kiki accepted.

Chapter Twenty-five

Guests couldn't help but look their way. They seemed to be having the most fun in the local gentlemen's club. Freddie and Slug seemed to be in a race to see who could finish their bottles of Hennessy Privilege and tossed the most singles in the air, while Kiki and Simone nursed their flutes of Moët. Simone knew he would be hammered before the night was over. In fact, this was the loosest she'd ever seen him. Usually, Freddie wouldn't finish a bottle of anything he was drinking. But she understood. After all, it was a celebration. She was happy for Slug and Kiki and was glad to have someone who could relate to her own happiness, being engaged.

The lights dimmed even lower, and the DJ drew the microphone to his lips. "I wanna give a shout out to my dawg Slug, the motherfuckin' thug!" the DJ began. "Congratulations my G, to you and Queen Kiki," he ended, then threw on Tupac's "All Eyes On Me."

The crowd roared as Slug and Kiki exchanged stares. He smiled and kissed her on the forehead. Just then, something nice and exotic came out of nowhere.

"You Slug?" she asked as she stood in front of the VIP section.

Kiki was in too good of a mood to trip. She knew Slug would handle it.

"Yeah, baby girl, but don't think you know me, though," Slug said, knowing it was true. He was sure he had never seen the girl before.

"I'm your engagement present." The girl smiled.

"What?" Her words made their way to Kiki's ears. She nearly rose up but Slug held her back.

"Look here." Before Slug could finish, Freddie stepped in.

"Chill, cuz, it was a joke." He broke out into laughter. The whole time Freddie was trying to keep his composure. But he couldn't hold it any longer. "I knew you was gonna trip," Freddie continued.

"Boyee!" Kiki punched him in the arm. Simone just shook her head.

Slug let out a light chuckle. He was all too glad to find out it was a joke. He thought somebody was trying to sabotage his engagement and get him killed. Slug leaned into the girl. "How much he give you, sweetie?" he wanted to know.

"Five hundred." The girl beamed.

"Since he paid you, he deserves the dance." He flipped it back on Freddie. "So, here's five more." Slug pulled out a stack of paper and peeled off five Benjamins.

"Nah, nah!" Freddie protested, throwing his hands up in a submissive manner. But the dancer had already made her way around and over to him. He peered over at Simone to see whether she was smiling. Surprisingly she was. He looked for approval from Simone. The dancer saw her shrug her shoulders and immediately sprung into action. The beginning of Bootsy Collins and Ice Cube's "Freak of the Week" could be heard from all the speakers, in the four corners of the huge room. She tossed her lean, long legs in staggering six-inch Louboutins across Freddie. By now, everyone's attention was drawn to their section. The crowd showed their approval as she danced her way into Freddie's lap, seductively.

Simone's wince showed just how unpleasant it was for her to watch the beautiful body, full breasts, flat stomach, and round, juicy behind dance all over her man. She realized she had made a mistake with her decision. She couldn't believe she had actually given permission. She was sure the liquor played a major part in her decision-making. The dancer's eyes were filled with ravenous lust, and desire fueled her bodily

movements. Simone noted the way the stripper looked at Freddie with sexual desire. She
wondered if Freddie knew who the stripper was
behind the blindfold.

Freddie maintained his composure despite
being slightly drunk as the dancer's soft behind
rubbed against his lap. He had almost forgotten
Simone was even present as he locked in on the
body slithering all around him. She nearly ran her
breasts across his lips. Despite the show, Freddie's attention was drawn to the main attraction
on stage. He immediately looked over at Simone,
who apparently didn't realize who the dancer
was. He knew it was her.

The dancer on stage walked around the pole twice,
before lifting a strong right arm and pulling herself up.
She wrapped her legs around the pole, and swirled her
way down. She threw her head back and let her hair fly
with the wind created by the twirl. She coiled around the
pole with one leg wrapped around it, and the other bent
in the air. She was an exotic acrobat, and no one in the
club worked the pole the way she did. It wasn't until the
DJ announced Tee-Tee the Diva that Simone's spider
senses went off.

She drew her attention to the stage and
watched as the girl on stage had tunnel vision for
Freddie. She also noticed how the girl became
even more confident about herself, and the

sexy performance. Simone was trying to place where she had seen the girl before. The dancer on stage stood up and performed a few more twirls around the other poles for the audience. Simone studied the interaction between Freddie and her. She studied his facial expression, the joy in his face when he saw who the dancer was. It was slowly breaking her heart, and she wasn't strong enough to handle it. She was tempted to smack fire out of Freddie, but she was a virtuous woman and knew he had an image to uphold and maintain in the streets.

Instead, she abruptly got up and exited the VIP booth. Freddie was so engrossed with the stage performance that he hadn't even noticed Simone's absence. The dancer he had paid for Slug had even ended her session, seeing that he was not interested in her. Simone sought safety at the bar. She knew it was her fault. She had never wanted to come to the gentlemen's club in the first place but she didn't want to be the party pooper or one who rained on everybody's parade.

The first thing she noticed was how the bartender was staring over her shoulder in the direction of their VIP section. When she turned and looked back, she saw that the stripper was headed back to the stage. She was heated. Her first reaction was to go over and black out on both Freddie and the disrespectful stripper, but she decided against it. She had far too much class for that. Besides, although she felt Freddie was out of pocket, she knew he didn't need any extra attention drawn to him. She pulled herself together and faced the bar. When she spun around, she noticed the bartender pathetically tuned into Freddie and the stripper on stage. Simone watched her down her fourth shot of a brown liquor.

Damn, do all these bitches got a thing for my man?

"Excuse me!" Simone hollered, slamming a hundred-dollar bill on the bar top and grabbing the bartender's attention.

The bartender's red eyes were apologetic as they met Simone's gaze. "I'm sorry, hon. What can I get you?" she asked, her speech slurred just a bit.

"Water," Simone said.

"I saw you in VIP. No charge," the bartender said. "You were at Freddie's table?"

"How do you know Freddie?" Simone retorted as she screwed the top off the water bottle.

"I'm sorry. Is that your boyfriend?" the bartender asked.

Simone thought quickly and answered, "He's my crazy-ass cousin. I'm just here to mingle. I'm Sade," Simone lied.

"Joy. Nice to meet you," she replied.

"So how do you know my cousin?"

The conversation was interrupted by the increased volume of cheers as Freddie made his exit off the stage. Simone took a look back for a second time. She rolled her eyes at the stage and turned back around. She scowled and put her focus back on Joy. She knew Freddie would be looking for her soon.

"We met here at the club."

"Are you all close?"

Joy sucked her teeth and said, "No."

"Aw, you're pretty. How come that didn't work?"

Joy grinned and replied, "Thanks, but I assume he was guarded because of a stripper who works here."

"I think he was telling me a little bit about her earlier," Simone lied again. She snapped her fingers at Joy and asked, "What's the girl's name again?"

"Tina. The one he was on stage with," Joy replied.

Simone swiftly turned around for a third time. This time, she took a good look at the stripper who headlined the entire performance. She nodded, as if she were giving approval. However, this particular nod was one that meant trouble for Freddie. Tina's face illuminated as clear as day as soon as the bartender said her name.

Childhood friend my ass, she thought. She looked back at Joy and asked, "And who is Tina to him?"

"Freddie told me that she definitely isn't his girl. Tina and I don't talk much, so your guess is as good as mine. But I assume she's a jump off," Joy told her. She wiped a wet, clean glass dry and fixed herself a drink.

"Let me get something with two syrup shots," a woman said, putting a ten dollar bill on the table.

"It's ten per shot. You're short, sweetie," Joy replied as she prepared to make the alcoholic beverage.

The woman added an additional ten dollar bill on the table. Joy nodded and picked up the twenty dollars. She turned to Simone, before grabbing a clean glass from the rack and said, "Nice meeting you! Tell Freddie I said hello."

Definitely not, Simone thought as she spun around in the barstool to look at the stage. Her eyes narrowed into spiteful slits as they caught a glimpse of Tina, exiting the stage. Simone began making a beeline back over toward the VIP section.

Freddie greeted her with a smile. "Babe, where'd you go?" he asked.

"I wanna go home!" was all she said.

Both Slug and Kiki were shaking their heads. They too had watched Freddie and Tina's non-verbals. Freddie knew he had gone too far and had exposed his hand more than usual. But between the Henny and the dancer who nearly made him nut in his pants, he had a great time and would be willing to accept the flack that came behind it once they got home. Rather than protest, he stood, hugged Kiki, and gave Slug dap. He went to snatch up the two bricks of singles he had sitting on the table with the last two remaining bottles of liquor, but Slug grabbed hold of his wrist.

"I'll take care of those, cuz." Freddie chuckled and nodded.

Moments later he was whisking Simone out of the club, but not before Simone and Tina made eye contact, as Tina sipped on her double shot of Peach Cîroc and iced tea.

***

Later, at the Bar

"Yeah, she said she was his cousin and her name was Sade," Joy relayed to Tina.

"That bitch ain't his kin; that's his main," Tina corrected her. "And her name Simone, with her stuck-up green ass," she added.

"So why she lie?"

"Snoopin' for shit she don't really want the answer to," Tina concluded.

"So this nigga has a girlfriend and couldn't say nothin' ahead of time. Ain't that some shit?"

"Ain't it though? Why is a grown man fucking with a little kid when he has a woman like me on the side?" She ran her hands down her own curves.

"I know you ain't bragging about being a sideline ho?" Joy giggled.

Tina grinned, rolled her eyes, and continued, "Bitch, whatever. Sideline or on the field. Freddie has been mine, for years now. Has been and always will be. Trust and know."

Joy shook her head as she took Tina's empty glass off the bar top. "You know you're a hot mess, right?"

Tina shrugged, a smirk fixed on her face. "Tee-Tee the Diva is the shit. And don't forget that. Freddie sure won't." She smiled at her friend and started to walk away.

Simone looked at Freddie and, before she could stop herself, she struck his face with an open hand. The sting was only heard by the couple, as no other guest even noticed the slap. Both Simone and Freddie were equally shocked by it. The only reasonable thing for Simone to do was to run. She turned away from the table and quickly brushed through the swamp of guests until she was in front of the exit doors.

The coolness of the air chilled her face, wet with tears. She hurried to the CLK, seeking refuge behind it. She knew Freddie was going to come after her; something just told her. She leaned on the side of the Benz and began to cry, not caring if she could be heard. Everything had just became too much. Tina, being on the run, et cetera. Being a part of Freddie's life had hit a low point.

I shouldn't have even come, Simone thought, wiping her face with the back of her hands. *Why would he even want to bring me with him? Fuck this living on the run shit!*

Simone wasn't feeling that special anymore. She was in a terrible mood, though she didn't want to be. Everything good about Freddie was thrown away. Freddie was under a limelight, and it was all negative press.

"Why'd the fuck you smack me? You lost your gotdamn mind?"

"I want to go home, Freddie!" she screamed. "I just want to go home," she repeated in between the breath that she was still trying to catch. She had cried way too many tears.

"Okay, baby. That's where I'm about to take you."

"No, I want to go back to Jersey. I don't want to be in North Carolina anymore."

Freddie sighed, and reached down to help her up. She snatched away from his grip and stood up on her own. She walked around to the passenger side, and got inside the car after Freddie unlocked the doors.

The ride back to the house was silent, until Freddie exited the freeway. "What's your problem?" he asked.

"That bitch is my problem."

"What did she do?"

"You! She did you! You did her! You're her sponsor!" Simone hollered, remembering the way Tina was looking at him. "And had I not come with you tonight, you probably would've fucked that nasty ho."

Freddie swallowed hard. He remained silent as she vented away her anger.

"That's what I mean when I say you don't keep it real. I feel so stupid!"

"I am!" he boomed. "Fuck Tina. You're the one I'm loving and fucking with."

"I just want to go home and think about this. I'd like a ticket back to New Jersey to-fuckin'-day."

"Babe, you buggin'. Please relax," he tried to reason with her.

"I want to leave today." Simone stood her ground.

Now it was Freddie who became pissed. "You better stop acting like a little-ass girl and grow the hell up. This ain't no fuckin' game. You just can't up and go back to Plainfield," he pointed out. "You think they're not looking for you too?" he reminded her. "We're in this together. I'm sorry I made you feel like however you feel and that she made you feel some kind of way, but that broad ain't no factor," he said all in one breath.

Freddie shook his head, silently embarrassed and annoyed as she continued to rant about it. He pulled the car in front of their place. Simone hopped out before Freddie could even put the car in park. Once they were inside the room, Simone began to put into her suitcase any clothes left out in the open.

"Simone, please relax," Freddie asked, nicely.

"Fuck you!" spat Simone in response.

This time, with a firm, hard voice, Freddie said, "Calm the fuck down!"

But she continued hauling clothes into her suitcase, like a madwoman. Freddie walked over to her, snatching his belt through the loops of his jeans. He grabbed her body in one arm and locked her hands in front of her. He took the belt and tied her hands together, and pulled the belt strap through a loop, causing the leather to tighten around her tiny wrists. Simone looked into his dark, smoldering eyes, unable to get any answers from his ferocious expression. A sense of fear swept through her body.

"I'm not gonna hurt you," he assured her. "I just need you to calm down. You wildin' so I'm restraining you." He chuckled.

But Simone found no humor in his joke. She sighed, asking herself to think reasonably about how to handle this. Calmly, she spoke: "I just feel like you're a different man now. Not the same Freddie I knew when we left Plainfield."

"Baby, I'm the same man."

"Well, I guess that's not a good thing, right?"

"Stop with this bullshit," he bellowed. "Chill. Relax," Freddie said as he threw his arms around her. Simone rested her head on his chest and let her tears fall on his chest.

I can't keep doing this, she thought. *My heart can't take it.*

Freddie kissed her on top of the head and began stroking her hair. "Tina or nobody else mean more to me than this right here."

His words were all that was needed to ease Simone's heart for the moment. Only he could soothe her pain, no matter who had caused it.

Chapter Twenty-six

Slug and Kiki got married quietly but the party that Saturday was anything but. The Boro turned out in full force to wish the happy couple a prosperous life.

"Nigga snuck and got married so we wouldn't see his whipped ass cryin' at the altar! I do!" A.B. yelled like he was crying, "Oh, baby, I do!" The fellas laughed and clowned a jovial Slug.

"Man, fuck you niggas, yo," he replied.

"Don't sweat what these niggas is sayin', yo. I'm proud of you," Freddie said, patting him on the back before adding, "You finally admitted to the world that Kiki got that ass wrapped around her finger!"

Slug laughed. "Oh, and Simone don't?"

"Hell no!"

They held the party at the rec center, thanks to Slug's mother who was still mad at Slug for getting married without letting her help plan the wedding. She scolded the couple good-naturedly with a smile. "Kionna, I can't believe you let Eric convince you to cheat me and your mama out of helping you plan the happiest day of your life."

"Miss Carolyn, I'm sorry, but you know Eric. Ain't no tellin' with him. So I figured I'd better take him up on his offer before he changed his mind. Now he's mine," she boasted with a girlish giggle. Even li'l Chris' father, Big Chris, showed up. He had moved to Charlotte, but when he heard that Kiki was married, he wanted to see for himself. She paid him no mind. Even li'l Chris gave him a hard time.

"You ain't my daddy! My daddy's name is Slug!"

Slug walked up and heard li'l Chris say that to Big Chris. The man looked like all the air had been let out of his balloon, totally deflating it. Slug knew why li'l Chris said what he said, because the cat really wasn't shit, but the puppy dog look on the man's face made Slug call li'l Chris to him.

"Li'l Chris! Come 'ere!"

Li'l Chris jumped at the sound of Slug's voice and ran over to him. Slug picked him up. "Dig, shawtie, don't play your pops like that. He came all the way down here to check you out."

"My mama said he ain't shit. You my daddy!" Li'l Chris pouted.

"What I tell you 'bout cussin'? I got to talk to yo' mama 'bout her dirty-ass mouth too, but dig: you my li'l man but, Chris"—he looked up at Big Chris, made eye contact, and spoke loudly enough for him to hear his next words—"that's your daddy. And trust me, he's gonna do better. So give him a chance. Not everybody's got a pops, shawtie."

Li'l Chris nodded as if Slug's word was law. Slug put him down and he went back over to Big Chris. Slug followed.

"What up, kinfolk?"

"What's up, Slug? Congratulations, man, you got a good girl," Chris said, extending his hand. Slug shook it.

"Yo, call me sometime, a'ight? I know it's paper in Charlotte," Slug asserted.

Chris had been looking for a job but with little success. "Good lookin', cuz."

Slug just nodded and left him to his son.

"Congratulations!" Freddie told Kiki after he hugged her. "Take care of my li'l cuz for me."

Kiki took one last look at her fantasy standing next to Simone. Freddie was slap yo' mama fine, but Slug made her happy, and that was all she really wanted.

"Thank you, I will. Now, when you gon' finish what you started with my girl right here?" Kiki asked with her hands on her hips.

Freddie looked at both Kiki's and Simone's inquiring faces. He cleared his throat. "Simone knows I marry her more and more every day in my heart," he replied, knowing that corny comment wouldn't get him off the hook with the sharpness of not one, but two likeminded black women. They both laughed.

"Hmm. That's all good, Mr. Smooth, but how about you take your heart and your ass down to the church or courthouse." Kiki chuckled.

"You really know how to put a nigga on the spot, don't you, Ki?" Freddie mused.

The party was in full swing and Simone and Freddie danced, enjoying themselves. Everything was all right until Tina caught his eye. She made eye contact with him and licked her tongue ring out at him, enticing him more than the mere sight of her did already. Slowly but surely, Freddie had gone back to his old ways, and Tina was the chief temptation on his list. As Simone got rounder, Freddie became less interested in sexing her. He still loved her, but Tina's luscious shape became more and more appealing. After Tina, more females got added to his hit list. But Freddie convinced himself he was doing nothing wrong. Home was taken care of, paper was coming like water, and the females flocked to him in droves. Once again, he was caught up.

Chapter Twenty-seven

Tina nodded her head toward the bathroom, then swung her ass in that direction. Freddie turned to Simone. "Be right back, boo. Let me holler at this cat."

"Okay, baby," was her easy reply, and he stepped off to the bathroom.

A few minutes later, Simone approached Slug while he was talking to A.B. and Shaq. "Slug, Kiki is ready to take pictures. Do me a favor and find Freddie, too."

Slug knew exactly where Freddie was but said, "Tell Kiki I'll be there in a minute. Freddie's talkin' to Mandrell."

As soon as Simone walked away, Slug jogged off to the men's bathroom and found it locked. He put his ear to the door and the slurping sounds he heard confirmed what he already knew.

Slug banged on the door. "Freddie! Ay, yo, bring yo' ass on. Simone lookin' for you."

Freddie's eyes were damn near in the back of his head. Tina was giving him head and driving him crazy with the way she worked her tongue ring. "A'ight, yo. Tell her I'm comin'!"

"Yeah, bet you is, nigga." Slug chuckled to himself, then hit the door one last time. "Hurry up!"

Freddie cleaned himself up and rushed over to the photographer. Kiki, Slug, and Aunt Ann were taking pictures. Aunt Ann's and Freddie's eyes met and she nodded knowingly.

"Come on, cuz. Me and you gonna take a few," Slug urged. He and Freddie flicked it up, then he, Freddie, Kiki, and Simone got together and posed.

Aunt Ann whispered in Freddie's ear, "I need to see you, nephew."

Freddie looked at her and replied, "Yes, ma'am?"

"Come on."

"Ma, where you goin'?" Slug called after her. "You ain't takin' no more flicks?"

"Mama tired, baby. Let me sit a spell wit' my nephew and I'll be ready."

Freddie and Aunt Ann sat in the back of the center watching the people dance and Slug take pictures.

"Freddie, I don't usually mess in you young folks' affairs, so I'll make it quick. Simone is a good girl. She come way down here wit' you after all you done did. She down here because of you, and what you doin' ain't right," Ann told him.

Freddie knew what was up, but wondered how and just how much she knew. "I'm sayin', Auntie, I ain't—"

"You ain't what? Comin' out a public bathroom with some home-wrecking heffer? I saw you, Freddie! So if I saw you, imagine who else saw you. Not only are you doing her wrong, but you disrespectin' that gal, Freddie. She's carryin' your child. Don't that mean anything to you?"

"Yes, ma'am, that's my world right there. What you saw, that don't mean nothin' to me—"

"Then why do you do it?" Ann asked, cutting him off.

Freddie couldn't answer. He had asked himself the same question repeatedly until he had just given up and accepted that it was just in him.

"Freddie, you may not want to hear this, but you gonna hear it. You actin' just like your father."

That roused his total ire. "My father? I ain't nothin' like my father!" He tried to control his tone because he was talking to his aunt. "I ain't leave my family for dead! I'ma be there for mine!"

Ann looked him in his eyes. "You think your father didn't provide? That is, until your mama got pregnant. Then he went back to his doggish ways, womanizing. You look just like your daddy, and you act like him, too. If you don't change your ways, you gonna end up just like him."

Freddie had never heard this about his father. His mother never talked about him. He didn't know his father was a womanizer, a Christianized term for what he himself was: a player.

"What happened to my father?" Freddie asked.

Ann rose slowly from her seat, then looked down at him. "Stabbed to death in his own bed. His lady friend did it." She watched his expression until the story had sunk in. "It's truly a thin line between love and hate, baby."

Freddie watched his aunt as she slowly made her way back over to the photographer. Simone caught his eye and waved, then she blew him a kiss, totally unaware of the situation unfolding around her.

Kiki watched Simone with pity in her eyes. She was so caught up in the web Freddie was weaving, she couldn't see her hand in front of her face.

"Slug, come here," she called him as he was talking to the photographer.

He walked over. "What up, Ki?"

"Slug, you need to talk to Freddie."

Slug sipped his Heineken. "About?"

Kiki raised one eyebrow. "Nigga, don't play stupid. Kionna don't miss shit when it comes to these triflin' bitches. Especially Tina nasty ass in the bathroom, Slug!"

"Ay, yo, mind your business, Ki. That's on them," Slug warned her. "Don't say shit to Simone."

"Oh, trust me. I dig my girl, but I done seen too many bitches blame the one who told 'em, thinkin' they want they man. You right, that is on them, but what I'm talkin' about is Tina. You know she known to set a brother up; that's what I'm talkin' about holler at him for."

Kiki was on point and Slug had to acknowledge that. He had been meaning to talk to Freddie but kept putting it off. Freddie was a grown man. And even though niggas was gritting their teeth, he could pull his own weight. But what Kiki had reminded him about threatened him as well as Freddie, and he damn sure wasn't gonna let Freddie's dick knock him in the dirt.

***

The only thing that came out of his talk with his aunt was another lavish gift for Simone, provided by his guilt. He copped her a 2003 forest green BMW 325i with a peanut butter interior. Simone couldn't believe it. She failed to see that the gifts always seemed to come after some unexplained absence, an act of infidelity that Freddie foolishly thought he could compensate for with material things. In reality, it was just creating a bigger void in their world.

But Simone was getting caught up herself. Subconsciously, she began to isolate herself. Freddie's transparent lies weren't the only blame, because for a lie to manifest itself there must be someone willing to believe it. Simone wanted to believe. She needed to believe, no matter what that tiny voice inside her head whispered. So she continued to ignore the obvious, until the day the obvious refused to be ignored.

Simone went to Nina Simone's hair salon for her weekly touchup. There were a few females there, including Tina who was getting her nails done. Tina eyed Simone evilly when she came in, but Simone only smiled at her hate. Nina could feel the tension in the room so she tried to keep Simone occupied with chitchat and idle talk.

"Didn't Slug and Kiki go to Cancun for their honeymoon?" Nina asked, as she streaked Simone's ebony mane with subtle red highlights.

"Cancun? Try Cancun and Hawaii," Simone replied.

Nina hummed with envy. "Damn! Slug doin' it up big, huh? It's good though. I'm glad they got married 'cause they been together like forever, yo," Nina said.

"And don't they look good together?" Simone commented. "Almost as good as me and my Freddie." She giggled, directing that last comment to Tina.

Tina sucked her teeth loudly at the mentioning of Freddie's name, so Nina tried to find a safer topic. "Simone, didn't you say you were from Jersey? I got family in Jersey," Nina informed her.

"For real? What part?" Simone inquired.

"She need to take her ass back to Jersey," Tina huffed, and her voice carried across the salon.

Simone turned her head in Tina's direction. "Excuse me?"

Nina could see it coming and tried to head off the collision. "She wasn't talking—"

"'She' has a name, and yes, I was talking about her," Tina hissed with much attitude.

"Tina, chill!" Nina told her. "Don't start no shit up in here, now!"

"Who startin' shit, Nina? I said what's on my mind and I don't bite my tongue for no-damn-body."

By now, the whole salon was all ears. Both girls were itching to put the other in her place. They didn't like each other from jump because they looked too much alike. Both were dark chocolate, Simone being only a shade lighter than Tina's Brazilian midnight complexion. Tina was easily the thicker of the two, but Simone's facial features complemented her more, giving each the ups in the beauty department. But that wasn't why Simone wanted to put Tina in her place. Simone felt like she had what Tina wanted. But she was about to find out Tina had already had it.

"Tina, you got a problem wit' me or something? You don't know me, so wassup? My car? My jewelry? My man?" she stated firmly, an obvious question seeking an answer.

Nina's heart dropped. She liked Simone but knew she had bitten off more than she could chew. It seemed like everybody knew about Freddie except her. But now that she had asked for it, she was about to get it.

"Your man?" Tina said, laughing as she stood up. She had been waiting for a moment like this. To her, Simone was a square bitch who thought she was all that and needed to be checked. "Your man, bitch? I don't have to want Freddie; I got

Freddie, I had Freddie, and I can have him whenever I want!" Tina stood in the middle of the floor.

"Simone, just leave, girl. You ain't even gotta stoop to her level," Nina tried to convince her. She hated for Simone to find out about Freddie like this. She could see how much she loved him, so she knew what was coming would hurt her badly.

"Naw, Nina. It's cool 'cause this bitch lyin'! You a sad bitch!" Simone spat.

"Sad? No, you sad and dumb! Everybody knows I'm fuckin' Freddie. That's why Nina tryin' to get yo' dumb ass outta here before your heart get broke. What? You think you the only bitch pregnant by Freddie? You better ask somebody!"

The word "pregnant" hit Simone like a hammer. The idea of another woman carrying Freddie's child enraged her. She quickly leaped up from her chair. Nina was surprised a woman four months pregnant could move that fast. She just barely got to Simone before she reached Tina.

Tina never moved. She just got into her bitch-stomping stance and held fort. "Naw, Nina. Let her go. I'ma beat the baby out her dumb ass!"

"Let me go!" Simone struggled against Nina.

"Tina, you need to leave for real! The nails are on me. You gotsta bounce up outta here!" Nina commanded, taking control in her shop.

"Ask Freddie, bitch!" Tina continued. "Ask him where he at when you call him talkin' 'bout, 'Bring me some rocky road.' Ain't that your favorite ice cream? When he comes home smelling like Pink, ask him about them scratches on his back, that 'T' I scratched in his back! Ask him!"

"Tina!" Nina thundered, now mad 'cause she hadn't left yet. "Fuck all that other shit! You in my spot and I said leave!"

Tina had said all she needed to, she could tell by the expression on Simone's face. Simone was no longer struggling to get at Tina. Every one of Tina's words had been like a fist, and it had knocked all the fight out of her.

"Yeah, bitch, who sad now? Tell our babies' daddy I said hello." And with that, Tina was out the door.

Simone didn't move. She didn't speak. She felt humiliated and couldn't believe Freddie had put her in a position to be humiliated in front of strangers.

"You okay, girl?" Nina consoled her. "I'm sorry you had to hear it this way."

Simone felt like a fool. The pain was too deep for tears, the anger too fierce for words. All she wanted to do was get out. Get out of the salon, out of Goldsboro, out of the clothes on her back, just out.

She didn't respond to Nina because she barely heard her. She just pulled away from her, grabbed her purse, and headed for the door.

Her first intent was to confront Freddie, but just the thought of seeing his face, hearing his voice, smelling his scent made her sick, physically sick to her stomach. She had to stop the car at a green light and quickly open her car door to vomit. "How could you, Freddie?" she begged into thin air. "How could you?"

The child she was carrying, which up until that point had made her feel so warm inside, now just made her feel full. Cheap and meaningless. He had given his seed to another woman. She couldn't face him. She felt like, if she saw him, she wouldn't be able to restrain herself from doing something she'd regret for the rest of her life. *Go home,* the little voice inside her urged. *Go home.* She knew the voice wasn't referring to the apartment she and Freddie shared; it was referring to Jersey, and she obeyed it without hesitation.

Chapter Twenty-eight

Freddie pulled up to their townhouse off Wayne Memorial Drive. It was a ritzy spot tucked away on the outskirts of Goldsboro, very different from the shack they'd occupied when they first arrived. He liked the apartment, but his extravagant taste that always stayed one step ahead of his pockets had him thinking about an eighteen-room mansion, and pushing a Maybach or an Azure. The money was good, but he wanted more.

He looked at Simone's empty parking space and checked his watch. He knew she had gone to the salon, but she was usually back by now. And since Kiki was on her honeymoon with Slug, he wondered where she could be.

Freddie came and went erratically, but Simone was like clockwork. He went inside to fix himself a bite to eat and get some sleep. While Slug was away, he was handling the operation, a fact he definitely wasn't feeling. It wasn't like he was on the block scrambling, but he hated handling packages, and delivering and picking up money. That was Slug's job according to their agreement, and he intended to check Slug about it when he returned.

Inside, Freddie browsed the refrigerator. Everything in it that he wanted needed to be cooked, and Simone had him so lazy he didn't feel like cooking. So he went into the living room, sat down on the couch, and called Simone on her cell phone. It rang four times before she answered it.

"Hello," she stated flatly.

"Ay, Sim—"

Click. The phone went dead and all that could be heard was a dial tone.

Freddie looked at the phone strangely thinking they must have had a bad connection. He pressed the speed dial again. This time the phone rang eight times, and Simone didn't answer at all. Something was wrong. He knew he'd heard Simone's voice, and he knew he had dialed right because he was using the speed dial. This time he dialed the number himself.

Simone had driven in circles for almost half an hour before finding her way to Wilson to get on I-95 North. The first time her phone rang, she knew it was Freddie, and she was all set to flip on him until she heard his voice. She felt that same sickness from before, but she felt something else, too: weakness. She felt like her heart was dangling like a puppet on a string, and hearing Freddie's voice made it jerk and spasm so she hung up. The second time, she refused to answer the phone. Instead she counted every ring until it stopped and she could breathe again. The third time it rang, she didn't want to answer and she refused in her mind to answer. But she answered anyway; she just didn't speak.

"Hello?" Freddie spoke into the phone, but she still didn't say anything. "Simone? Yo, Simone. You there?"

"What do you want, Freddie?" Her voice was ice cold and Freddie could feel the chill through the fiber optics.

"Whoa, what the deal? You okay?" he asked, but knew she wasn't.

"I'm leaving, Freddie," was all she replied.

Freddie jumped off the couch. "Leaving? What are you talkin' about? Where you goin'? Why you leavin', boo? What the hell is—"

"I'm leaving you, Freddie!" she screamed into the mouthpiece, cutting him off. "Don't worry about where I'm going!"

"Hold up, hold up!" Freddie's head was spinning and he felt sick. Despite his foolish behavior and player ways, Simone truly was his heart.

He was crazy with fear not knowing where she was and having no way to see her at that point. "Please, baby, let's talk! Please! Where you at?"

"Congratulations."

"Huh?"

"I said congratulations. I saw Tina and it turns out that I'm not the only one who's . . ." She couldn't even say the word. Just thinking about it clouded her vision so badly she had to pull over to the side of the road. "Freddie, why are you doing this to me?" she asked with so much pain and anguish it brought tears to Freddie's eyes. "What did I do to deserve this, Freddie? Didn't I love you? Didn't I?"

"Boo." *Damn,* he thought. This was definitely serious. "Simone, listen to me. I swear to you, ma, Tina is a fuckin' liar! I ain't fuckin' her, boo, I swear." Freddie was lying through his teeth. But if a lie was going to keep the only true thing in his life, so be it.

"Freddie, you're lying!" she cried, but wanted desperately to believe him.

"Simone, I swear to you, baby! That bitch see what we got, all those bitches see what we got, and they'll do anything to break up our home, boo, to ruin what we've worked so hard to build!

Together! Don't let them succeed, baby, don't let them succeed! We a family, and I don't want my son to grow up without a father like we did!" Freddie tried to persuade her. Neither he nor Simone ever knew their fathers, and they had vowed that when they had a child, they wouldn't let that happen. He thought about what his aunt had said about his father and felt a sickening sense of déjà vu, wondering if his father had gone through this same thing with his mother.

"And I don't want my baby growing up with a triflin'-ass nigga for a daddy!" Simone retorted between sobs.

"Come back, Simone!"

"No!"

"Please, baby! Don't let it end this way!"

"It's over, Freddie!" she said, not even convincing herself.

"Then I'm comin' to Jersey! I know that's where you're going and I'm coming, come what may! Even if I gotta sleep on your porch!" Freddie said.

"Then you going to jail!"

"What else I got, if I lose you?" It was the only real thing he had said during the whole conversation.

Simone looked at the blue interstate sign beckoning her: I-95 North. *Home.*

"Please, Simone! Come back! Please!"

The strings to her heart jerked and twisted, and reluctantly she gave in.

As soon as Freddie hung up the phone, his pain turned to rage. He was too far gone to try to convince himself that he'd try to change his ways, but he was gonna check these bitches.

Tina saw Freddie's number on her caller ID. She picked up, already talking. "Freddie, listen, I—"

"What the fuck you tell Simone you pregnant by me for?" If Tina had been standing in front of him, he would have choked her.

"I am!" Tina yelled.

"That shit ain't mine!" he cussed her.

His comment kinda hurt Tina. "It could be! And why my baby gotta be shit, Freddie?"

Freddie laughed. "'Cause you don't even want it! Ain't you 'posed to be havin' an abortion?" he reminded her.

"I don't know now! I might just keep it!" she said, wishing she hadn't told Freddie she might not keep it and hating even more that he had thrown it in her face.

"Word up, Tina, don't get this shit twisted. Either play your position or leave it for somebody who can. Simone is my wife and we just got a beautiful understanding. Don't let your feelings fuck that up!" Freddie warned.

"Whatever," she replied, sucking her teeth.

"So what you gonna do? 'Cause I ain't for all this drama, yo," Freddie said, laying it down.

"I said whatever. You just better check that bitch, 'cause if she come in my face again—"

"Look, fuck all that! I gotta handle some shit, yo. You got some money?"

Tina didn't respond.

"Tina!"

"I ain't cash my check yet," she said, sucking her teeth again.

Freddie checked his watch, trying to time Simone's return. "I'll be through there, a'ight?"

"When?"

"Just be there."

Freddie hung up. Her little short-ass check wasn't nothing to Freddie, but it was the principle. She had violated, and she had to get broke, literally. One of them trick-ass niggas she was fucking was gonna have to pay her bills this month because Freddie was going to claim every dime she had.

Simone walked into the house an hour later to find it full of flowers and balloons. The sweet fragrance of the assorted blooms filled the air, but she smelled nothing. Freddie came out of the bedroom, smiling as he approached, but Simone felt nothing. She was just numb, drained of what once seemed utterly important. Even the glow of her pregnancy had diminished, like the sun hiding behind thick, gray clouds.

Freddie took her left hand and produced a black ring box. He opened it to reveal a $5,000 diamond ring. Its sparkle hit the dead iris of her eye; she didn't react at all. Freddie gently slid the huge rock on her finger.

"I know you confused, baby, but I swear you all I need, all I want. I told you I'd get you another ring, and I pray you know it comes from my heart."

Freddie placed his hand on the back of Simone's neck and kissed her. Her tongue tangled with his out of reflex, not desire. He slid her shirt up and kissed her swollen belly, his tongue probing her belly button. Then he carried her to the bedroom where he'd covered the bed with rose petals. He got undressed and took Simone into his embrace, but she felt nothing. She wasn't even wet. Freddie had to use his tongue to lubricate her, and while he was inside her, she remained numb.

He collapsed on top of her, kissing her gently. "I love you, Simone."

Chapter Twenty-nine

The next morning, Freddie awoke to the strange feeling that he was being watched. He rolled his head around and saw Simone sitting on the bed watching him. She was wearing a white nightgown, and was leaning against the headboard with a pillow in her lap. Her face wore no expression.

"Good mornin', ma," he greeted her, and kissed her on the knee because it was the closest part of her to him.

"Morning."

"You okay? You sick or something?" Freddie asked, not feeling quite right.

She shook her head but kept looking at him.

Yo, shorty buggin'. "Then why you lookin' at me like that?

"Does it make you nervous or something? I can't look at you? I can't look at my man?" she inquired sarcastically, the timbre of her voice a little cracked.

She need some space. He rose up and kissed her on the nose. "Nervous? For what? Yo, you hungry? I'ma fix you something to eat, a'ight?" Freddie offered, finding a reason to get out of the room. He got up, brushed the rose petals from his naked body, threw on a pair of shorts, and exited the room.

Simone sat back against the headboard and sighed. She slid her hand from under the pillow and looked down at the large chef's knife in her grip. She examined her own reflection in it.

She had been staring at the scratches on Freddie's back. Many were faint, but she could tell that two, now scarred over, had been deep enough to draw blood. They formed a perfect T. *"That 'T' I scratched in his back!"* Tina's voice echoed in her head. Simone had wanted to plunge the knife deep into his back and leave scars of her own. She envisioned herself stabbing him for every scratch. But when she held the knife above her head, she froze and couldn't do it. She couldn't bring herself to hurt him, couldn't bring herself to cause him pain, even though her heart was filled with pain he had caused. She thought of the I-95 North sign and knew she could never leave him either. Simone felt trapped. While Freddie was running to escape incarceration, she had run into one. Her love had become her prison.

Chapter Thirty

Slug returned from his honeymoon feeling refreshed and relaxed. Cancun and Hawaii had been lovely. He had never seen water so clear, so beautifully blue. The only water he was used to were pissy public pools or the polluted saline of Myrtle or Atlantic Beach. He had heard on TV about the soothing sounds of the waves, but thought that was just TV shit until he and Kiki sat on the beaches, watching the sunset, their bodies wrapped around each other intimately.

"What you thinkin' about, Slug?" Kiki asked, snuggled in his arms and feeling the tide coming up to her knees, caressing her warmly.

"Goldsboro Junior High."

"Huh?" She chuckled. "Why junior high?"

"That's when I read that shit about Columbus tellin' muthafuckas the world wasn't flat and they ain't believe him."

"So?"

"I woulda been one of them muthafuckas." He chuckled, making her laugh. "Bein' in the hood all your life make you think that's all there is sometimes."

"For real."

He stayed silent for a few. "We gotta get outta there."

Kiki rose up on her elbows. "For real, Slug?" she asked, her excitement building.

He nodded. "That ain't no place for li'l Chris to grow up, or any other kids we have. Muhfuckas either end up dead, in jail, strung out on crack, or stay fucked up and broke. Fuck that, yo. I'll hustle blood to come up, but after that we out."

Kiki threw her arms around him. "Thank you, baby."

"I ain't makin' no promises when, but my word, shawtie, we gettin' out the hood."

Kiki said a prayer that they would make it out.

That was the mentality Slug came back with: not necessarily trying to get out of the game, but knowing he needed to. As soon as he hit town, the serenity melted away under the scorching ghetto sun. He was back to the alert street nigga the streets had molded him into.

Slug cruised the Boro in his restored '72 Cadillac Eldorado convertible. It was pearl white, an exact duplicate of Boss Hogg's Caddy from *The Dukes of Hazzard* except for the gold Daytons. He'd had it restored while he was on his honeymoon, and he picked it up when he returned. Everything was normal. Money was straight and he was on his way to see Freddie, to have the talk with him that he had been putting off.

They agreed to meet in Herman Park where cats congregated and played ball. By the time Slug arrived, Freddie was already there running on a three-on-three pickup game. Slug didn't come to ball; he came to chill. He got out of the big Yak with his white Kangol cap tilted, sporting a Carolina blue wife beater, white shorts, and a pair of Carolina blue And Ones with no laces. He leaned against the gleaming Caddy, shaking hands and smacking asses that came within range.

"You better stop, Slug," flirted one delectable cinnamon sister in a pair of coochie cutters, "before I tell Kiki." She smiled.

"Shit, you don't even believe that," Slug replied. "She might whoop your ass just for tellin' her." He chuckled and watched her ass wiggle away.

Freddie finished his game and approached Slug dripping with sweat. "What the deal, cuz?" Slug dapped him.

"Ain't nuttin'. You?"

"I'm chillin'," Freddie replied.

"Yeah?" Slug smirked like he knew something.

"Yeah," Freddie repeated, a little defensive. "'Fuck so funny?"

"What's this I hear about Tina being pregnant and telling Simone it's yours?"

Freddie wiped his face with his shirt. "Bullshit, yo. Ain't nothin' to it."

"You sure?"

Freddie felt like Slug was interrogating him. "What the fuck, yo? Yeah, I'm sure."

Slug lit up a Newport, took a drag, and exhaled smoke through his nose. "Look, cuz, you need to check yourself. Shit—"

"Check myself? What—"

Slug cut in, "Listen to me. I been meaning to holla at you on the real. Ain't nothin' like a woman if she get it in her mind to get you fucked up. And Simone know too much about you, too much about what's poppin' wit' us, for you to be lettin' these chickenheads blow up your spot, cuz."

Freddie nodded. "I know and I feel you. But like I said, it's straight," he assured him.

"Naw, it ain't, 'cause you still fuckin' wit' Tina. And I'm tellin' you, cuz, that bitch is conniving. Her M.O. is settin' niggas up."

"Fuck I look like, Slug. A lame? You think I'ma let a bitch rock me to sleep?" Freddie prided himself on how he handled women, and he felt like Slug was questioning his expertise.

Slug blew a stream of smoke into the air. "Nigga, you ain't gotta be a lame. A woman can rock any nigga to sleep if he slip."

"You sayin' I'm slippin'?"

Slug took a step closer to Freddie and softened his tone. "Freddie, look around you. You don't see it, but you makin' enemies. Broads ain't the only ones who catch feelins'; niggas do too. And you runnin' up in niggas' girls and baby mamas. You settin' us up for some ol' circus drama we don't need."

"Man, fuck that! Let these bitch-ass niggas catch feelin's, son! They want it, they can get it." Freddie's voice boomed and caused a few heads to turn in their direction. "You worry about yours; let me worry about mine! Matter of fact, you need to handle your muthafuckin' business and remember your position!"

Slug was taken aback by the word. "Position?" he echoed.

"Position. Honeymoon or no honeymoon, the grind is your responsibility. I don't touch shit. Don't forget the hand that feeds you, nigga! Wit'out me, you'd still be a nickel-ass nigga!"

By now, the attention of half the park was on Slug and Freddie so they were locked in. And neither of their egos would let them back down. Slug tossed his cigarette aside and pulled his shorts out of the sag he wore them in. "First off, young'un, you talkin' to a grown-ass man so lower your muhfuckin' tone. Second, don't try to shine on me 'cause you can't check yo' bitch, nigga." Slug spoke with force but didn't raise his voice.

Freddie threw a quick left hook that caught Slug behind his right ear. He dazed him but didn't drop him, and Slug threw up his southpaw. He shot Freddie a furious flurry that used all of his boxing skills, dipping and dodging, and throwing a straight right that busted Freddie's lip. A crowd had gathered around the two cousins going blow for blow, toe to toe, until Slug got up under Freddie, scooped him, and slammed him onto the hood of Shak's Benz 500 series.

"Ay, yo, hold the fuck up!" Shak protested as he and A.B. rushed to break up the fight because they were on his car.

They struggled to pull them apart, A.B. grabbing Slug, and Shak restraining Freddie. "Y'all niggas chill! Y'all family!" A.B. barked.

They finally got the two men apart; they had been locked tighter than two red-nosed pit bulls. They huffed and puffed, glaring at each other, Freddie with a busted lip and Slug with a bleeding nose.

"Nigga, we can do this all night," Slug said, winded, with his hands on his knees. "That still won't change the fact that you slippin', cuz. If you gonna play, play. Just don't let these tricks play you." Slug stood up, dropped his shorts back in his sag, got in his car, and drove off.

Chapter Thirty-one

"Freddie. Freddie, you 'sleep?" Simone asked, shaking him.

If I wasn't, would you have to ask? "Not now," he said gruffly. "What time is it?"

"Two o'clock," Simone answered, sitting on the edge of the bed, smiling at him. Her glow was back and she seemed to be getting bigger by the minute. Things between them had been rocky at first, but she had come around and returned to her old loving self. The only thing different was that all she seemed to say lately was, "Freddie, I need some money."

Freddie sighed. "For what now, Simone?"

"To get some baby stuff," she replied.

"What happened to all that dough I gave you two days ago?"

"I went shopping," she lied. She was getting good at it, almost as good as Freddie.

"And bought what?" Freddie probed.

"Come on, boo." She smiled and wrinkled up her nose in the cute way that she did. "Don't be like that. Kiki is waiting for me."

Freddie just studied his smiling fiancée. Something wasn't quite right. Her smile didn't reach her eyes, but Freddie didn't see that. "Take what I got in my pants, a'ight? Just let me get some sleep, yo," he said and rolled over on his side. He hadn't gotten in until close to four.

Simone kissed him on the cheek and grabbed his pants. She emptied both pockets like a professional pickpocket, then said, "That's all?"

"Simone!" Freddie barked.

"Okay, okay." She stuck her tongue in his ear. "I love you, daddy. Sweet dreams." She said it like she was rocking him to sleep and he nodded off.

Since his fight with Slug, things hadn't quite gotten back to normal. To the undiscriminating eye, it was all good; they still hustled together and could still laugh and joke. But deep down, something had been lost that couldn't be retrieved.

While Simone was hitting up his pockets, he was hitting up everybody else's. He tightened down on the chicks he was dealing with. He didn't really need the money but neither did they, in his book. He also didn't need to do what he did to Slug.

"Ay, yo, I hollered at my peeps. They said shit is hot up top so they gotta go up to eighteen five," Freddie informed Slug as they drove back from Raleigh. "So, yo, instead of fifty-fifty, I gotta see sixty-forty, yo. Feel me?"

Slug smiled knowingly. "Yeah, cuz, I feel you. I feel you."

It seemed as if everything in Freddie's life was changing for the worse, everything and everyone except for one person: Gina. Freddie had begun to rely on her more and more, to get away from all the bullshit and stress he himself had created. They spent every other weekend together. One weekend was for business; the next was always just because.

This weekend was just because. Gina flew into Douglas International Airport in Charlotte where Freddie was waiting for her. They checked into the Hyatt and spent the day at Carowinds, an amusement park on the outskirts of Charlotte. It was a blazing Southern day, so the water rides and breathtakingly exhilarating roller coasters were greatly appreciated. Gina felt like a young girl again, eating cotton candy, getting it stuck on her nose, and letting Freddie lick it off. Freddie even won her a large, stuffed toucan with a rainbow beak. It was so big, she had to hold it in both arms.

Being with Gina was like being free for Freddie. There weren't any games, there weren't any lies, so he could just be himself. It was like a breath of fresh air. They went back to the hotel to shower off the perspiration of the day, and then relaxed in the well-air-conditioned room, skin to skin while sipping on cognac: Grand Cru for him and Rémy Red for Gina.

"I gotta give it to you, Freddie. You surprised me this time. I didn't expect that," Gina admitted, rubbing his nose with hers. "I haven't been to an amusement park in years. I had a lot of fun."

"Yeah, me too," Freddie agreed. "And I ain't had fun in a long time."

"You okay?"

Freddie shrugged. "Mo' money, mo' problems." He sipped his drink.

"So I guess the life of a drug dealer ain't as easy as you thought it would be, huh?" Gina asked, but it was more like a statement.

"Naw, G, it ain't that. Shit couldn't be sweeter."

"Then it must be Simone," she surmised.

"Something like that."

"Well," she began, kissing him softly on the forehead, "I hope you don't think I'ma lay here with you naked"—she kissed both eyelids—"and listen to you talk about Simone"—she kissed him on the nose—"when I'm trying to make you forget about her." She finished with her tongue massaging the inside of his mouth.

"And if you succeed?" he asked.

"Then you'll be all mine like you're supposed to be. Haven't you figured it out by now, Freddie? I'm the only woman who can handle you because I'm the only woman who truly knows you."

Freddie smiled. "Then if you know me, you know that 'only woman' ain't even in my vocab."

"Well, that's Simone's problem. As long as you wit' her, I'm her problem. But once you're mine, any other woman is my problem. So if you cheat on me, I'll kill you." She chuckled, but her eyes narrowed like a panther's. Freddie caressed her cheek and Gina kissed his palm.

"Be careful what you ask for, yo."

Gina was becoming Freddie's refuge and he felt attracted to her in ways he never had before. He leaned over and kissed her. "But tonight, it's just me and you, and I want to treat you like a queen."

"Like a queen," she teased with one eyebrow raised. "I am a queen."

Freddie started with her right foot, massaging it along the arch, rolling his thumb down and across the ball of her heel. She had been on her feet all day, so his gentle touch relaxed her. He ran his tongue along the bottom of her foot, tickling her and making her squirm with sensual delight. He worked his way up, gently brushing the tips of her toes with his tongue, ever so slowly finding his way to her ankle and inner calf. Gina gripped the covers and let a soft moan escape from her throat. Freddie parted her thighs, slid a pillow under the small of her back, and began nibbling his way closer and closer to her sex. Freddie had never eaten her out before, so when she felt his tongue licking and sucking on her extremely swollen clit, her eyes widened and all her breath was taken away.

"Fr . . . Freddie, what . . ." was all she got out before she found herself trying to squirm away from his wickedly delicious tongue. She scooted back until she was pinned against the headboard, and then she clawed the walls. Freddie's tongue explored her inner sweetness so deeply that it made her knees weak, and then he brought her down on his face. Gina was in another world.

"Oh, Freddie. Okay, okay, I give. Oh, baby, I give."

Freddie didn't know what she had given, but Gina knew. Deeper and deeper his tongue went until he felt her leg lock and spasm. She screamed his name as her stomach jumped and she heaved and hollered from the intensity of her orgasm.

Freddie rolled her over onto her back, spread her legs, and rubbed his hardness against her softness before penetrating her. Gina screamed like a virgin, "Oh, Freddie, I love you. Oh, I love you."

His slow grind and nipple tongue tease had Gina under his control; he took her rhythm and made it his own. She wrapped her legs around his back and cried into his chest. He licked her tears away only making her cry more. "I'm yours, Freddie. I'm all yours. Whatever you ask, I'll do. Whatever you want, I'll be," she whispered, sucking on his earlobe. "I'm all yours."

Chapter Thirty-two

"Welcome to McDonald's. May I take your order?" the crackling voice asked through the loud speaker.

Simone leaned out of her car window a little and said, "Yes, give me two number ones with a Sprite, no ice, and a strawberry milkshake, and one number three with a Diet Coke."

The cashier repeated the order, informed her of the price, and told her to drive around. Simone turned to Kiki in the passenger seat and asked, "Girl, do me a favor and pay for our orders. I ain't bring no money out with me."

Simone and Kiki had gotten to be good friends. Marriage had mellowed Kiki out somewhat. She was still ghetto and she still loved to fight, especially Slug, but her demeanor was more serene. She was coaching Simone on the do's and don'ts of being pregnant.

"Sure, boo," Kiki said, going into her purse and handing Simone a twenty before adding jokingly, "Girl, you don't never have no money. Let me find out Freddie got you on a budget." Simone pulled up to the window and paid.

"Naw, I just went and paid the bills. I guess I just forgot," Simone lied smoothly as the man at the window handed her the food. She handed the bags to Kiki and drove off.

"How is Freddie anyway? I hardly ever see him since we moved out to the country," Kiki said, nibbling on a bouquet of fries.

"You never see him? I ain't seen him since Friday morning," Simone confessed sourly. It was Sunday afternoon.

"Friday?" Kiki asked, looking away on purpose and focusing her attention out of the window. "Is everything okay wit' y'all?"

Simone glanced at her with a reassuring smile. "Yeah, girl. Why'd you ask?"

"I was just, you know, checking. 'Cause, shit, if I hadn't seen Slug since Friday, Roy Jones wouldn't have nothing on me." The girls laughed.

"Naw, Ki, it's all good. Me and Freddie, we got an understanding."

Kiki let it go but she knew there was more to it. Not every smiling face is a happy face, and something was different about Simone. What

Kiki didn't know was what was different. She didn't know that her friend was only a shell of her former self, but she had learned a valuable lesson from Freddie: how to be a player.

Chapter Thirty-three

Gina walked through the terminal of Newark International and all she could think of was Freddie. Everything she saw seemed to remind her of him. It was like the song by Luther Vandross, "Think About You."

She had just arrived back in Newark, and she could hardly wait to return to North Carolina in fourteen days. Gina glided with a confident stride and a satisfied air, heading to the reserved parking area where she'd left her black Benz G wagon over the weekend. The traffic on I-9 was terrible, but she was too preoccupied with her thoughts to mind. She thought about the long drive out to Wayne but decided to go see her Uncle Lou on Clinton Avenue.

She pulled up in front of Lou's deli and spotted her uncle's Lincoln LS parked down the block. She went inside to find Stephanie, Lou's lady friend of the last thirty years, behind the counter.

"Hey, Step," Gina greeted her and kissed her on the cheek. "Lou in the back?"

"Ain't he always," Stephanie retorted sarcastically. "Him, Woody, and the damn checkers. Can't you hear 'em?"

Now that she had mentioned it, Gina could make out the gruff voices of grumpy older men and giggled as she went into the back.

"Woody, don't start that bullshit! Now we been playin' checkers for damn near fifty years, and we ain't never played jumpin' backward!" Lou huffed, sitting on an upended milk crate.

"Bullshit! I ain't jump backward, you blind motherfucka! Put yo' glasses on! I double jumped, and you can jump backward when you double!" Woody exclaimed, rocking on his crate.

The two sixty-year-olds were lifelong friends and constant companions. Although Woody wasn't in Lou's profession, he benefited from it greatly because he owned a construction company. Lou made sure he stayed flooded with contracts. The two men sitting in the back of the small deli were a case study in microeconomics. They represented the fueling force behind the national GNP: crime and construction.

Gina walked in and kissed Lou on the cheek.

"Hey, baby girl! How are you doing?" Lou asked sweetly. Gina was his dead brother's child, but he had raised her as his own.

Gina looked down at the heavyset man. He was extremely short and extremely wide, with the frame and temper of a bulldog. Despite the weight he held in the streets, he was usually dressed as he was now, in a pair of Dickies work pants, a shirt, and a pair of black work boots. The only telltale sign of his wealth was his huge diamond pinkie ring, gold Rolex watch, and diamond-encrusted gold tooth.

"I'm good, Uncle Lou. And what are you two arguing over checkers for?" she asked, totally amused.

"It ain't the checkers, sweet thang, it's your blind-ass uncle," Woody informed her. "If he knew how to play, we wouldn't be arguing."

"And hello to you too, Mr. Woody. How are you?" she asked, giving him a kiss too.

"Better now." He grinned like a sly old fox, eyeing Gina's wide hips filling out her Apple Bottom jeans. "All that brown sugar! Lord, I love you, woman! You can have all my money, just let me smell it!" He cackled.

"Watch yo' mouth, dirty-ass nigga," Lou warned playfully. "That's my niece you talkin' to. Besides, old as you is, just the smell'll give you a heart attack." Lou and Gina laughed.

"Then I'll die happy," Woody said, folding his arms across his chest like he was in a coffin, a satisfied grin covering his face.

"You too much, Mr. Woody." Gina blushed.

Lou was studying the checkerboard. "I guess you got my message."

"No. I just got back in town," Gina replied.

Lou looked up at her. "So you don't know?"

"Don't know what?"

Lou slowly eased himself off the crate. "I'll be right back, Woody. Lemme talk to Gina a minute. And don't cheat."

Sshhit! Woody thought as uncle and niece walked out the back door.

The door led out on to a large vacant lot that was filled with the usual ghetto debris. Lou looked around casually, but Gina knew her uncle, and his observations were never just casual.

He glanced at her. "You look good, baby girl. I take it that nigga takin' care of you, huh?"

At the thought of Freddie, she couldn't help but blush. "He's doin' all right."

"Hmmmmm," Lou hummed skeptically. "I bet he is."

Gina knew what he meant but she let it go. She knew he didn't want to be giving Freddie weight. It had taken a lot to convince him so she knew to leave it alone. "You said you sent me a message?"

Lou put his hands in his pockets and spit onto the ground. "The feds."

"The feds?" Gina repeated, looking around at the cars and visible windows. "Here?"

"Naw, not here, yet." He turned to face her. "Some people out in Elizabeth I deal wit' been dealin' wit' some people down in Willingboro, and a couple of them jokers caught a case. They don't know me and I don't know them, but you know the feds play domino rules: one fall and lean, the next fall and lean."

"They say anything yet?" Gina inquired.

"No, but they will. It's one in every bunch. Everybody wanna join the help yourself program. So, listen, I'ma be shuttin' down for a while. I ain't takin' no calls and I ain't makin' none. So I can't do nothin' for ol' boy anymore."

Gina had figured as much when he began explaining the situation. She knew there wouldn't be any more deliveries. Her heart sank when she thought about Freddie, what he was going to do, and how he would take the news.

Lou saw the concern on her face. "Baby girl, I know you wasn't expecting this, but there's nothing I can do about it."

"I understand, unc. It's just that Freddie's depending on me, so . . ." Her voice trailed off.

Lou studied her for a while, then asked, "You really love this joker, don't you?"

Gina looked him in the eyes and answered, "I do, unc."

He sighed hard. "Well, what about the girl he down there wit'? Didn't you tell me he got a girl wit' him? What about her?"

Gina lowered her eyes. "I can't make him choose."

"It seems to me he already chose," Lou surmised, but Gina didn't respond, so he continued. "Baby girl, I raised you, so I know that when you got your heart set on something you're determined to get it. And you know I don't approve of this joker. He ain't got nothin' but larceny in his heart, but you gonna have to learn for yourself. But, listen, if this nigga really worth your heart, then he gonna have to choose. And if he choose right . . ." Lou looked out over the lot again like he was planning his next move. "If he choose right, I know some good peoples in Jamaica. I got some interest in a sugar company down there. Let me see what I can do about getting y'all down there."

Gina's spirits jumped into her eyes and she hugged her uncle. "Thank you, Uncle Lou! Thank you!"

"Hold on before you thank me. I said let me see what I can do. Besides," Lou said, holding her gently by the sides of her face, "the trip is for two. You and him, baby girl. You may not be able to make him choose, but I can. Let me know okay?"

Gina knew her uncle's offer was the answer to Freddie's problem. He'd be free from Dante, the police, and the game. With the money she had put away and her uncle's connection, they could grow old in Jamaica together without a worry in the world. It was the chance of a lifetime and she prayed that Freddie would see it that way too.

Chapter Thirty-four

Simone pushed her shopping cart through the Winn-Dixie supermarket absentmindedly. She shopped by rote, grabbing the things she knew they needed without thinking about it. Her mind was on the mess her life had become, the mess she had let it become. She told herself at JFK that she was making a mistake, but she ignored her mind and followed her heart. Now she was trapped. She glided along to the checkout counter and waited as the extremely slow new employee rang up the person in front of her.

"Excuse me, miss," the older brother in front of Simone asked the checkout girl politely, "but since when is Tide detergent $20.35?" He smiled, being patient with her obvious inexperience.

"I'm so sorry. I'm . . . Oh, okay. Let me start over," the cashier said. But she was a little flustered, so the manager came over.

"Vickie, you okay?" he asked.

Simone saw that this might take awhile, so she looked at the other lines. This was definitely the shortest. She rubbed her swollen belly and leaned on the cart. The manager helped the girl ring out the older man, who departed with a "God bless you" and left. His departing comment made Simone smile. That's what she liked about the South. Everyone was so friendly; at least, at first they tried to be. Had this been Jersey, the cashier and the customer would probably be fighting right now.

The thought made her giggle as she moved to be rung up and the manager looked up at her and smiled. "I'm glad to see somebody is having a good day."

Up until then, Simone really hadn't looked at the manager, but when he spoke, she got a better view of him. He was around six feet one inch, with a caramel complexion and a short, close cut full of waves. He wasn't heart-stoppingly gorgeous, but his bright white smile was warm and inviting.

"Oh, no, I just was thinking about something," she stuttered in reply.

"Well, that smile just made my day," he flirted. He saw her swollen condition, but she was alone, and beautiful. Simone was well aware of his advance, so she busied herself unloading the cart. The checkout girl began to grab the groceries, but the manager stopped her and said, "I'll take care of this for you, Vickie," and she stepped aside, feeling like a third wheel.

"I can tell by your accent that you aren't from around here," he said, scanning groceries.

"Umm, no," Simone said, brushing the hair out of her face. "I have coupons," she continued, trying to keep the encounter professional.

He took the coupons and the hint. "That'll be $73.89," he told her, and Simone took out her wallet. Two twenties and a five were all she had. She cussed herself mentally, and tried to figure out what to keep and what to put back.

"Is there a problem?" he asked, still trying to use his megawatt smile.

"No, no problem," she answered. Reflexively, she grabbed her Visa and handed it to him. "I'm a little short on cash. Could you just charge it?"

"Sure," he said, taking the card.

Now that he wasn't looking at her, she looked at him. Simone watched his hands, and noticed his clean fingernails. She noticed his wristwatch and his choice of color. She studied his profile. He was definitely cute. Very cute. And she liked his personality, the way he flirted: not pressing, but persistent.

He turned back to her with a quiet expression. "I'm sorry, but your Visa won't go through."

Simone felt a little embarrassed, remembering that she hadn't paid her bill since she had left New Jersey. She had no choice now but to put some things back. "I'm sorry to be so much trouble, but I'm going to have to put a few things back."

"Oh, it's no trouble. It's my job."

She finally got her bill down to under fifty dollars and got ready to push the buggy out, when the manager came around the counter and said, "Please, let me." He smiled.

"Oh. Thank you," Simone replied. She felt funny letting him push the cart for her and being in a man's company, but she was tired, so . . .

"So you go to Essex County College? What are you taking?" he asked, pushing the cart through the parking lot slowly. Simone started to ask him how he knew and he read it in her expression. "I saw it on your keychain."

She glanced down at her keys. She still had all of her old keys from Newark; she had merely added her new car and house keys to them. "Oh, right. Umm, accounting."

"Oh, you like to count other people's money, huh?" he joked, making her laugh, something she hadn't done in a while. "I'm in school myself.

I'm going to Wayne Community College for filmmaking. I'm hoping to transfer to the NC School of the Arts in another year or so."

Dreams, Simone thought, also thinking of her own, and what had happened to them. "Well, I wish you luck."

"I appreciate that. And hey, maybe I'll look you up. As beautiful as you are, you deserve to be up in lights."

Simone was sincerely flattered by his comments. She definitely didn't feel beautiful; she just felt heavy, physically and emotionally. She hadn't been much into fashion lately, either. She just kept her hair up in a ponytail. So often that Freddie had the nerve to say one day, "Why don't you do something wit' your hair, ma?" So she kept it like that, more out of spite than convenience.

She didn't know how to respond to the manager's comment, so she was glad that they were close enough to the Benz to chirp the alarm.

"Is this your car?" he asked, a little surprised. After the rejected Visa and the short money, he expected anything but a CLK.

"No," she said and he looked confused. "I mean, yes, it's my car, but no . . ."

It felt like her whole life could be summed up in that unfinished statement. Nothing she had felt like hers anymore.

He could tell she was a hustler's girl. The car was probably some drug dealer's and she was just driving it. He was probably her baby's daddy, too. But he could sense in Simone that everything at home wasn't all roses. "Are you okay?"

Simone nodded, avoiding eye contact, trying to fight back tears of confusion.

"Look, I know this is none of my business, but I can see you have a lot on your mind, and maybe, sometime, you may need someone to talk to, so"—he reached into his pocket, took out a pen, and wrote his name and number on her receipt—"if you do," he said and shrugged, "I'm a real good listener."

Simone looked at the paper and could read it in his hand: *Brian*. She was no stranger to flirtatious brothers. Every day she caught smiles and comments, but she always brushed them off and kept it moving. She truly saw no one but Freddie. But she had never let it go this far before. No other man had gotten two sentences out of her. She had never hesitated before, but now she had.

She took her receipt from Brian's hand and slipped it into her pocket.

Chapter Thirty-five

Gina bounced her crossed right leg on her left knee and checked her watch for the thousandth time in the last ten minutes. She was waiting for Freddie in the Hampton Inn in Rocky Mount, North Carolina. It was the drop-off weekend and Freddie was on his way, expecting the drop.

She had talked to him several times since she had spoken with her uncle, but she hadn't said anything about the cutoff. She didn't like talking over the phone, but that wasn't the only reason she hadn't said anything. Gina wanted to tell him in person, to use everything she had to convince him to come away with her and leave the States. She felt that the only thing that would stop him was his feelings for Simone. She tried to convince herself that he didn't love Simone as much as it seemed, and she imagined him accepting her offer of freedom openheartedly, without reservation. She believed in her heart that the love he had for her could be and should be so much more. He wanted him to love her the way he did Simone, but better.

"I love you, Gina. You've always been there for me. And I know now that I wanna be with you," she imagined him saying, then taking her in his arms, and holding her so tight she could hardly breathe.

Gina stood up and nervously smoothed the front of her multicolored sundress, checking her reflection in the mirror. The knock at the door made her jump. She took a deep breath and crossed the room to the door. She peeked out of the curtain and saw Freddie standing there, smiling back at her.

"Hey, sweetness." He beamed. "You gonna let me in or what?"

Gina unlatched the chain lock and opened the door. Freddie stepped in and wrapped his arms around her, palming her ass, slapping it to feel it shake. "It's like candayyy!" he sang playfully. "What the deal, ma? You good?"

"Now I am," she replied, wrapping her arms around his neck and tonguing him down. "I missed you."

"I missed you too, G," Freddie echoed. "You hungry? You wanna go get something to eat or just be something to eat?" Freddie teased her with the tip of his tongue.

"No, no, I'm okay," she told him, but her tone told him otherwise.

"You a'ight, G?" Freddie questioned.

"Uh-huh," she said and pulled away from him. "I, umm, just need to talk to you about something."

Freddie watched her pace to the far wall; then she turned around. "Freddie, how long do you plan on doing this?"

"Why, what happened? You ain't run into no trouble on 95, did you?"

"No, I . . . I just need to know. Freddie, you know you can't do this forever, and you can't run forever. As long as you are involved, anything can happen, and you need to think about that," Gina stated.

Freddie approached her. "Dig, ma, I feel you, but let me worry about that," he crooned, and tried to embrace her, but she evaded him again by stepping away.

"No, Freddie. I have to worry because I'm involved too. Have you ever thought about that? What if something happens to me?"

He reached out and caressed her face. "Is that what this is about? You're right, ma, and I'm sorry. And I have been thinkin' about it. I was thinkin' maybe we could get somebody to mule it. You wouldn't have to meet them or nothin'. You could just leave—"

Gina sighed and rubbed her forehead. "No, Freddie, that's not what I . . ." She sighed again. "It's my uncle."

"What about him?"

"Some people . . . They caught a case, and he doesn't know what they'll do, so he's gonna chill for a while," she finally got out.

"Chill?" Freddie asked, seeing the pieces but not the puzzle. "What do you mean, chill?"

"I mean, I can't bring you drops anymore," she informed him.

"Wait, wait, let me get this straight." Freddie paced back and forth. "You said some people caught a case. You mean his people?"

"No."

"So what that got to do wit' him?"

"He's just being careful, Freddie. You know everybody's snitching these days."

"Can't he hit you once more? I know you said no more than five, but double up just this once. We could mule it and—"

Gina could hear the hysteria building in Freddie's voice. He had become addicted to the paper chase. "I'm sorry, Freddie, I can't." It broke her heart to say it. "It's not my fault."

"Not your fault? I gotta live, yo! I eat off this shit! Fuck I'm 'posed to do now?" Freddie sat on the edge of the bed, rubbing his hands together.

"What about all the money you've made so far? I know you ain't spent it all. Don't you have enough to live on until we figure something else out?"

"A hundred thousand ain't shit!" he barked. He had been spending money like water and had only managed to squirrel away a nutshell. Freddie was used to the best and wouldn't settle for less.

Gina sat next to him on the bed and put her arm around his neck. She ran her fingers through his curly hair. "Baby, listen. You didn't expect this to last, did you? I told you, anything can happen, but I've got some money put up. A lot of money. The type of money we could retire off of, go away, leave the States, and leave this all behind. My uncle has friends in Jamaica."

The laugh started low and built up until Freddie was laughing aloud. "You slippin', G," he said as he stood up. "Your game is gettin' weak, yo."

She stood up too. "It's not a game, Freddie. Really. I'm serious. Leave with me. We can get away, before it's too late."

Freddie studied Gina with amusement. She had been reeling him in, slowly but surely, making him depend on her, not only financially but emotionally; and she almost had him. He had been feeling drawn to her, and now he could see why. "You had this planned, didn't you?"

"No, Freddie, I—"

"You had this whole shit planned! Put me on, string me along, then freeze me out!" He chuckled menacingly. "I expected better from you, G."

Tears streamed down Gina's face. "I didn't have anything planned, Freddie. But I don't apologize for the way it turned out. You know how I feel about you and I just want the best for you."

"And that's supposed to be you, huh?"

"It's not Simone. She could never love you like I can."

"What about my unborn child, huh? Who's gonna love my son? You think you can buy me from my seed? Can you give me one? Can you?"

Gina broke down into an all-out sob. "Please don't do this to me, Freddie. I just want to help you."

"Help me? Bitch, fuck you and your help!" Freddie roared. "You cuttin' me off! Naw, I'm cuttin' you off! Fuck you, you barren bitch!" Freddie spat venomously and turned to the door.

The love in her heart wouldn't let him go. She couldn't stand the pain of seeing him turn away. After all she had done for him, for him to just turn his back. Her pride refused to accept his leaving, and each individual emotion combined in an explosive mix that launched her at Freddie's back.

"Nigga, you ain't never gonna leave me!"

Freddie had just opened the door when her body crashed into his, slamming him against the door. "Gina!"

But she was all over him like an enraged tigress. "I'll kill you if you walk out that door!" she vowed, swinging wildly.

Freddie's ire rose to boiling as he fought to get her hands off his neck. She was stronger than he had expected, so he had to fight fire with fire. He backhanded her hard enough to make her spit blood, then hit her with a merciless blow to the stomach, which instantly took the wind out of her and made her crumple to the floor at his feet.

"Freddie, why? Why, Freddie?" she groaned, and coughed, and balled up into a fetal position. "Why'd you do this to me?"

"Bitch, you did it to yourself," he coldly replied. "You did it to yourself."

Freddie opened the door and slammed it behind him, leaving Gina balled up on the floor.

She lay there crying tears of pain, which became tears of anguish, and finally tears of rage and revenge. It was apparent to her that Freddie was so far gone that he had forgotten who she was. But as Gina lay in a fetal position all she could think about was how, soon, his memory would be refreshed.

Chapter Thirty-six

"Hey, Ben," Detective Crawford called, sticking his head into Detective Wilson's office. "Got a minute? I think I may have some good news for you."

"Good news? I remember that concept vaguely. Come on in, Andre."

Crawford entered the small, messy office carrying a few faxes in his hand. He proudly handed them to Wilson. "It's about the cop shooting and homicide a few months back," Crawford informed him.

"Believe me, son, I haven't forgotten. Every time I see Officer Williamson in that wheelchair, I'm reminded of this Holmes bastard," Wilson sneered. Freddie had managed to elude Wilson for close to a year, and that infuriated him. He was used to making arrests within days. "What am I looking at? All these funny codes and numbers. I'm in no mood for riddles, son."

"It's not a riddle; it's a Visa printout," Crawford informed him. "Remember the girl? You asked me to keep track of all her credit cards."

"Yeah?" Wilson answered sourly. "Didn't they go bad months ago?" He was wondering what Crawford was getting at chasing dead credit cards.

"Well, it turns out that, for whatever reason, Ms. Jackson tried to run the card. It was rejected, naturally, but it still registered with the credit bureaus." Crawford smiled and Wilson's whole demeanor changed as he got up on his feet.

"Son of a bitch! Goldsboro, North Carolina! There it is in black and white! Son of a bitch!" His eyes went to the words "Winn-Dixie." "Winn-Dixie? What is that? Sounds like a supermarket or something."

"Exactly."

Wilson couldn't have been happier. "Do you know what that means, Andre? That she tried to use her card at a supermarket?"

Crawford's brow curled up. "No."

"Think! When people go food shopping, they usually do it close to home. Had this been in Raleigh at a clothing store, it would have been like trying to find a needle in a haystack. But this tells us he's definitely in Goldsboro, probably in that very area."

Wilson grabbed his suit jacket off the back of the chair. "Get on the phone to Goldsboro PD and fax 'em a shot of our man, Freddie Holmes," Wilson ordered.

"Where are you going?"

"Home." Wilson smiled. "To pack for the trip to the Dirty South." Then he was out the door.

Chapter Thirty-seven

Slug sat in the back of the Soul Bowl, a famous soul food joint that boasted the best Southern cuisine. He ate there every afternoon and this afternoon was no different. He was enjoying his meal of fried catfish, turnip greens, yams, and cornbread, with a side of coleslaw and French fries. He hadn't seen Freddie in days, since Freddie told him they had been cut off.

"What you mean cut off, cuz? Just like that? 'Fuck you do?" Slug asked.

"I ain't do shit!" Freddie exclaimed. *"They on some ol' bullshit, son!"*

Slug knew there was more to it than Freddie was letting on, but he decided to let it play out. Then a few days ago, he got word that dudes in Wilson were moving major weight. Slug didn't put it past Freddie to cross him out, but he didn't expect it. He hoped he hadn't. Family or no family, if Freddie had cut him out, then it was Freddie who had violated, so no one could blame Slug when he served justice.

Then again, his mental channel changed, maybe it was all for the best. Slug was sharper than Freddie was, and he understood the game's tide. It rolled in and you got wet. The trick was not to get washed away when it rolled back out. Slug understood this, so he had been stacking. And now that he was married, it was time to make a power move to the 'burbs, mow lawns, and parlay. The feds were everywhere, and it was just a matter of time before his name came up, on a humble, and he couldn't see doing a fed bid. He knew Kiki couldn't handle it. She loved him, but she wasn't cut out to bid a stretch. She was the type of woman who needed constant attention, and he planned on being around to give it to her. If Freddie had cut him off, he could make it on his own.

While he was filling his mind with thoughts and his belly with Ms. Jones's good cooking, he heard the jingle of the bell attached to the front door. He looked up and filled his eyes with the full figure of a woman who looked like she had been raised on a steady diet of grits and cornbread, but she wasn't fat by a long shot. She wasn't from around here, either. Her Coogi dress hugged her curves and the split up her left side revealed a succulent, mahogany-toned thigh. Her Manolo Blahnik boots had a four-inch heel sharp enough to stab someone with, and they were clicking in his direction.

She wore a pair of dark Chanel sunglasses that hid her eyes, like Aaliyah used to, and her layered bob accentuated her features. "Slug." She said his name like she knew him well enough to be comfortable speaking it.

"You askin' me or tellin' me?" he drawled smoothly, wiping chicken grease from his mouth.

She smirked. "May I?" she asked, referring to the chair to his left. Slug nodded and she sat down, taking off her sunglasses, revealing the eyes of a woman with an agenda.

"You don't know me. But I know you, and we both know Freddie."

"Freddie?" Slug questioned as if he'd never heard the name before.

"Freddie. The 'five a month' Freddie. Ring any bells?"

Slug now knew whom he was talking to: the connect. He should've figured it was a woman. Now Freddie's attitude about getting cut off made all the sense in the world. Freddie had fucked up, and Slug was about to find out just how bad.

"Don't you mean 'used to be five a month' Freddie? That river done run dry, li'l mama," Slug said, taking a bite of turnip greens.

"Well, that depends."

"On what?"

"On you," she stated, making ironclad eye contact.

"I'm not sure I'm following you, li'l mama," Slug replied, wanting the picture made clearer. She understood perfectly.

"As they say, one monkey don't stop no show. What Freddie lost could be your gain," she explained. "But for you, Slug, whatever the quantity, I'll guarantee it, as long as you traffic it. And I'll give it to you for the same thing Freddie was getting it for: fifteen."

Slug chuckled. "Son of a bitch. Ol' boy said you was chargin' eighteen, and then you went up to twenty." Freddie had been playing him the whole time.

"Looks like Freddie was playing us both," she replied, with an undeniable bitterness that Slug had to question.

"Both?"

She hesitated before she answered. "Ever been in love, Slug?"

He held up his left hand, showing Gina his wedding ring. "Either that or rooted."

She leaned in closer. "Be good to her, Slug. Because there really is a thin line between love and hate."

"I'll keep that in mind, but, uh, what's the catch to your proposal?" Slug wanted to know. "I mean, no disrespect but as fine as you are, still, I know you ain't no fairy godmother and it ain't my born day, so what's the catch?"

Without blinking or stuttering, Gina stated firming, "Kidnap that bitch Simone."

Her words caught Slug off guard. His mind thought she would say something about Freddie, but shorty wasn't playing fair. She was hitting where it hurt.

"I'm not asking for her to be hurt, but if she is that's not my problem. I just want that bitch snatched up, and I want you to ask for a hundred thousand dollars," she demanded, remembering the amount Freddie told her he had saved. "I want every dime he's got, every dime he made off me." Her top lip quivered and her voice trembled slightly with a rage that made Slug glad he wasn't in Freddie's shoes.

"You sho' know how to hurt a nigga, don't you, li'l mama?" Slug commented, sucking the meat out of his teeth and pulling out a Newport.

She smiled seductively and narrowed her eyes in an aphrodisiac-like gaze. "I know how to hurt a man," she cooed, then reached out to touch Slug's face, "but I know how to please one even better." Then she licked her lips slowly.

Slug moved her hand away from his face. "Dig, shawtie. I damn sho' wish I could find out, but uhhh, no offense, but I see what dick do to you, so I ain't even tryin' to put myself in that position."

She smiled, appreciating the weight of his statement. "I like you, Slug."

Chapter Thirty-eight

Gina was working both ends of the East Coast. While she was working out the deal with Slug to kidnap Simone and take all of Freddie's paper, she had a plan working in New Jersey for Freddie.

"I'm comin' yo! Damn!" Cream yelled as he rolled lazily out of bed. He rubbed his face and checked his Cartier watch on the dresser; it was well past noon. He looked around for his wife as the door buzzer rang again. "Kandi, get the fuckin' door!" He got no reply. "Where that bitch at?" he asked out loud as he went down the steps to the front door of his two-story house.

"Kandi, you down here?" Still no reply. He opened the door to the foyer and glanced out the peephole, but he didn't see anyone. "Who da fuck playin' games, yo?" he asked, irritated that he had gotten up to answer the door, but whoever had come was now gone.

Cream opened the door to see if he could catch whoever it was before they left, but he saw no one. All he saw was a car turn the corner. He peeped down the street, but still saw no one.

That's when he looked down at his feet and saw an envelope. He bent over and picked it up. It was sealed but there was no address, no writing on it period. Cream ripped it open and found a picture inside.

It was Freddie.

His blood pressure went through the roof and he scanned the streets again, thinking somebody was playing with him. He looked at the picture again, and then he turned it over. Some handwriting caught his eye:

Goldsboro, NC. You owe me ten grand.

Cream couldn't believe it. They had been looking for him for months, and now, out of the blue, someone had delivered Freddie to Cream's doorstep, literally. Cream ran inside to call Dante.

Chapter Thirty-nine

Dante was at his crib with a thick, topless redbone in a purple thong. He was taking pictures.

"Come on, ma. This is for my dudes in the feds. Bend over that chair and let 'em see that ass," he ordered.

She bent over and stuck her ass out real far, as if to kiss the camera with it. "You like this?" she flirted, mimicking fuck faces for the camera.

"Word. Hold up. One more. A'ight, spread that pussy and stick your finger in it," Dante said.

"Tay, you nasty," she responded, but did as she was told.

Dante was hard as a rock. "A'ight, take one wit' my dick in your mouth, yo." He grinned.

"No, Tay! I'm not taking any pictures like that." She pouted and sat down on the couch.

"Chill, yo," he said, approaching her and pulling out his dick. "I ain't gonna take it of your face, just of your mouth."

She looked up at Dante's dick in front of her face. "Just my mouth, Tay!"

"That's what I said, ain't it?" he answered as she slipped her juicy lips around his shaft.

"Luk diz?" she asked, with half her mouth full of Dante's stiff, pulsating dick.

"Naw, the whole thing," Dante said, making her deep throat him while he took pictures of her whole face.

His Blackberry rang.

"Damn," he cussed, dropping the camera while the redbone continued to brain him. "Yo," he barked into the phone, upset at the interruption. "Who this?"

"Cream, yo! Ay, Tay, you ain't gonna believe this shit! I know where that dude Freddie at!"

"Word? Where?" Dante asked, almost ready to cum.

"He down South, son. Down in the Dirty, slippin'!"

"Ay, yo, word to Mannie! We goin' down there today, yo, today! Be ready!" Dante yelled and hung up.

"Who was that?" the redbone asked, now licking around the head of his dick.

"Your clown-ass husband. Hurry up, Kandi, yo. I got a trip to make."

Chapter Forty

Simone had long since stopped caring about who Freddie was fucking. She disregarded the hickies, the nights he didn't come home, and the mornings he returned. She even ignored the numbers she found in his pockets, which, instead of throwing away, she laid on his nightstand. The only change was that she made him wear condoms whenever they had sex, which was more and more infrequent. The only thing they had in common was the joyful anticipation of their coming child. She and Freddie would share the experience of their unborn kicking inside her. She would beam proudly, and Freddie would beam, equally proud. Simone didn't carry her grudge with an attitude; she just accepted the situation. If women were stupid enough to give him money, she was cool with spending it.

That morning she had been lying back on the couch, watching *Brown Sugar* on DVD. "So when did you first fall in love with hip-hop?" She loved that movie. While lying there, she heard a knock at the door. She struggled up from the couch thinking Freddie had lost his key again or that maybe it was Kiki. She looked out the peephole and saw a man dressed in brown and a UPS truck in the parking lot.

"Yes?" she said through the door.

"Delivery for Simone Jackson," he replied dryly.

Delivery? She hadn't ordered anything to be delivered. Then she thought that maybe it was a surprise from Freddie. He did still pamper her. She opened the door. "I'm Simone. Where do I sign?"

"Right there," was the last thing she heard before the delivery man held a rag up to her face. She felt herself struggle momentarily. Then there was total darkness as she faded out of consciousness.

Chapter Forty-one

Detectives Wilson and Crawford had been in Goldsboro for two days, held up in the Goldsboro Police Department. Little sleep and two-day stubble told the story of the endless cups of coffee and fast food they'd been through. The Goldsboro Police had been extremely helpful, but so far the detectives had been unsuccessful in tracking Freddie down. The only picture they had of him was five years old. At that time he was sixteen with cornrows and no facial hair, so he couldn't be identified by any of the detectives. The closest they came was when the narcotics squad got involved.

"I swear I've seen this guy before," Jakes, the redneck who had taken Freddie's money, swore. "I just can't place where," he stressed.

"It's an old picture," Crawford explained, studying the large white man.

Crawford was no racist, and was a city man head to toe, but like most African Americans, he had Southern roots. He could remember the elders in his family congregating and reminiscing about the days before they had migrated from the South. Looking at the sheriff, Crawford was convinced he was the type of man they'd be talking about when they spoke about being called *boy*.

He probably thinks we all look alike, redneck cracker.

"He's probably cut his hair, maybe even grown some facial hair." Wilson joined in. He, too, had picked up on the sheriff's nonchalant attitude toward his partner.

Timmons looked from Crawford to Wilson. He took the picture. "Can we get a copy of this? I'd like to show it around to a few of our informants."

"Sure."

"Thanks," Wilson offered for both him and his partner. He knew Crawford was somewhat in his feeling, and he had every right to be. There was no doubt in his mind Timmons was being a dick because of the color of Crawford's skin.

Within a half hour, Timmons had gotten something back.

Wilson thought they'd hit the jackpot when one of the informants turned out to be one of the crackheads who helped move Freddie's furniture. They rushed the apartment the crackhead had told them about, only to find it empty and abandoned.

Another dead end.

Wilson and Crawford had already been by the Winn-Dixie and surrounding stores showing Freddie's and Simone's pictures, but to no avail. The only hint of a lead they got was from Brian, the Winn-Dixie manager.

"Sorry, Detective. I can't say that I've seen him before," Brian replied.

"Well, what about her?" Crawford asked, holding up Simone's picture again. "She tried to use her Visa in here about a week ago."

Brian was rigid, struggling not to let it show. He recognized Simone's face as soon as he saw it, and his heart sank. He hoped she wasn't wanted, just affiliated with a wanted man. He hadn't heard from her, and now he knew her situation. The police wouldn't get anything out of him, or so he thought.

"No offense, Detective . . . Crawford, is it? But this is a huge store and I see a lot of faces. I'm just here to do my job and go home," Brian said with a slight edge in his voice that Crawford missed, but Wilson didn't.

Wilson knew he knew the girl. It was written all over his face the minute he laid eyes on the picture. But he didn't know Freddie, which meant Freddie didn't know he knew Simone.

"Okay, sir. I understand. But if you see her, I ask that you give us a call at the Goldsboro Police Department," Crawford instructed.

"Sure," Brian said. He was turning away when his eyes met Detective Wilson's momentarily. Wilson hadn't said a word the whole time, but Brian didn't like the way he was looking at him. He was happy to get away from his gaze.

"He knows her," Wilson told Crawford while they walked back to the rental car. "I'll bet my pension on it. I don't know how or why, but he's more than a casual acquaintance."

"Maybe he's a family member." Crawford shrugged. He, too, had gotten the same impression, now that Wilson mentioned it.

Wilson shook his head. "No, because he doesn't know Holmes."

Crawford looked at him. "You think?"

Wilson shrugged. "Who knows. Maybe Miss Simone is into a lot of extracurricular activity. Whatever the case, we need a list of all his calls for the past six months, and hopefully we'll get a tap for any future ones, too."

The dragnet was slowly tightening around Freddie.

Chapter Forty-two

Dante and Cream had reached Goldsboro as well. Their crew arrived in town in two rentals. Dante and Cream were in an Explorer, and two shooters were in a Ford Focus filled with a mini arsenal. Both shooters were Puerto Rican females who were known to get down. They were heroin addicts, but you couldn't tell by looking at them because they were Angie Martinez/Jennifer Lopez–type dimes. But make no mistake, their guns did go off, loudly and often.

They rode around to all the hot spots, dropping Freddie's name, trying to find him.

"Yeah, yo. I told son I was comin' through," Dante told one cat in a green Range Rover, acting like they were friends, "but I ain't know when I was gettin' out, so I decided to surprise him."

But no one gave Freddie up. Those who didn't know him couldn't tell, and those who did wouldn't. Eventually, word got back to Slug.

"Two niggas in a Explorer?" Slug asked.

"And two bad-ass Spanish *mamis*," the Range Rover cat informed Slug.

Slug thought it might be connected to Gina in some way, but with Freddie, you couldn't tell. Maybe they really were looking for him. Slug had no idea because he no longer trusted his cousin. But since he had already made the first move, he felt he had the upper hand. So if Freddie had exported an army, he was ready to go to war, chess move for chess move. Because he already had his queen.

Chapter Forty-three

Simone awoke in a darkened apartment with a splitting headache. She found herself lying on a couch while two men with black bandanas tied around their faces watched her. She stiffened with fright, remembering what had transpired.

"Just be cool, li'l mama. If your man act right, this'll all be over in a minute," one of them said, then turned to the other. "Call your folk."

The second man grabbed the phone and dialed. After a moment, he spoke into the phone, "It's done." Then he hung up.

Simone looked from face to face, scared to death. "Please let me go. Whatever Freddie did, I didn't have anything to do with it. Please," she begged.

"Just like a bitch," the second cat hissed. "As long as shit is sweet and the money is comin', it's all good. But soon as shit get gangsta, they all fo' self!"

The first man laughed. "Be cool, folk. Just make the call to Freddie."

***

Freddie was on his way back from Wilson when his cell phone rang. He turned down his Sam Scarfo CD and answered it. "What da deal?"

"Yo' girl, nigga." The voice cackled.

Freddie sat up straight in the seat. "My what?"

"Listen."

Freddie heard muffled sounds. Then it felt like a hand squeezed the blood out of his heart when he heard, "Freddie!"

"Simone?"

A thud hit his stomach and he had to pull over to keep from wrecking his car, as a sudden dizziness filled his head.

"Freddie, they came to the house! They . . ."

"Simone!" he hollered into the phone, but the only reply was a menacing laugh.

"Damn, dog! This pussy that good, it got you hollerin' like that? Shit, you don't act right, I might just have to see for myself."

"Muthafucka! You touch her and I'll kill you! I'll kill you!" Freddie screamed and pulled out his gun like they were right in front of him.

The second man laughed again, eying Simone's chocolate thighs. When they kidnapped her, she only had on a T-shirt, a bra, and no shoes. "Damn. Li'l mama got some pretty feet, dog," he said as he ran his gun up Simone's thigh.

"Please, don't," Simone begged, seeing the lust build in his eyes.

He pulled her shirt up and saw that she wasn't wearing any panties. "Damn! And no panties!" He cackled.

Freddie was sick to his stomach. "I'ma kill you, nigga! I'ma kill you!" He kept repeating it, tears welling up in his eyes.

"Nigga, you ain't gonna do shit but come off that hundred grand, ya dig?" he demanded.

"I . . . I hear you," Freddie replied. "Just don't touch my fuckin' girl!"

"Nigga, I already did," he boasted, and jabbed a finger inside Simone's sex. Then he held the phone to her screaming mouth.

"Freddie, please!"

Freddie opened the car door and vomited.

"You still think it's a game, dog? Huh?" the kidnapper taunted.

"Naw, man." Freddie broke down. "It ain't a game."

"A hundred Gs, partner. I'ma call you at the phone booth outside Darnell's in one hour. Have my scrilla and you get yo' bitch back." Click.

Freddie laid his head against the steering wheel, mind racing, trying to figure out who could have done this. They had kidnapped Simone, and it was killing him. He straightened himself up for the drive. They could have the money even though it was all he had. But he swore on his unborn that these fools would pay for this with their lives, whoever was involved.

Freddie drove straight to the crib, running red lights with complete disregard. He was in kill mode. He would gladly trade his soul in exchange for the people responsible. To have them on their knees, begging for their lives, which he lusted to take.

Inside the apartment, he busted the safe and emptied it. He knew he had a little over a hundred grand by a thousand or two, but he had no time to count it. Besides, he had $2,500 in his pocket, and three Gs stashed in the CLK. He was going to give it all up without hesitation. Simone and his unborn child were worth that and more. Simone alone was worth that. No matter how grimy he was or how bad things had gotten between them, he truly loved Simone with all his heart, and he'd do anything to make sure she was safe. Until she was safe, nothing else mattered to him.

Freddie stuffed the money into a shopping bag, balled it up, jumped back into his car, and jetted out to Darnell's gas station.

When he arrived, he checked his watch nervously. He had ten minutes. He looked around for any shady faces or out-of-place sights, but besides the usual crowd of bums, drunks, and nickel hustlers, Darnell's was normal.

All kinds of things went through his mind about what they had done to Simone. The thought crossed his mind that if he paid them, they might deliver her dead body. In a kidnapping, there were no guarantees, Freddie knew. Maybe she had seen something she shouldn't have seen, or heard something she shouldn't have heard, and they wanted to make sure they weren't going to be identified.

Suppose they had . . . Freddie hated imagining that someone was raping his heart, taking what was his without permission. He envisioned Simone screaming out his name, and him being unable to hear her, help her, or save her.

He knew it was all his fault. The life he had led, the enemies he had made, all of it contributed to the present situation. He vowed that if he got Simone back safe and sound, they would leave Goldsboro. To go where, he didn't know, but as long as they were together . . .

The payphone rang and he answered before it had finished the rattle of the first ring. "Let me speak to my girl," Freddie demanded.

"Easy, dog. You'll get yo' pussy back in the same shape if, and only if, you got my scrilla," the voice taunted.

"I got it, muthafucka! Now put her on the phone! I ain't givin' you shit 'til I hear—"

"Freddie," Simone sobbed, "why is this happening to me?"

"Baby, it's gonna be okay. Did they . . . hurt you?"

"You mean, did we fuck yo' bitch?" the man asked, taking the phone from Simone. "Not yet, nigga. But if you don't put the money inside that green Dumpster on the side of the store and leave, we gonna bust this pussy wide open, and then kill her. Ya smell me?"

"Bitch-ass nigga, why you ain't come at me? Come see me! Come see me, you fuckin' bitch-ass nigga!" Freddie barked uncontrollably, but the kidnapper hung up. Freddie made the drop, then jumped back into his car and skidded off.

Chapter Forty-four

Slug was playing pool at William Alston's poolroom when he got the call. "Yeah."

"We got the scrilla."

Slug didn't respond.

"What you want us to do wit' li'l mama?"

"Fuck you mean 'do'?" I told y'all niggas to leave her alone. You got the scrilla, cut her loose," Slug ordered and hung up.

He felt bad that Simone had gotten caught up in Freddie's bullshit, but he didn't regret it for two reasons, or at least that's what he tried to convince himself of. One, he did it for the money. With his cut of the ransom and what he had already put up, he had enough to kiss the game good-bye and get out the Boro. Second, from the look in Gina's eyes when she propositioned him with her scheme, if he had said no, she still would have gotten it done. And ain't no tellin' what total strangers would've done to Simone at Gina's request.

Slug studied the spread on the table and thought about the irony of life. Everybody wanted to be a shot caller. "Nine in the corner," he told his opponent before he sank the shot, cross table.

And once a shot was set in motion . . .

"Combination, ten into the twelve, twelve side pocket."

The only thing that controlled it was finesse, the amount of force behind it.

The twelve ball teetered, then dropped.

Too much force and you could scratch yourself out of the game. Too little, and you could miss the shot that could win the game.

"Eight ball, bank," Slug announced, a Newport hanging out of his mouth, his eyes squinting against the smoke. The clack of the cue ball hitting the eight rang out across the pool hall. It careened and tumbled off the bank, then rolled as if magnetized into the winning pocket. Slug smiled.

"Bank, nigga."

Chapter Forty-five

Simone sat in downtown Goldsboro on an old bus stop bench. The sun had set so the streets were all but deserted and all the stores were closed. Her face was outlined with salt from all the tears she had shed.

There were no more illusions or facades to hide behind. Freddie's actions had cost her more than love; they had almost cost her her life. They had waved guns in her face, snatched her out of her own house, off her own doorstep, and taken her prisoner. She could still feel the man's finger inside her, violating her womanhood while he laughed at her pleas. He taunted her with threats of doing worse and she was helpless to stop him. It seemed as if her unborn child had sensed the danger and was lying dormant, not kicking or moving, so out of character.

Simone was all cried out. There would be no more tears. She sat stone-faced and half-naked at a public bus stop, like she had been abandoned and discarded. This was how Freddie found her when he skidded up to the corner and jumped out, gun drawn. When they got the money, they told Freddie where he could find his Simone. He went there, holding his breath, not knowing exactly what he would find.

"Simone! Are you okay, baby?" he inquired intently, checking her from head to toe. She stood and Freddie tried to embrace her, but she didn't hug him back. She just stood there like a lifeless doll baby wrapped in his arms.

She pushed him away firmly, but calmly, and said, "Just take me to the apartment, Freddie."

He was so happy to have her back, he failed to realize she called it "the apartment" and not "home."

Chapter Forty-six

Dante and his crew of shooters sat up in the Motel 6 plotting their next move.

"Man, this country-ass hick town ain't but so big. Where the fuck is this joker at?" Dante wanted to know, pacing the floor. He had waited a long time to avenge his brother's death, and now that he was this close, he wasn't about to give up. He was growing impatient.

"At least we know what kind of car he's drivin', *papi*," the brunette hit woman offered as consolation. They found that out from a local hustler whose baby mama had been letting Freddie juice her on the regular for all she had or could get her hands on. He had seen through Dante's game, and he had nothing but hate in his heart for Freddie.

"And who the fuck is this Slug muhfucka?" Cream asked, mouth full of pizza. "We find him, we beat Freddie's whereabouts the fuck outta him!"

"Whoever Slug is, these bamas damn sure ain't tryin' to point him out," Dante commented.

"Fuck it, let's ride out some more. We bound to see this CLK Freddie pushin'," Cream suggested.

"Fuck, yo," Dante spit. "I ain't leavin' 'til this cocksucka' bleed. That's my word on everything I love!"

Chapter Forty-seven

Detective Wilson had the same thing on his mind. Nobody shot a cop and got away with it in his book.

"Look, man, I done told you all I know," the skinny, damn near toothless crackhead said, sitting in an interrogation room with Wilson and Timmons. He was the same crackhead who had moved Freddie's furniture, but he had caught a felony larceny charge, and he was trying to duck the habitual offender category looming over his head by giving them Freddie's.

"I don't know where he live no more. All I know is him and Slug makin' paper. A lot of paper. And he push a Benz."

"What about hangouts? Where's he pushin' the stuff?" Wilson asked eagerly.

"He don't. Neither one of 'em do. The only place I can tell you he might be is Pop Bogs or the Blue Note. All the major dealers be out there on Saturdays."

Wilson looked at Timmons, who shrugged and said, "It's worth a try."

"So, if y'all catch him, y'all ain't gonna forget about me, is you, Timmons?"

Timmons looked at the dirty crackhead with disgust. He hated a black man on drugs, but he hated a snitch even more. "Take yo' ass back to the cell."

Chapter Forty-eight

Simone and Freddie rode home in silence. Freddie wanted to ask her if she recognized anything, heard any names, and most importantly, ask what they had done to her. But her facial expression was one he hadn't seen before. He knew the ordeal had been traumatic, but he prayed she'd be okay.

When they reached the apartment, Simone went straight to the bedroom and slammed the door. Freddie started to go to her but decided not to. She was home safe. He could hear the bathwater running from behind the closed door and thought it best to leave Simone to herself.

He turned his attention to payback and picked up the phone to call Slug. Things hadn't been good with them at all since the fight, but they were blood, and he knew Slug would ride out with him.

"Hello?" Kiki answered the phone.

"Ki, this Freddie. Where Slug at?"

"He ain't here, Freddie. Call him on his cell. How you doin'?" she asked.

"I'm cool."

"Simone there?"

Before he could answer, Simone walked out of the bedroom fully dressed and carrying a small suitcase. Freddie didn't even bother to answer Kiki and hung up.

Simone dropped her keys onto the coffee table. "Let me go, Freddie," she stated firmly, a look of resignation in her eyes.

"Go where? What you mean, boo?" Freddie asked, knowing full well what she meant. He tried to take her hand but she stepped away from him. "Baby, I know that what happened—"

"No, Freddie, you don't know. You couldn't know. They didn't have a gun in your face; you didn't . . ." She sighed. "I don't want to talk about it. I just want you to let me go."

Freddie was beside himself with fear. Any man who's been confronted with the loss of everything, the only thing he's ever cared about, can understand. Those who haven't can't understand until they have.

His mind raced and his tongue stuttered, "You right, ma, I don't know. But I do know that whoever did this is gonna pay. I swear to God, they're gonna pay for what they did to you."

Simone laughed without smiling. "You just don't get it, do you, Freddie? There's nothing you can do to pay them back for what they did to me. Ever!"

Freddie grabbed both of her hands and said, "Then let's get away. You wanna leave? Cool, I'm feelin' you, but let's leave together. Let's go somewhere and start all over, get away from all—"

Simone walked away from him. "So you can do the same thing all over again, Freddie? So I can lie in another bed, alone? In another strange place, hearing your lies and your apologies? I can't do this anymore, Freddie. I don't love you anymore."

"Please, boo, don't say that," he whispered, trying not to cry, "I know I fucked up. I know there's nothing I can do to make this all go away, but please don't take your love from me. It's all I got." Tears welled up in his eyes and Simone had to turn away to keep from being magnetized by his open display of emotions.

"I can't do this, Freddie. Can't you see? It's over, Freddie. Just let me go," she repeated her demand.

"How could you leave me, baby? How? I gave up everything I have for you, to get you back, Simone," he begged.

"And I gave up everything I am for you! How dare you ever say that, Freddie! I gave up my life, my dreams, my body! They were going to rape me, Freddie!" Simone cried.

Freddie went to her and embraced her, and she found herself hugging him back. "I'm sorry, Simone, I'm so sorry. Please, boo, I'll make it better. I will, I promise."

At the word "promise," Simone cringed and pushed him away. "No, Freddie, no! I don't love you. I hate you! Do you hear me? I hate you! Just let me go!"

To hear his heart turn on him was too much for Freddie's pride to bear. "You wanna go? Go! I ain't stoppin' you!" He paced the floor, realizing his love was leaving, but he had to salvage his manhood to survive. "You wanna leave? Leave! Fuck you waitin' for? Huh?"

"Yes, Freddie. Let me go," she whispered to herself.

"I gave them everything! Everything! And now you wanna leave? Bitch, breeze. I can make another baby. Can you make another Freddie?"

He was purposely trying to hurt her, not knowing that's what she meant by let her go. Freddie's words stung her, but she knew it was what she needed to break free.

She reached down and picked up her suitcase. "I . . . I need a ride to the bus station."

Freddie tossed the phone at her feet. "Call a cab," he hissed dryly and turned his back to her.

"Thank you," she whispered and turned for the door. The first step was the hardest, but she forced herself, step by step, until she was halfway down the street.

Freddie stood in the middle of the living room, cold and alone. Simone had walked out the front door with his heart. So he had no choice but to be heartless. He wanted to go after her, beg her to stay, and he knew she would. He knew the power he had over her, but without the love, it wouldn't be the same. Simone was right. It was over.

He grabbed the half-pint bottle of Grand Cru Rémy Martin cognac he had left on the kitchen counter days ago, cracked it open, and tossed it up. The smooth elixir slid down his throat, burning his chest. He didn't take the bottle down until it was half empty. His head was spinning as he tossed it up again, and drained it this time. Then he dropped it on the floor. He staggered over to the full-length mirror on the wall and looked at his reflection.

"I shoulda let 'em have that ungrateful bitch," he said, trying to remain cold because it was the only way he could remain numb to the pain he was running full speed from. "I'm muhfuckin'

Freddie," he staggered and slurred. "Naw, Simone!" he yelled, "I ain't fucked up. You fucked up. 'Cause you'll never find a muhfucka like me. But you a dime a dozen!"

He wished she was still there so he could cuss her, humiliate her, and demean her. Then he smelled her Gucci fragrance and it sent him for the Crown Royal.

Simone was gone. There was nothing he could do about it. And his money was gone, too. He had to do something about that. Fifty-five hundred wouldn't last him the weekend. He had to make a power move, and he knew just where he needed to start.

He stumbled over to his cell phone lying on the floor and went through his contacts until he reached the Cs: Cynthia, the white broad he had conned out of three Gs a few months back. He hadn't called her since, but he was glad he'd kept her number.

"Hello?" she chimed.

"Cynthia," Freddie slurred, and she knew exactly who it was.

She was standing in her bedroom in her slip, getting ready for a white-tie event. She glanced into the bathroom where her husband was busy at the sink. "Freddie," she whispered with nervous excitement, "is that you? Why haven't you—"

Freddie cut her off sharply. "Check this: I ain't in the mood for no muthafuckin' questions 'cause I'm a grown-ass man, a'ight?"

"I know that, Freddie, I just thought—"

"Didn't I just tell yo' dumb ass I'm a grown-ass man? I don't need anybody to think for me. You can either listen or hang the fuck up!"

Cynthia swiftly left the bedroom, closing the door behind her. "I'm listening, Freddie, but you don't have to talk to me like that," she said, trying to sound firm, but Freddie already knew he had broken her. If he hadn't, she would've hung up.

"Then understand where I'm coming from and I won't have to. Look, Cynthia, there's some things I need to share with you, some secrets I need you to keep. But I gotta know I can trust you, that I can count on you. I ain't sayin' jump when I say leap, I'm sayin' come when I call. Can you do that? Can I count on you for that?" By the time Freddie finished, Cynthia was a wrap.

"Oh, of course, Freddie. You can count on me. What do you need me to do?"

"I need to see you tonight," Freddie told her.

Cynthia thought about the $1,000-a-plate charity banquet she was supposed to attend, and then she thought about the golden dick she had been fiending for. The decision made itself. "Where?"

"Get a room somewhere. Wilson; get a room at the Marriott. I'll call you in an hour, a'ight?"

"Okay, Freddie. Whatever you say," she responded eagerly.

"And bring some money."

"How much?"

"Surprise me." He smiled and hung up. He purposely left the amount up in the air to determine what level they were on, and how he needed to put it down to elevate it. To Freddie, Cynthia was just the beginning, his door to that country club, jet-set pussy. It was time to step his game all the way up.

Freddie went and got dressed in his beige, white, and brown velour Coogi, a matching beanie, and a pair of brown and beige Gators. He threw on his jewels, earring to pinkie, not forgetting his Gucci frames.

He stepped in front of the mirror to admire himself. "Damn, you a pretty muthafucka!" he told himself. "What? Them niggas thought they could break me? A hundred grand ain't shit. As long as bitches got pussies, I'ma get paper."

He wanted to shine on whoever had kidnapped Simone. He wanted all of them to know who they were dealing with. Freddie decided to stop through the Midnight Lounge on his way to Wilson, so all of them would know he couldn't be broken, that he was unbreakable. He jumped into the BMW M3 and headed for the club.

Freddie pulled up to Midnight and hopped out of his M3. He was so drunk, it was a miracle he'd made it that far. Normally, he would be on point coming to the hot spot, checking his surroundings as he and Slug cruised through the parking area. But because of the liquor and Slug's absence, he hadn't noticed that he had just passed two detectives. Fortunately for Freddie they hadn't noticed him either. They were looking for the platinum CLK. His inadvertent choice of whips had gotten him past the police surveillance.

He entered the crowded club staggering noticeably. He looked around, knowing that whoever had played him was at the club and probably watching him, and they were. Slug and the kidnappers, J-dog and Bruno, were all together in the body-infested establishment.

"There go that pretty muhfucka now, folk," Bruno said, watching Freddie move through the crowd.

"What up, folk?" J-dog asked Slug, ready to set it.

"Ain't shit up, folk. He still family. Ain't no need in pressing the issue. Y'all cats take that twenty grand and be out."

J-dog gave Slug a pound. "We gonna miss you, baby boy. Holler at your manz and 'em sometime, dog."

"Fo' sho'," Slug told them, and then they walked off.

Freddie spotted Slug and smiled at him. He came over to the table and sat down. "What the deal, cuz?"

"You," Slug replied and they shook hands. "You a'ight, cuz?"

"If I ain't, I'm gonna be, yo," Freddie boasted. "Why you ask?"

Slug shrugged his shoulders. "Look like you got a lot on your mind, folk."

"Simone left me, duke," was all Freddie said. He started to tell Slug about the kidnapping, but decided against it. What's done is done, and he was now ready to move on.

"What you gonna do now?"

"Relocate," he stated simply. "And step the game up."

"I feel you, cuz," Slug said, pulling on his Newport. "I was thinkin' the same thang. 'Cept I'm leaving the game where it stands, yo."

"The game's all I got, son," Freddie replied.

Slug nodded and looked away. He felt sorry for Freddie. He was trapped, but he had trapped himself. Family was family, but at the end of the day, a man's gotta stand on his own.

"Be easy, cuz, I'll be right back," Slug told him and got up, headed for the bathroom.

About that time, Dante and Cream walked up in the club looking around.

"Yo, duke, spread out. If you see that lame, don't do shit. The guns are in the car, but these his people, so we know somebody's strapped. We spot him, we lie until he bounce, and work him then, a'ight?" Dante laid it down and Cream nodded in understanding. They split up and began looking for Freddie.

Cream bumped into Tina, who was heading the other way carrying a bottle of Grand Cru. She saw Freddie lying low in the corner and went over to him instinctively. She slid into the booth next to him, kissing him on the neck, and caressing his thigh. "What's poppin', stranger? What's the matter, you ain't got time for Tina no more?" She pouted with her sexy bottom lip poked out.

"Naw, I just ain't got time for no games, yo," Freddie answered.

Look who's talking, she thought, but instead she said, "What's that supposed to mean, Freddie? You think I'm playing games with you?"

"It means shit's fucked up right now and my paper ain't straight. So until it is, I'm keeping everything official and everyone around me official, yo," Freddie shot back at her, grabbing the Grand Cru and turning it up.

"And I ain't?"

"Are you?"

Tina smiled. "Freddie, I'm about the same thing that you about. But you got the game fucked up lettin' that square bitch carry you when a real boss bitch, like me, was born to take care of you." She ran it down, checking game with science.

Freddie just stared straight ahead, his thoughts a blur. Tina stuck her hand in his pants, grabbed his dick, pulled it out, and began pumping along the whole shaft.

"Let Tina take care of you, baby," she purred, and lowered her head, taking him into her mouth. Freddie put his head back and did something he hadn't done in years. He cried from the heart. He cried for his mother, knowing all she had put up with from his father; he cried for his father because he couldn't be a real father or a real man. He cried for everything he had put Simone through, and he cried for his unborn child that he now feared he'd never know. He also cried for how he had treated Gina and played Slug. But most of all, he cried for himself.

Cream saw Tina's head bobbing, sucking someone off over at one of the booths. "Damn, these country broads are some freaks!" he mumbled in disbelief, but his attitude changed when he saw who she was going down on. "Oh shit!" he exclaimed, pushing through the crowd looking for Dante.

Chapter Forty-nine

Dante was in the bathroom taking a piss at the urinal and, right next to him, Slug was taking a piss too. The two men acknowledged each other's presence then went on with their business.

Slug finished first, washed his hands, and headed out. As he was leaving, a guy walking in said, "What up, Slug?"

"What up," Slug replied.

Dante almost pissed on his shoes trying to get his pants up. He didn't even wash his hands as he rushed out, trying to follow Slug. Cream ran up to him.

"I found Freddie!"

"Where?" Dante asked, forgetting all about Slug.

"In the back wit' some bitch blowin' him!" Cream snarled, imagining that Freddie had had his wife doing the same thing.

"Come on. When he come out, we'll be waiting for him."

Timmons checked his watch and looked at Wilson. "You ready to call it a night?" Before Wilson could answer, he saw Cream and Dante hurry out of the club and walk over to two women in an SUV.

"I know that ain't . . ." Wilson began, then he looked over at Timmons. "I don't know how he got past us, but Holmes is inside!"

He and Timmons got out of the car and headed for the door.

Chapter Fifty

"What's the matter, boo?" Tina was looking up with a wet mouth. Freddie had gone limp, but he hadn't cum. That's when she saw his tears. "Freddie, what's wrong?"

Freddie brought his head down and shook it. He started to push Tina away, to push it all away, but his eyes froze.

The first bullet whizzed through the air, shattering the bottle of Rémy Martin Grand Cru VS on the table and piercing the soft flesh of Freddie's upper left side, separating two of his ribs. The burning sensation ignited his insides letting his intoxicated mind know he had been shot. But he wasn't surprised. How could he be when he saw it coming, saw them coming, from across the crowded club.

The second shot caught him in the neck. His blood splattered all over a screaming female beside him who was scrambling to get away.

Yes, he saw the bullets coming. He could see them in his eyes before he saw the glint of the cold steel in the shooter's hand. When their eyes first met, his instincts went into survival mode. He saw murder and knew he was the victim. As he reached for his pistol, something happened. Something just made him stop, and he accepted what was taking place. He was tired.

Even the fourth bullet, the last shot he felt, seemed to move in slow motion. From the barrel of the gun, he followed its *Matrix*-like trajectory as it zeroed in on him. He watched it come dangerously close to a woman's ducking head, break a glass in a man's hand, and finally lodge itself deep inside his own flesh. Simultaneously, Freddie's mind was sent to that place where pain can no longer reach.

His last sight was of those eyes and the determination in them. He knew it was coming; no one can run forever. His last thought was, *damn, why did it have to be me?*

Chapter Fifty-one

Simone trekked along the busy thoroughfare of Wayne Memorial Drive, carrying her small suitcase. She was finally free. The things Freddie had said made her feel used and depressed, but she had needed to hear them, had needed to hear him say them to her to let her go.

She had lied to Freddie; she did love him. And she knew in her heart that she always would. Deep down, she wished Freddie would pull up beside her, beg her not to leave, embrace her tightly, and declare his undying love. But it didn't happen.

Simone was in no condition to be walking, so when she reached the corner gas station, she called a cab from the payphone. While waiting for it, she saw Freddie drive by in the BMW he had bought for her. She could hear Jay-Z's *In My Lifetime, Vol. 1* pumping out of the open windows. He didn't look in her direction, just kept his attention straight ahead, bopping his head to the music. He looked like he didn't have a care in the world, like he couldn't care less about her leaving him. She noticed that he had changed clothes. She couldn't tell what he was wearing, but she knew it was different from what she had just seen him in.

Simone guessed at where he might be going: Tina. That made her blood boil. She imagined Tina in her apartment, in her bed, maybe even in her clothes, taking her place. The cab pulled up and Simone got in. Her mind was set to go to the bus station, but she heard herself say, "The Midnight Lounge." She had to see for herself, confirm what she already knew to be true and see Freddie with her.

Simone arrived at the club, asked the cab driver to wait for her, and then disappeared inside. The club was packed, as usual, and the thump of the music hurt her ears. It made her grab her stomach in a motherly embrace. Recognition flashed across the faces that knew her and, in her condition, they wondered what she was doing there. Simone even started to wonder herself. Freddie had obviously gone on with his life, and it was time to get on with hers.

That was her thought before she saw Freddie in the corner booth, and he wasn't alone. Tina was with him. Seeing her hugged up under Freddie and whispering in his ear brought back all of her anger, frustration, and grief. For six years, she had made Freddie her world, and to see him hugged up not even an hour after she left made her forget everything. All she felt was hate.

That was, until she saw Tina's head lower and begin to bob slowly up and down in Freddie's lap. "I can make another baby. Can you make another Freddie?" he'd said. Simone just snapped.

Quietly and calmly, she began her approach. She only had the gun because of the kidnapping. She saw the small .380 on the dresser and grabbed it out of fear. Now, here in the club, she felt the weight of the steel in her hand.

Simone took aim and it was like Freddie could feel her from across the room, feel her pain. He lowered his head and looked directly at her, and she fired.

She had aimed for Tina's bobbing head, but instead hit Freddie. Tina screamed and scrambled to get up. She fired again and watched the blood from Freddie's neck splatter all over Tina's back. Tina fled for safety and the club erupted into a frenzy. She fired the last two shots in rapid succession, each one tearing away a piece of flesh from the man she loved.

The pushing and shoving of the escaping clubgoers brought Simone back to reality and she knew she had to get out. She made her way toward the door amid the other clubbers, then stepped outside and into the waiting cab.

"What the hell!" Wilson exclaimed, watching people run, screaming, from the lounge.

"They shootin', yo!" somebody shouted.

Wilson and Timmons pulled their pistols and aggressively pushed their way inside. "Police! Out of the way! Move!" They looked around, scanning the place for the shooter and listening for more shots. All they heard was a girl crying over a body slumped in a corner booth.

"Oh, my God! Oh, my God! Freddie, please don't die!" Tina begged hysterically.

Detectives Wilson and Timmons ran up on the scene. Wilson saw the man he had been looking for. "Get an ambulance!" he directed.

Chapter Fifty-two

Dante and Cream were sitting in the Explorer, hecklers on their laps, eyes glued to the door, when people came bursting out.

"Fuck is goin' on?" Dante asked, getting out of the car, scanning the faces, and making sure Freddie wasn't one of the people running away.

Cream got out and stood beside him, gun in hand. A girl ran by and Cream grabbed her arm. "What the fuck goin' on?"

"Somebody got shot!" she said, then snatched her arm away and continued running.

"Yo, Cream, go see what's good," Dante said, sending his boy to gather information.

They didn't have long to wait. The ambulance arrived along with several squad cars, and they cordoned off the front of the club. But that didn't stop the curious from huddling around. The EMTs, along with Timmons, Wilson, and Tina, walked out of the club, and then came Freddie on a stretcher, oxygen mask affixed to his face. Tina clung to his side. Cream looked into Freddie's face and felt mixed emotions. He was glad that Freddie was the one who had been hit, but he hated the fact that he hadn't been the one to hit him.

"No, miss, you can't—" The paramedic tried to stop Tina and she flipped.

"No! I'm going! I'm his wife! I'm going, motherfucka!" she ranted and raved as Wilson silently nodded an okay. They all piled into the back of the ambulance and the door shut.

Slug stood outside in shock. He had heard the shots, but didn't know who got hit until now. He looked around the crowd and his eyes found Cream. Slug never forgot a face. He remembered Cream from the shootout in Plainfield, and he knew instantly that these had been the cats asking about Freddie.

His mind told him that these were the dudes who had gunned his cousin down. Regardless of everything that had happened, Slug wasn't about to let this violation go unpunished.

Cream ran back to the SUV and got in. "Son, they fuckin' shot Freddie!" he exclaimed, disgusted.

"Who?"

"Fuck, I don't know. But that was him in the ambulance." Cream hit the dashboard in frustration.

"He dead?"

"They ain't have a sheet over his face."

That was all Dante needed to hear. He started the truck up. "Then he ain't dead." He signaled for the two girls to follow. "Let's go find this fuckin' hospital." Dante pulled out onto Ash Street with the Ford Focus behind him.

"Yo, Tay, what are we gonna do when we get to the hospital?" Cream asked. He wanted Freddie too, but he wasn't down for no wild cowboy shit.

"Fuck you mean? We ain't leavin' 'til this nigga's dead, fo' sho'. I ain't come all this way for nothing. Word to—"

Dante never got a chance to finish his sentence. As he sat at the light, he didn't see the two CBR 900s that pulled up on both sides of the Explorer. J-dog and Bruno simultaneously raised their guns and let off a barrage of shots into the SUV. Dante and Cream never even had a chance to react. They jerked and twitched violently as the bullets filled their already dead bodies.

But Cream and Dante weren't the only ones caught off guard. J-dog and Bruno didn't know that the two girls in the Focus behind them were with the cats in the Explorer.

"Mira, aqui!" the J-Lo lookalike yelled and opened fire with a Mac. Her partner in crime

was synchronized perfectly with her, twin .40s blazing. Their shots hit metal and flesh, sending sparks and soft tissue flying in all directions. J-dog and Bruno lay tangled in their motorcycles.

The blond Boricua walked up on a half-dead Bruno and stood over him. *"Muerte, punto!"* she sneered, and emptied the rest of her clip. Then she checked on Dante and Cream. They had both met their Maker.

"Mami, vamanos!" the other Latina yelled, hearing the sirens in the distance. They both jumped into the Focus and disappeared into the shadows.

Chapter Fifty-three

The first things Freddie saw when he opened his eyes in the hospital were a bright white light, and two blurry faces. As his vision returned and his pupils focused, he saw that the two faces belonged to two smiling men he had never seen before but recognized instantly: cops.

"Welcome back, Mr. Holmes," Wilson announced triumphantly. "You almost got away from us, for good. But thank God for the miracle of modern medicine. Wouldn't you agree?"

Freddie just looked at Wilson, stone-faced.

"I didn't think you would. But I can't say that I blame you, because where I'm sending you, you're going to wish you were dead," Wilson taunted, then began with the all-too-familiar words, "You have the right to remain silent . . ."

Epilogue

One Year Later

Trenton State Prison was the end of the road for anybody in the New Jersey prison system with twenty-five years or more. Nothing but concrete and steel, it was where dreams died and inmates prayed for miracles. This was where Freddie was expected to serve out his twenty-eight-year sentence. He had been charged with three murders and one attempted murder. Three murders because the gun he killed Mannie with had two previous bodies on it. He easily beat the first two bodies, but copped to one count of second-degree murder and attempted murder for the cop he shot.

He lay back on his bunk, looking at the letter in his hands. The return address simply read: SIMONE JACKSON.

He smiled. He had been down for almost nine months and Simone hadn't written him one letter. She had sent numerous pictures of his daughter, Fredica Simone Jackson, and had sent the beautiful bundle of joy up to see him with his mother, but she had never written him prior to the letter he held in his hand.

Freddie was almost afraid to read the letter, satisfied with the daydream of what he wanted it to say but knew in his heart it didn't. He had written her countless letters, and this was her first reply. There was a scent to it.

Hello Freddie,

How have you been? I received all of your letters, and to answer your question, Fredica Simone and I are doing fine. Did you get the last pictures I sent you? She is growing so fast, it's amazing! Every day I thank God for her little fat-faced self. Everyone says she looks like I spit her out. I must admit, she does look a lot like me, but those are definitely your dimples and your eyes. Every time I look into her eyes, I think of you, the good times that we shared, and it makes me smile.

I am also glad that you are doing well with your college courses. I always knew you had it in you. Remember I used to try to get you to go back to school? I'm glad you're doing it now. Never stop learning, regardless of where you are.

After all the times you wrote me, I guess you're surprised to finally hear from me. But I felt there were some things that I needed to say to you, for you and for myself to have closure. You said in one of your letters that you're sorry for everything you did to hurt me and that you don't blame me for what I did to you. Believe it or not, Freddie, I don't blame me either. I'm not trying to rub it in or be an evil bitch, but you owed me at least that. Do you remember what you said at the airport? What you vowed to me? You pledged on your soul to give me your life. Do you remember, or were those just sweet words you're so good at talking?

You say you don't hate me and I don't hate you. I feel sorry for you because I don't think you deserve all that time. It was a no-win situation for you, and you did what you had to do. But ask yourself this: if you hadn't had sex with that girl, would you have even been in that position? Think about that, because until you change that part of yourself, you haven't changed at all, like you claim.

As for money, I'm okay. I'm working in Elizabeth and going to school at night.

Plus, I have some money put up, which I have you to thank for. All that money you were giving me I was saving, saving for us, until "us" became our daughter and me. With what I saved, plus the $25,000 Slug and Kiki gave me, I bought the house that you now have the address to. It's hard but I'm making it.

And lastly, as to my personal life, you need not be concerned about that and I don't need any advice from you as to what kind of man I need. There will never be another you, because no one will ever hurt me like you did. No one will be playing daddy, as you put it, either. I will continue to send you pictures of our daughter, and I'll send her to see you with your mother at least twice a month. But please don't think you can use Fredica Simone to set things right between you and me. They are as they are meant to be.

I'm praying for you, for your strength and wisdom, and I pray you can get out because our daughter deserves that. She deserves to have her father in her life. Stay strong, Freddie.

Sincerely,
Simone

***

Freddie sat up on the bunk and laid Simone's letter beside him on the pillow. She was right and there was nothing he could say. He had made many promises to her, promises she had bet her life on, and he had let her down. He must have been a fool to think that, after all that, she'd do twenty-eight years with him. Freddie didn't even know how he could do twenty-eight years. One day at a time, he guessed.

Slug hadn't written him once since his incarceration and that angered him. But knowing Slug had hit Simone off with the amount of money he had made him grateful to Slug in his heart. He had no way of knowing it was his own money, the money he had paid Simone's ransom with, nor would he ever.

Freddie thought about what Simone said about the time he got. He didn't feel he deserved it either, but looking back on all the people he had used, abused, or manipulated, he realized that justice had truly been served, and he had to accept it.

His thoughts turned to Gina. He hadn't written her or heard from her at all. He really didn't have anything to say. Until now.

Freddie crossed his small cell to his desk and took out his notepad and pen. His attention was caught by the series of pictures of Tina on his desk. Tina had hopped the fence months ago, after she learned what he had been on the run for. She wrote for a few months, then the letters just stopped. The only reason he kept the pictures was because they were nude and panty shots in all seven of them. He chuckled to himself as he grabbed his pen.

G,

I don't know if you'll ever read this or if you even want to hear from me. I'm sure you know where I'm at and the bid I got. You've always got your ear to the streets (smile).

I'm not gonna stress this scribe with all kind of apologies or whatever because I know you know I am sorry for how I treated you, but you probably don't want to hear it. It's all good, though. I just wanted to tell you that I finally learned the measure of a man. The measure of a man is taking responsibility for your own actions, good and bad. When you do something good, it's only the result of the lessons from doing bad. And when you do bad, you accept the consequences. I ain't doing this time for murder, but for the life

I led that led me to that. I understand that now.

I just wanted you to know that I truly appreciate all that you mean to me, and I'll forever value the time we spent together. I don't expect to hear back from you, but I just wanted you to know at least this.

Freddie

Freddie sat back and tilted the chair until he was looking at the ceiling. Twenty-eight years. He was twenty-two and would be approaching fifty when he got out. He set the chair down on all four legs and looked at the notepad. He felt he had a story to tell, and he definitely had the time to tell it. He took up his pen, and this was how it began:

The first bullet whizzed through the air, shattering the bottle of Grand Cru Rémy Martin on the table, piercing the soft flesh of my upper left side, breaking two ribs. The burning sensation ignited my insides, telling my intoxicated mind that I had been shot.

The End

ORDER FORM
URBAN BOOKS, LLC
97 N. 18th Street
Wyandanch, NY 11798

Name (please print):_____

Address: _____

City/State: _____

Zip: _____

QTY	TITLES	PRICE

Shipping and handling-add $3.50 for 1st book, then $1.75 for each additional book.
Please send a check payable to:
Urban Books, LLC
Please allow 4–6 weeks for delivery